M R Green was born in Berkshire. He loved to read as a child and always wanted to write but never did. As a boy, he loved to play video games and watch Sci-fi films. After his GCSEs, he got a job in a retail store, and of course this was just a stop gap until he found something better. That urge to write a book never left him and he thought about it more as he got older. In his mid-twenties he decided he was going to give it his best shot, while still working at the same retail store he started to write. He did most of his writing and idea forming before his shifts and on his lunch breaks.

I would like to thank Ahmad Odeh, Adam Sandland, Simon O'Brien and my family for all their support with my work. I couldn't have done it without you guys. Also, all of those hours of Dungeons and Dragons have really helped.

M R Green

THE STORIES OF CANTOON – THEIR BEGINNING

AUSTIN MACAULEY PUBLISHERS™

LONDON • CAMBRIDGE • NEW YORK • SHARJAH

A CIP catalogue record for this title is available from the British Library.

ISBN 9781398402232 (Paperback)
ISBN 9781398402249 (ePub e-book)

www.austinmacauley.com

First Published 2022
Austin Macauley Publishers Ltd®
1 Canada Square
Canary Wharf
London
E14 5AA

Prologue

Over a thousand years ago, Planet Cantoon was a success. It was a prime example of what a colony planet should be. It was one of the few gems that the Galactic Empire really cared about, but only because new metals and minerals that were scarce on most worlds were not so on Cantoon. The planet was flooded with equipment and people to harvest the huge amounts of natural resources. An advanced communication base was built on one of the twin moons, so the colonists would always be protected from their enemies. It was, however, one of the furthest planets away from the civilised 'known' space.

Without warning, the Galactic Empire's core was ruthlessly attacked. Two out of three of their systems were reduced to cinder in minutes. Eight planets and trillions of lives ended without any justification. The Galactic Empire would attempt to fight this enemy from the darkest reaches of dead space. They never knew where this nightmare came from, but this threat's technology far surpassed their own.

They deliberately cut communication to all of their manufacturing colonies with a two-worded message: 'Be Safe'. Because, that was all the time they had left.

This was done so that the data streams would not be tracked and followed. There were contingency plans for times of crisis but a number of newer colonies were not given these instructions, Cantoon was one of them. This was due to the moon base being unmanned since the start of the Galactic War. At the time, the factions continued to work, each having their own tasks and routines.

When the colossal cargo ships no longer returned to orbit to take away their produce, tensions started to rise. Many suspected that they had been forgotten but few chose to believe it. An entire planet full of people began to push and pull against each other, and this was just the start.

The Factions formed their own republics, and they chose their own leaders. No matter how many times each faction tried, none of them could make contact with the empire or even the moon base that floated above them. Hostilities were kept to a minimum because of the slim chance that the moon base was still keeping its watchful eye across their world.

The first flash point was when the base, and a large part of the moon itself, was destroyed. No single faction admitted to the act, but this proved they were on their own. The planarity police known as the Protectors, were far outnumbered by the rest of the factions but they knew they could bring order to this world. If only the others would stop and listen to them, if the others would just give them what they wanted.

They would be made to listen, because the Protectors had looked after this world, so by right it will be theirs.

Chapter 1

Planet Cantoon had spent the last twenty years, once more gripped, in the struggle of global war. The frontlines moved like the changing of the tide, anything that couldn't be taken by one side or the other was left in ashes. It would seem that this war had also slowly ground to a halt, and maybe this time a treaty would not be signed. No land or technology would be traded because blood is all that would be required.

One nation, more aggressive than the rest would not accept any proposal, they would take what they were destined to own. This was their world after all, and they had always fought the hardest for its survival. The Bellatorum would go to any limit and would sacrifice any number of soldiers, because in their opinion, anything was justified. This war, the fifth war, will be the last. Even if it meant they would destroy what was left of this planet to claim victory, it had to be done to enforce their peace over all.

*

The Boneyards were where new recruits were broken into shape. Each Boneyard trained their flesh in its own way.

Depending on the quality of the finished product, they would be sent to the frontlines or onto further training.

454376AHF was wide awake and counted the joints in the ceiling tiles again. From his bed, he could easily count fifty-seven joints. There were always fifty-seven, but he counted them again to make sure he was right. He was barely past thirteen years of age or so he was told. He'd had no childhood to speak of, or any part of one that would be considered normal, but what was normal?

He could strip down any pistol he was given, clean it and put it back together in minutes. He also had a basic understanding of unarmed combat and first-aid. Those two lessons were set one after another, so the victors had to support their rivals after their defeat.

Come on, something happen. He thought with a jaw clenched.

He glanced down the row of bunks to the main set of doors. light from the corridor seeped through the slatted windows. With the dim amber glow, he could just make out the other fifty bunks. A head popped up two beds down. They had a brief conversation in simplified sign language.

"What you doing 45?" It wasn't normal sign language. This was something they had invented themselves.

"I have a feeling something is going to happen. I can't sleep for thinking about it."

At the end of the previous day, one topic was odd, even for them. They were shown how to release a harness. It was a five strap, like something you would get in a sports car. They were shown once, told it was important and not shown again. After this, they went back to normal, drills, fighting and weapons testing.

"Should I wake the others?" asked the lad with a wave of his hand. In the dim light, his pale blue eyes seemed to stand out more. 45 only needed to think about it for a couple of seconds.

"Yeah, get everyone up. I want us to be ready for anything."

The boy rolled over and grabbed a battered metal cup from under his pillow. No one was allowed to have items in the dorm room, but this guy could get most things anywhere. 45 was always quietly impressed. With metal cup in hand, he stared at the door and waited for the Minder's footsteps. As the faint pat of hard sole on concrete came near to the door, he slapped the cup into his bed frame. He pulled the cup under his covers and rolled over.

The Minder would have continued on his patrol but the noise forced it to swing the door open. As the reinforced material hit the door stop, it made an even louder bang. The armoured figure checked the room for movement, his stun baton crackled and flashed but it was not required for the moment.

Behind the mask and the yellow glassed eye slots a low clicking noise seemed to increase then fade. He was perfectly still; it didn't look like the Minder breathed. With a flick of its hand the baton disappeared back into its holster, and then he left. Everyone in the dorm was awake and blinked their attention to 45.

The Minder, like all the others that patrolled this site, was a 3rd generation modified soldier. Their brain was more machine than organic but this was combined with a perfectly honed body. Underneath their black armour, they were all the same, but no one other than their mechanics would ever know this. They didn't speak directly to anyone because they didn't have the capability, and digital communication was far more reliable over long distance.

The problem with these reused soldiers was that they were trained and equipped to fight in any battleground on their planet and then suddenly, they were not doing that. This huge amount of information was loosely wiped from their minds and then they were told to guard a building.

No matter how many times this happened some of this information would stick and then the Minder could decide to use it at a random moment. It is considered unwise to anger a Minder, sometimes it's best to not even look at them.

They were recalled due to the infamous Battle of Central Lake; when five thousand of them received a bad signal by command and tore each other to pieces, along with anyone else unfortunate enough to be in their path. At the time, they were escorting captured civilians from a taken city, none survived.

45 raised his hands and clenched his fists, when the rest of the dorm copied him. He started to signal what he wanted them to do.

"I know that something is going to happen tonight but I don't know when. We all need to be on guard." Each one of them got ready in their own way, some remained in the same position while others rolled on to their sides and left one leg sticking out of their bed. 45 had saved their arses on many different occasions. Over the last few years, he had become the dorms unofficial leader, which he quite liked, but still kept to himself.

After an hour, he had started to think that just maybe he might have made a mistake. He would get so much shit for this in the morning, getting everyone up half way through the night for nothing. Then he heard footsteps followed by voices. Whomever it was, was trying to be quick and quiet.

The lad with the cup hadn't taken his eyes off 45 the entire time he was awake. 45 signalled and the lad struck the cup once. There was a low click followed by a blinking sound. The lights flashed a couple of times before the room was fully illuminated, the doors swung inwards with a double handed shove.

"Get up, you lot, we have a..." by the time their handler had looked up every bed was empty. He scanned the room and as always was secretly impressed, every one of them stood at the end of their bunks, eyes forward, arms straight. Their handler was called Tom. He was not to be called anything else.

Tom, like all the other adults they had ever met, wore a uniform. He was a stocky man with short grey hair and scar that joined the corner of his mouth to the bottom of his right ear. Other than the one silver eye, he looked normal, but like anything they had come to know, looks were always deceiving.

"Wow, I was told this dorm was good." A second person had followed Tom into their room. She was taller, leaner and from general posture looked far more dangerous. She was dressed in what they would consider formal clothing. White shirt, black trousers, black tie and fitted jacket. The clothing didn't move as she walked, which usually meant that it was armoured in some way. Her hair was tied into a plait which hung down her back. Her boots sounded heavy against the floor and her hand never moved more than an inch from her sidearm.

She tapped her finger on the trigger guard almost like she was counting in seconds. By her demeaner and her minor facial expression, 45 assumed that she looked down at them, and he was right. In her world, these so-called people couldn't get any lower.

"Are they in the required bracket?" She asked.

"For the new guidelines, yes," Tom replied, "given so, I would recommend more experience to make them perfect." Tom smiled to himself and puffed out his barrel chest.

"Are there no problems or redundancies that need to be taken care of?" She made a conscious effort not to look directly at any of them, they were not worthy of her gaze.

"There are none from this dorm." Tom was very proud of this dorm. This dorm would be the greatest yet, fuck it, he could even get a medal.

"Good, move them to the Slab." The woman waved her arm towards the door.

The room remained still because not one of them understood what the adults had said to one another. Tom barked orders in a language they could understand. He walked up the dorm like he always had. He made sure everything was, in his own right, perfect. The boys were dressed and their holdalls were packed in under a minute. The woman shouted something from the doorway, it sounded like a garbled hiss than a collection of words.

"No room for any extras, dump all your bags." Tom's voice boomed across the dorm. She must have watched them pack but she still waited until they had finished before giving the order.

Every male except one, dropped his bag. Maybe he misheard or didn't want to let it go, but Tom was nose to nose with him in a second. "Drop the bag or do I have to lose my temper?" As Tom spoke his face crept into a slanted smile. His teeth gave off a faint silver tint.

Tom wasn't one to swear, he wasn't the type to get angry. 45 had heard him use bad language twice, and after each time the person he swore at didn't come back. Before Tom had finished his words, realisation had struck, the bag dropped to the floor with a fabric thud. He lowered his eyes so he didn't have to face Tom's gaze. Tom smiled and his silver eye seemed to rotate a little in its socket.

"Good, form two lines. When I say, go straight to loading area two, do not stop, do not mess me around, that is an order. Do you all understand?"

"Yes sir!" They were as one voice as they shouted their answer. Tom placed two fingers to his temple and listened. It was only seconds before he snarled to himself and turned back to the woman.

"I'm required to help move the seventeens. A fight has broken out and there have been some casualties."

"That's the last dorm of the upper bracket, isn't it?"

"Yes, it is," Tom felt his jaw clinch, "they just need discipline." He knew what was coming, that higher condescending tone that the transfer bigots used. It wasn't that he disliked them, he just wished he never had to see them.

"I know you didn't agree, but that's why the required limit was so severely reduced."

Tom had been forced to listen to her enough and to be fair, he hadn't been that interested in the first place. A dorm was going to make him look bad, and that's all he cared about. The two lines had been formed and now the final instructions were required.

"They know which route to take so just give them the order to go." Tom left the room, the double doors swung behind him. As soon as they had shut her demeanour changed.

"I fucking hate this place and the smell is disgusting. Why couldn't I get the female dorms for a change?" She walked the room for a few moments and gave them a sideways glance.

"Get going then!" They didn't move, they didn't understand. "I hate speaking low, why can't you shits learn my language." She stopped, breathed and spoke clearly. "Move out! Head straight for Area Two." She exaggerated this with a forceful flick of her arm, the other hand still tapped her trigger guard.

The dorm began to march through the doors and into the corridor, the first two out held the doors open. When the last of the dorm had passed, the door holders re-joined the lines.

As 45 walked through, he glanced at the polished metal post and saw his reflection. He couldn't remember when this habit had started, it was just something he did now but this would be the last time he saw this room. He was of a slim build but still strong, his crisp blue eyes and straight jawline set him apart from most.

The corridor was like all the others where they lived. Every surface was painted battleship grey and the floor was covered in coloured lines. Each line led to a specific location and the boys followed the green one. They marched down the line in perfect unison.

They passed dorm after dorm; a Minder stood ready at each one. The Minders were in any sense of the word, guards. The males couldn't see their faces because of the helmets but their eyes glowed amber or yellow. They never spoke directly to any of the residents. Even during a fight, whether it was a win or a loss, they still made no sound.

As the lines passed the last of the upper dorms, one set of double doors smashed open. They stopped as shattered glass tumbled across the floor. The lines split down the middle and hugged each wall so people other than them could get past.

Minders stormed past as the last of dorm seventeen broke into a full-blown riot. Two males armed with handmade blades attacked the Minder at the door. They repeatedly stabbed him in the neck and eyes. Dark red blood sprayed across the floor and walls. More Minders arrived and the flash and zap of their weapons lit the air.

The seventeen dorms, unlike the rest, had been given quite extensive combat training, which each of them used effectively. As more of the dorm piled into the corridor, seventeens and Minders fell in equal numbers. One of the rioters, that was covered in more gore than the rest, charged towards the two lines.

"We will save you from our pain!" He screamed, blood run down his face and past his broken teeth. The line turned and started to rush back up the corridor, 45 somehow managed to be the closest as the male grabbed his arm with a vice like grip. In hindsight, if 45 had known what the rest of his life intended, he probably would have welcomed this and let the guy stab him.

Two bangs rang out, 45 watched the males left eye vanish with one shot and the other blew a hole through his forehead. 45's attacker staggered back two steps before he slumped to the floor. The guy's death grip almost dragged 45 with him. 45 wrenched his arm free and tried to regain his composure. He wanted to take his eyes off the body, but the quickness that the colour drained from his skin controlled his gaze. He stepped back from the pool of blood.

"What the fuck are you doing? You have insulted me with your actions, you will stand down!" The woman that was in their dorm screamed over the noise of battle. Several males tried to rush towards her but didn't get very far. She picked her targets with lethal precession and three more bodies would be dragged to the incinerator this day. "Hold fast or I will execute you all!"

The corridor fell silent as an army of Minders poured into the area. The males from dorm seventeen were dragged away, either for recruitment or liquidation. No one was sure which was worse. 45 hadn't realised he'd been sprayed blood until the woman pointed it out to him.

"I said get moving, go to the Slab. This will not be delayed any longer, clean yourself up as you move." She turned to the Minders and gestured to the bodies with a disgusted nod. "Remove these and recycle them, but rip off their numbers first. The records have to be kept accurate."

One of his dorm mates shoved 45 to get his attention and he stumbled forward. He didn't recognise him at first but it was Terry. Terry's eyes made him stand out from the others, as they were pale green.

45 had been shown images of death and the butchering of animals, but not someone two feet from his face. If death could be that quick, how could you prepare for it?

They reformed their lines and marched around the bodies. Exit number two was behind three separate doors, each manned by a Minder. They queued and waited before they were led outside into the night air.

45 looked up into the cloudless sky. Millions of stars gazed back down at him, he knew what a star was but none of their names, or if they were even named at all. He'd never been outside at night before. It didn't change the taste in the air, the factories still pumped out their smog somewhere in the distance.

He didn't bother to look around as he knew there was nothing new to see. He was in their home city next to one of the towering exterior walls. If this had been during the day, he would have been able to see the buildings near the city centre disappear into the sky. He knew he would never be able to get that far into the city as that was not his role in life.

He had heard of several people that had tried to escape from their compound but they were caught, each one was not seen again. Even if they did make it out, where would they even attempt to go? It was better to accept and stay. 45 was more impressed by the sight in front of him. He had heard the name a lot, but this was the first time he had seen the Slab, and it was bigger than he could have imagined.

The Slab was a huge transport vehicle. The width alone took up five lanes of the highway. It looked like a gigantic beetle with its sloped armour and flat front. Doors lined the sides just above the rows of wheels. This vehicle was only usable at night due to the population of the city being under curfew after eleven o'clock.

"You stand there and follow on, are you trying to be stupid? You up front, eye's straight and no noise." A new uniform they had never seen before walked the lines as more dorms arrived. He spoke their language like it was his own. His long black hair was tied behind his head, a streak of white flowed down one side. His pale chiselled features where off set by his yellow-tinted eyes. They would look better suited on an animal than a person.

They waited in the cold, not one of them knew why they hadn't been ordered onto the Slab yet. The woman that had fired in the corridor strolled out of the closest building flanked by two more of the same uniform. Screams followed them but these were ended by muffled gun shots.

The man that was among the lines spotted them and strolled over with a smile and a wave. The next conversation went straight over 45's head.

"We should have left by now. What's taking so long?" He asked as he looked past them at the old building. It was falling apart, even this exact exercise of rounding up these people was a complete waste of time.

"There was a problem with a few of the higher numbered dorms. Some of the selected were very reluctant to go." Said the woman. A male with the same uniform nodded with agreement. He had a deep gash across his cheek which would need stitches, his blood had flowed down the front of his coat and arm.

"How many have we lost?" He asked the question but didn't really care for the answer.

"Across the whole academy? Maybe thirty recruits, give or take a few that were missed." She waited for the rage to show its ugly face but it never came. He sighed as if he had misplaced his keys or forgotten to tie his boot laces.

"We can always make more, losses are expected and many will be removed over the next couple of years," he looked down the lines of recruits.

"Any reports from the girl's dorms?"

"No problems that I have heard of yet. I believe they have already boarded their Slab and are on their way." She was too used to people starting to scream when they didn't get what they wanted and this man's calm manner made her nervous.

"We need a fresh start anyway. This method of training takes far too long," he sighed one last time.

"Ok, I'm tired and this whole situation is getting dull. Get them boarded and secure. It's too late for this shit and we only have a couple hours before the sheep start using the highways again."

"The Seventeens are still being processed due to the current incident." Her feelings for those people were not relevant, she had a job to do and that was all she cared about. The man had already started to walk up one of the boarding ramps.

"I don't give a shit if I'm honest so I'll get the wagon to pick them up. The research team always needs live targets." He spoke without slowing his pace or even a turn of his head.

"You heard what he said so get them all on the Slab." The woman shouted at the Minders as the male member of her team turned to her.

"Never met him before and I've done this run for ten years now. He seemed unnaturally calm for this sort of job, I'm more used to screaming and tantrums."

"Neither have I, but I think that's the head of Organic Research, Tyler Smith from the nearest academy. The same site that this lot is being taken to. If that is him then I hope I don't meet him again. He has a reputation for getting results no matter the cost. I don't have much hope for this lot," she shook her head.

"They might as well just execute these ones now and be done with it. Anyway, I'm hungry and could use a drink, maybe a shot of black."

*

The Slab was loaded with its cargo and so far, without incident. Each dorm tried their best to stick together as this was all they knew. 45 managed to get seated with most of his dorm. He didn't speak to them all and some he didn't even know their names. They just did what they had to do to get through each day. He tried to forget the corridor and think of better times, but none came to mind. The only person that he would call a friend sat next to him and spoke so low that only 45 could hear him.

"You thought of a name yet?" He had taken the name Jake. Jake heard Tom scream it at someone else once and kept it for himself.

"Not yet, I haven't had time to think about it." Jake smiled at 45's response. 45 was always thinking, it was like he never stopped.

"There's not much time left. I heard that when we get processed, they make you pick a name. If you don't give them an answer within a certain time limit, they give you one. I was told a certain squad leader was given the name Cockface until he reached a higher rank and was able to have it changed."

45 almost laughed, he tightened his jaw to stop himself but it still came out as a snort.

"You've still got blood on you," Jake gave a slight nod to the side of 45s face, "Just there." 45 raised a hand and touched the splatter.

"I know, I think some went in my mouth." He saw a flash back of the guys' eye as it disappeared into his skull. He would remember that pop sound for the rest of his life. Everyone went quiet as Minders began to walk up the aisles. One of them stood next to 45s seat and stared at him for a full ten seconds. 45 wanted to look round and meet its gaze but he knew it was better for him not to.

There wasn't much room but 45 still shifted in his seat to extend the distance between him and the Minder. The Minder must have gotten bored or been told to go somewhere else as it walked back up the aisle. As the Minder made another circuit of the Slab a minute later, he dropped a strip of cloth into 45's lap.

"I don't understand them at all. You ever heard one of those creepy bastards speak?" Jake said as he watched the Minder leave, Jake looked down as the Minder stopped and looked round at him. He prayed that it did not hear him as the last set of bruises he had received were almost completely faded.

"Nope," 45 said as he tried to clean as much blood off himself as he could. The seating inside the Slab was the same as a passenger plane, two seats then an aisle one after another until all available space was filled. Over a hundred males sat there.

They had tried once again to keep similar dorms together, but in the end, it didn't really matter. The woman from the corridor incident walked onto their floor. She stood on a platform at the front and cleared her throat, she was given the signal and started her rehearsed speech.

"We are taking you to your new living and training area. The old academy has been shut down so this is a clear out.

When we get to our new destination you will be processed and tested. You will be put into new dorms depending on your initiation results. You will not disappoint us."

She glared across the room and no one met her gaze, no hands were raised and no questions were asked. In the silence, she made her exit and went to get another drink, she was quickly joined by the other members of her team that had made similar speeches.

"I wondered why they were grabbing everyone at once." Jake said. 45 was more interested in the blood stuck to the inside of his ear.

"What do you think is going to be built in place of the academy then?"

45 shrugged, he wouldn't see it or be there so it didn't mean much to him. The section they were seated in started to get restless as it felt like they had been sat still for ages. They heard the engines rumble into life and felt everything rise up slightly.

From the outside, the Slab raised its hydraulics and the monstrous wheels began to turn. The nights in the city were always quiet. The 11pm curfew for all non-military personnel were a main factor for this. The residents of the city were also not allowed pets as this encouraged independent thought, which was heavily controlled in their society. On the plus side, road kill was never a problem.

Chapter 2

The driver of the Slab sat in front of two dozen screens. Other than the screens, he was surrounded by flashing lights and control panels. No one other than him knew what half of these buttons did, even though most of them weren't used any more. It didn't concern him as the screens were the most important part of his task.

The camera feeds covered the whole of its exterior and the road into the distance. There wasn't a square inch that wasn't covered and if there was a problem, he would know about it. The driver didn't really drive the Slab, he just made sure there were no issues or delays.

His left eye rotated in its socket. This mechanical eye processed ten times the information his right could, and it fed this into the augmented part of his brain. He ran his hands through his scruffy hair with a sigh and a stretch. It had been a long night and he just wanted to get into his soft bed and go to sleep.

He grabbed his favourite mug, because he knew a coffee would make him feel better, especially at the strength he was going to make it. He snapped two coffee capsules and dropped them inside, and then another two. The cup began to fill up as the powder turned to liquid and expanded.

As the Slab thundered down the highway its huge wheels passed within inches of a lamp post, but no alarms sounded to indicate a possible problem. His coffee was almost ready, he could smell the liquid as it bubbled. The Slab listed to the left and tore the next lamp post clean out of the ground. The Slabs wheels twisted the metal post onto itself and spat it back onto the tarmac.

The people within the Slab didn't feel a thing as the hydraulics reacted to the object and reset. Several lights flashed red as an alarm sounded and the driver flicked his eyes across the screens in a second.

"Fuck sake." He tapped on several buttons without even a sideways glance. Its wheels kissed the next lamp post as the Slab corrected its position. The warning for proximity only flashed on when the hazard had already passed. The driver slid his finger down a panel and lowered their speed to a crawl.

With a sigh, he dialled the number for emergency support. A face appeared on the main screen. He seemed a little too happy to have gotten a call in the middle of the night. His smile was excessively big as he grinned from ear to ear. His eyes looked like they were hidden behind a set of dark goggles, but these were, in fact, in place of them.

"You have reached sector 27 maintenance. How can I help on this fine morning?" The person on the other end recognised the driver immediately. He was about to have a joke when the driver tapped his index finger next to his eye.

I'm being watched. Is what that gesture said. The driver looked at the clock and it wasn't even past 4am.

"Good morning maintenance. The Slab is moving down highway 272 and we have had a minor incident. We have struck lamp post G782."

"That's not good news driver, is the damage causing an obstruction?" The goggles flashed different colours as he spoke. Data flowed from an external source straight into them.

"Yes maintenance, the debris is across three lanes, east bound."

"Thank you for your report, there are already droids and a group of lows on the way. You may need to get your AI recalibrated so this doesn't happen again." His smile remained big and toothy.

"That will be my first priority when we arrive at the facility. Thank you for your time on this matter." They exchanged a nod and the screen switched its feed to an external camera.

"Fucking prick, hate that guy," he sipped his coffee and with a sputter, spat the contents onto the floor, "arsehole people." He turned and tipped all of the liquid into the bin. He was going to find out who had mixed up his drink capsules again and have them shot. He pressed a couple buttons and slid his finger up a panel. He watched the power levels increase until the Slab was at full speed again. The main door behind the driver slid open and Tyler walked into the room.

"Do we have a problem?" The driver's seat spun 180 degrees so he could face his guest. "Only a minor problem sir, the Slab's intelligence is having issues. I've had to report a lamp post it just tore out of the ground. The whole unit keeps listing to the left. I had performed multiple checks but the system checks keep coming back clear. So, at this point I cannot confirm if there even is a fault at all."

"Have you sent the report away?" Tyler asked as the driver lent across his control panel and pressed a big green button.

"Yes Sir!" The driver said with a nod. He wasn't sure if these reports had to be sent as he was convinced no one read them. He once signed one report with the name 'Bairy Hollocks' and nothing ever came of it.

"Don't slow down again, you hear me. We have been delayed enough as it is without this adding to my timeframe." Tyler scanned the room as he spoke. He had forgotten the original reason as to why he was heading towards the driver's cab.

"Yes sir," the driver saluted and bowed his head. Tyler returned the gesture with a wave of his hand as the door closed behind him. The driver's seat spun back to its original position. He tapped at his keyboard to turn off the impact alarm and then turn on the air conditioning.

Cooled air flowed into the room from two vents. The driver wasn't sure if it was the humid air making him warm up or Tyler. The far-left screen flashed red and showed two warning messages. He turned his head to one side then shook it with a sigh, he always disliked this machine.

Procedure is to slow down and check the fault.

Procedure must always be followed without fail for risk of injury or death.

His finger was almost on the speed panel, but he was ordered to not slow down. It was strange as he had never felt this sick before, his mouth tasted of bile and his eyes watered. He pressed his index finger to his temple.

"Engine room respond?" As the driver waited for a response, he pulled an empty bin towards him, the urge to throw up seemed to increase as he waited.

"Yes Colin, what's the problem?" the voice was almost drowned out by engine noise and other people's voices. The more he listened, the more they sounded closer to screams then speech.

"Engine four is showing a fault. It's not showing full power at my end, also, the system thinks there is a fire in the control room."

"Why have you not slowed us down first?" Asked the Chief Engineer. Colin heard him pick something up and throw it with immense force. The sound of an impact was followed by a cry of pain.

"I have been ordered not to. This has come straight from Research Head Tyler." Colin spat into the bin as his feeling of sickness doubled.

"There are no fires in the control room because that is where I'm standing. Hold on let me check on the engine." The Chief Engineer screamed something in the Low language. All the driver could hear was the rhythmic drone of the machines. This went on for about two minutes. He didn't understand the low language as he had no reason to learn the filth.

"There are no problems with any of our equipment so I will reset the warning systems from here. That should remove the messages off your screen. All pressure, hydraulics, and fuel flow are in the green, even the temperature is at a stable level for once. Is the AI reporting a fault that's not really there?" The driver watched as both red messages turned green with a satisfying click and vanished.

"It's possible, thank you for your help with this matter." He no longer felt sick as he didn't need to slow down anymore.

"Have a safe drive, if you need us, we are always here." The connection between the two went dead. Colin sat back in his seat and kicked the bin to the other side of his station. He thought about what just happened.

This machine is falling apart, should have been decommissioned years ago.

Colin groaned as three more screens flashed red at him. One of them told him that the driver was not in his seat. He shook his head and reached for the speed panel but caught himself just before his finger touched the control. He glanced between the screens and the panel before he pulled the bin between his legs once more.

"This is going to be a long trip," he sighed and reached for another set of capsules.

Chapter 3

The recruits, as they would be now known, had a rather pleasant trip. There was the odd incident between the upper dorms but nothing that a hard jab with a stun rod couldn't fix. 45 overheard one of the others ask to go to the toilet but was told there wasn't one.

Thanks for that, now I need to go.

"You thought about what's coming next?" Jake asked, he wasn't too good with the obvious. He ran his fingers up the inside of the harness and gave it a tug. 45 wasn't really paying attention as he counted the number of seats on his row again.

"We are going to be tested and put in dorms depending on what our results are. Our academy was all military so I'm going to guess it will be anything within that bracket." He turned so their eyes met. "But I am guessing Jake, don't take what I say to heart." Jake already had as this was what he did.

"Ok, ok, I got it. So, what you are saying is we might not be in the same dorm anymore?" Jake shook his head. He had already felt his hands begin to sweat at the thought of it.

"That's a possibility yes, but don't worry about it now. If you have to worry about it, then start near the time or you will just stress yourself out." Jake nodded. He didn't really understand, but 45 had a way with words. Metal speakers caked with rust threw out sound and dust all at once.

"Approaching drop-site in ten minutes, prepare to disembark." The voice was electronic, something that could have come straight from a sound board. The next voice was that woman's again, 45 wished he could put a name to it.

"We are running late. The Slab will be evacuated in less than two minutes. As an incentive to move quickly, the last one to leave will be executed." She said this like it was an everyday occurrence.

To say, this started a surge of panic was an understatement. 45 watched the section he was in degrade into chaos. This was all watched on hidden cameras to the amusement of the research team. They took notes to see who took charge or who couldn't handle the pressure.

45 took a lot of their interest as he remained still while others tried to rip apart their seats or harness. Some of the recruits broke finger nails and teeth as they tried to break free. 45 looked around for any Minders or other personnel, but there was none that he could see. They had been left on their own.

He looked up at the newly installed surveillance camera. It seemed to turn towards him as the lens focused.

Who is watching us? 45 thought to himself.

"What do we do?" Jake was about to join in with the madness, but he turned to 45 as he knew he had already worked out a plan.

"The seat won't unlock till we stop. They need to calm down, they're wasting energy for no reason."

Jake raised both of his arms and began to open and close his fists. He kept this up till more of their dorm noticed and joined in. Nearly half of the section had stopped and followed Jake's movement.

"What do we do?" Jake still had his hands up.

"I'm not in charge." More of this section joined in with Jake's hand signal.

"Yeah, I know, but what do we do?" 45 sighed, why was it always down to him to make a decision.

Could no one else have an idea for once? He raised his voice so everyone could hear him in their section.

"The seat harness will unlock when the vehicle comes to a halt, so stop wearing your selves out. When we get the signal undo your strap and head for the door, aisle seats first then the rest. Don't block others and don't stop. Is everyone with me?"

"Yes!" The sound came from thirty of them but sounded like one word. Any of them that weren't in 45s dorm followed suit as there was no one else to follow. 45 stared into the back of the seat in front. He knew eyes were on him and he tried to not let it become a distraction. Jake kept his voice low so only 45 would have heard him.

"What about the people at the back? One of them is going to be last."

"Someone always has to be the last one, Jake. That's just the way it is as they are the rules that we have been given. We just have to be quicker than the rest of the Slab and get our section out first." 45 gave a quick look around the section and there were a number of, what he thought were, older recruits.

Why has no one else wanted to lead!

The electronic voice cracked into life. 45 gripped his harness with both hands and waited. The Slab had already stopped and lowered its hydraulics in preparation for the unloading ramps to extend.

"We will disembark in 5. 4. 3. 2. 1." The LEDs on their harnesses turned green. 45 pulled the latch, pressed a button and twisted the whole buckle, it fell apart with ease. It was going well as 45 got to the aisle, no one blocked, no one slowed down. He saw a pair of arms flailing about in an aisle seat ahead of him. The lad had placed his feet against the seat in front and tried to force himself out but all this did was take the skin off his arms.

"Help me, my harness is stuck, help me please!" 45 just wanted to run past him, he had no ties to this person and he knew nothing about him. The lad glanced round and they looked straight at each other.

Something clicked in his brain and 45 couldn't stop himself. He side-stepped into the row and stood in front of him. 45 grabbed his harness, the light on the main buckle blinked red. He shouted at a couple boys from his dorm and Jake joined in as well. Together they tried to rip the harness. It didn't even stretch as they all pulled, it wasn't going to break.

It's not going to snap. I didn't bring a blade and neither did Jake. Why did I make this my problem?

45 dropped to his knees and scanned the floor for anything sharp but it was swept clean. As he stood, he saw a number of his dorm were stood still and watched him work. He waved them on to get them out of the Slab. They hesitated for only a moment before they made their way outside. There weren't many people left in their section and they had to go as soon as possible.

"What's going on?" A guy that looked older than them seemed to appear out of nowhere.

34

"The fucking seats jammed Frankie, get me out of here, please." The lad pleaded with his friend. 45 tried to think of an idea but he kept coming back to the unbreakable straps.

Leave the straps and think of something else.

"Sorry brother, I'm not getting killed for a faulty seat. We can't take you with us."

"I'm begging you, please don't leave me here. I don't want to die because of a fucking seat." The lad pleaded with Frankie but he was about to walk away when 45 grabbed his arm.

"Take the seat." They turned their attention to 45.

"What did you say?" Frankie said accompanied with a strange look. Frankie had thought 45 had asked him if he wanted a sweet.

"Take the whole seat, everything we use is repairable so the seats could have a release latch." Frankie was already on his back and pulled himself under the seat.

"I think I have something don't let the seat fall on me." There was a loud crack and the seat wobbled. Frankie wiggled out from beneath it and grabbed hold of one side. Between the five of them they carried the lad and the seat out the closest exit.

They got some astonished looks as they carried their passenger down the ramp. 45 knew they could be the last ones out of their level. They dropped the seat on the concrete as an adult in uniform walked over to them. Maybe because it was dark, but at first 45 didn't recognise Tom.

"Hi ya boys, what's all this then?" 45 stepped forward before anyone else had a chance to speak.

"His harness jammed so we brought the seat with us." Jake was about to join in and support his friend when he saw the signal that 45 had made behind his back. Jake stopped and faced forward.

"Well, the problem is, your group left at the same time and the last person needs to go." Tom had a glint in his eye that 45 had never seen before.

"That was me." 45 had already said it before his brain had worked out why.

"And which one of you had the idea to remove military property?" Tom asked as he looked between them and then down to the seat. The damage was done so 45 didn't hold back. He didn't think it could get any worse.

"That was also me. I thought it was better if we didn't leave anyone behind." Tom's face said it all as it turned red.

"Well you said it yourself, you were last off, you fucked up kid." In the blink of an eye, Tom drew his side arm, aimed it at 45's face, smiled and pulled the trigger.

*

Two corridors down from where the driver sat was a security door shadowed by four Minders. In this room, twenty people stared at monitors. These monitors were hooked up to dozens of cameras positioned throughout the Slab, some hidden and some you just couldn't miss.

"When's the announcement going out?" One researcher asked another. Their uniform was mostly white with a black trim, on their lapels was an embroidered blue cross within a circle.

"About four minutes, why?" he said with a grin.

"I forgot my popcorn. I was hoping I could go get some." Both of them laughed, maybe a little louder than they should have as Tyler walked over.

"Everything set?" He asked and leaned in to look at the monitors. The researcher went rigid and sat upright.

"Yes sir. All exits and corridors are covered, and we have more cameras in the seating areas than before." He pressed a button and every camera feed that he was in charge of flashed onto his screens.

"Have you picked out an example for your area yet?" Tyler picked up the researcher's prep work to make sure it was up to standard. After a quick glance he dumped it back onto the desk.

"Yes sir. Aisle seat so he's harder to ignore." The researcher pointed to the screen so Tyler could see his choice.

"Why not pick one of the smaller ones instead?" The researcher remembered what happened last time and had changed his choice accordingly.

"If they're too small and with enough force they can be pulled through the harness. Both of his shoulders dislocated but that's not what we are going for here."

"Very true." Tyler nodded and smiled. He liked this researcher more than the rest. "What do you call yourself and what is your number?"

"My name is Jimmy, sir, and it is 17689REA." Tyler nodded again and made a mental note of the number. This was stored with the rest of his digital data.

"Good work, look forward to hearing from myself."

"Thank you, sir." Tyler walked back up to the other end of the room and sat down into his chair. It took more than a few steps to get there.

"That was lucky." The researcher next to him blew out a long exhale of breath.

"That's a nice way of putting it, the broadcast is going out now."

"Approaching drop-site in ten minutes, prepare to disembark." That electronic voice made the researchers teeth itch. Tyler typed something on his keyboard with one of his slanted smiles, the one people learned to hate. He tapped the side of his head before he spoke.

"You're all good to go, make sure you all give them your best smiles and then wait for the screams." *Lights, camera, action.* Tyler's smile grew more twisted with those words.

"We are running late. The Slab will be evacuated in less than two minutes. The last one from each section will be executed." Jimmy smiled to himself.

The chaos was always something to look forward to. His screens covered sections C and D and his task was to look out for extraordinary leadership or problem solving. He also looked for any loose meat to be cut free, these were the cowards and possible risks.

He glanced between his screens. Section D was a complete mess but section C was the polar opposite. One lad had his hands up and signalled to the rest. Most of the section followed his lead. Jimmy clicked through his camera feeds until he could get a better look at his face.

He brought up all of Jakes information and then pulled up all of 45's. At first, he thought Jake had taken the lead but soon realised that 45 was giving the orders. He checked the details on a few more of the boys. Quite a few of them seemed to not be stressed as the rest or not at all, it was odd that all of the good ones came from the same dorm. He checked section

D and wished he hadn't bothered, some sat there screaming while others just cried.

"Pathetic," Jimmy couldn't help the way he thought, it was just a job. He felt the Slab begin to slow. Now this is where everything got really interesting.

"Anything of importance to report?" Tyler called from his chair. Jimmy forwarded one of the section C camera feeds and all the necessary information and went back to his job. Section C emptied like a dream, no one fought as they left their deck in an orderly fashion.

Section D was a lost cause as a riot started. Several of the males had started to attack anyone that came near them. He never really understood why this happened to some of the recruits. All they had to do was leave the Slab and not be the last ones out.

There was always one section that degraded into anarchy and this time it had to be one of his, how boring. Jimmy turned back to section C to see what they would do about the locked harness.

"Would you look at that." Jimmy spoke more to himself as the same two boys stopped to help. They pulled at the straps and more joined in. "That's not going to work and you're running out of time lads."

"Anything good?" the guy that sat to his left leaned over.

"Possible two Category 1s and about thirty Cat 2s."

"That's not statistically possible is it." He thought Jimmy was taking the piss until he saw the feed.

Well, fuck me.

"What dorm is the majority in section C." Tyler shouted from his chair he couldn't help but smile. A mass of clicks echoed as every one's fingers struck their keyboards. Each person wanted to prove themselves to be the best and quickest in front of Tyler Smith.

"Thirty are from dorm 13C. The last few are scattered throughout the Slab," he started reeling off the section numbers "and two are in D."

Jimmy checked the feed and scanned the mess. He picked up their locaters and, in the chaos, they, without incident, fled their section. Three more researchers called out possible candidates. Jimmy turned back to the camera on C.

What are you doing? Jimmy thought as several of them yanked at the harness to free his pick.

"Why haven't they left him yet?" Said another researcher into Jimmy's ear as she leant over to see what was happening. Her sections had left their sacrifice behind without a second thought.

"It's him," Jimmy pointed to 45 on the screen, "he stopped to help and others joined."

"The harness won't break, they are wasting their time." She wanted to look away as she had seen this all before but for some unknown reason she couldn't.

"Double check that you are all still recording, I will be checking when I get back to my labs." Tyler shouted from his chair. He also watched section C with great interest and amusement. Jimmy glanced at his third screen and his recording was stable. The audio wasn't that important.

"Are they taking the seat? Well shit, they are taking the fucking seat." said the female researcher but Jimmy had missed it. All he saw was five lads struggle with a chair and carry it out of section C and down the exit ramp.

"Well done boys, well done, best show in years." Tyler stood up and clapped his hands. "Jimmy, send a Minder to make sure no one shoots those two from section C. I can guarantee someone will try as they left as a group, and the rest of you." Everyone froze, was this good or bad, judging by the tone of his voice no one was quite sure. "Good work, you may be hearing from me in the near future."

Jimmy let out another long exhale of breath as he issued the guard orders to a Minder close by. What an evening he had had so far! Jimmy had assumed the best part of his night would have been when he swapped the drivers drinking capsules again.

Chapter 4

45 had closed his eyes and thought this was it, this was his end. He heard the two-gun shots but felt no pain. He forced his eyes open and stood in front of him was a Minder. The Minder had taken both bullets to the gut. He didn't show any signs of pain nor did he bleed. Tom's eyes bulged and his skin tightened over his face. He opened his mouth to scream at the Minder but stopped himself as he pressed a finger to his temple.

"Yes sir, all is taken care of, what about the other stragglers. Do you want me to deal with them?" Tom nodded twice and leant round the Minder and winked at 45, but he spoke to the group.

"All's good now, you lot have passed this little test." He took what looked like a metal key from his pocket. This slipped into the central clasp on the faulty harness, and it fell open.

"Form your lines and get ready to be processed." Tom's smile was clearly over exaggerated. "Good luck!"

45 tried not to look towards the Slab as he heard more gun shots from inside its shell.

"Oh dear, I guess some didn't pass the tests," 45 turned towards Tom, their eyes met and Tom's smile didn't fade, "off you go then." For better or worse that was the last time 45 saw Tom. In hindsight, compared to the rest of the people he was going to meet, Tom wasn't that bad.

"Yes Sir." Jake grabbed 45's arm and pulled him into a line and lowered his voice to a whisper. "What the hell just happened? He shot at you." 45 just shook his head.

"I have no idea what that Minder was doing. I should be dead." 45 said as Jake nodded. Jake thought about the two shots and where they ended up.

"That Minder didn't make a sound or even flinch. They must still be lodged inside it somewhere." 45 couldn't think straight, and he'd only just realised how cold it was. A hand grasped 45's shoulder, he turned and it was the guy that had been trapped in the chair.

"Thank you, I owe you my life. I will repay you someday." He walked past and joined another line.

"You made a friend," Jake looked around and Frankie nodded back at him, "make that two." 45 let himself smile before he spoke.

"Jake, there is a chance that we may never meet them again. We do not know what is going to happen inside that building."

"That's true, but the more people that like you the less chance that someone's going to stab you in the back."

It's normally the people closest to you that do the most harm.

45 chose to keep that to himself. He scanned his surroundings for the first time and only now noticed how big the building in front of them was. It must have been forty floors high and he could only guess at how many floors were underground.

He couldn't see many windows but it was still dark outside. They filed through large steel shutters and into corridors. There was a bleep noise as he passed through a metal detector and into a large hall.

Just past the metal detectors, they were grabbed by more people in uniforms and split up from those around them. 45 nodded at Jake as they were told to join different lines. These lines followed a hand rail system to booths. Each booth had a window and an intercom system. Without the glass being smashed, nobody would be able to get to the person inside. There were twenty booths and rails that led up to each one. Before they had been split 45 squeezed Jake's arms.

"You will be fine, just follow the training and do what they ask." Jake nodded once as he ground his teeth. He wasn't fond of change and 45 had always been there with him, and now he wasn't.

The line 45 joined seemed to move quite quickly, then grind to a halt for five minutes before moving again. A lad that looked maybe a year older than 45 stood behind him and couldn't help but ask.

"What are you going to call yourself then?" 45 didn't turn as he answered.

"I haven't thought about it." He really hadn't, this was the most thought he'd given to his name since he knew he had to pick one over a year ago.

"Well your turn is coming up so think of something or," the lad pointed past the side of 45's head, "he will pick one for you." An older man with glasses sat in their booth. His face was covered in scars and from where 45 stood both of his hands looked metallic. Now 45 was closer he could hear what was being said.

"Number?" he asked.

"452364BHF," a male replied.

"Selected name?"

"Erm," the lads eye went wide as he fought to remember the name he wanted.

"If you don't pick one I will and I'm shit with names."

"Erm, Charlie, please."

"Your data has been saved Charlie. Follow the line and you will be moved to the testing area, NEXT!" He screamed.

The questions that the man asked never changed. 45 tried to catch anything from the other booths but the hall was too noisy. Two lads were between him and the booth. For the first time that he could remember he felt nervous.

Why am I nervous, this makes no sense? 45 thought as he tried to control his breathing.

"NEXT!" one more and it was his turn. Now he was close to having his first panic attack as his heart thumped against his ribcage, this feeling was brand new to him. 45 could feel the sweat run down his back. He clenched his fists to stop the shake in his hands. He started to count the metal rivets that lined the edges of the glass window.

"NEXT!" 45 walked up to the booth and stopped at the designated mark. "Number?" from the wrists to his fingertips the man's hands were all metal. The plating slid inside itself near the joints as he tapped on a kinetic keyboard. 45 then realised he hadn't answered and the man was staring at him.

"Sorry, it's 454376AHF," he tapped at his keyboard. 45 thought that the clicking that his fingers made was awesome, his nerves long forgotten.

"Selected name?" 45 remained silent as his mind went blank.

"If you don't pick one I will and I'm shit with names," still, 45 had nothing to say.

"Ok then." The guy turned in his seat and looked at the wall to his left. It appeared his eyes scanned down a list but it could have been anything. His eyes stopped and he smiled to himself and turned back to his keyboard.

"From now on your new name is Quakers." 45 felt something like nothing before in his life. Time seemed to stop, he felt his heartbeat slow to nothing and felt relaxed, like getting into a hot bath at the end of a stressful day. He would have to guess at the feeling as he had never done that before.

He wished he could stay at this point for eternity but that was not meant to be. A presence was with him, and this presence gave a push, just enough to get him shifted in the right direction.

"Wait I have a name," The guy stopped just before his metal fingers touched plastic, "Please, I'm sorry to waste your time."

"Go on, I've not got all day."

"Vandeaga."

"Spell it please."

"V.A.N.D.E.A.G.A."

"Your data has been saved Vandeaga, follow the line and you will be moved to testing, NEXT!" Vandeaga almost hesitated but started to follow the line.

"Oh, and Vandeaga, that's a good name I've never heard it before." The man gave him a mini salute. It was more of a gesture of goodwill than a mark of respect.

Vandeaga, where did that come from? He had also never heard that name before. He didn't know now and wouldn't for a very long time.

He followed the line at his feet and soon joined the others, once again they queued shoulder to shoulder. He glanced round to see if he recognised anyone, but he didn't. They slowly filtered into another hall.

This one was lined with countless stainless-steel chairs. He tried to count down one line then multiply by the other, but he couldn't see them all and lost count near to a thousand. Vandeaga sat down and tried to think of something other than the Slab incident but he couldn't. He still couldn't believe Tom was going to shoot him in the face.

"Thank fuck that shits over with," a guy that could have been Vandeaga's senior slumped down in the chair next to him, "Almost forgot my own name." He stared ahead like he hadn't addressed anyone other than himself. He turned to Vandeaga and pointed at his face.

"You've got blood on you."

"I thought I got most of it off, it can wait." The lad just nodded as he didn't really care.

"What are you aiming for?" He asked in such a way that made it clear he wasn't interested, he just wanted to pass the time.

"What do you mean?"

"I want leadership or ghost squad. It all sounds like a laugh." He drummed his fingers on his thighs as he spoke.

"I hadn't thought about it before now." There were moments that this information was given to them but it wasn't required for a test so Vandeaga didn't pay it much attention.

"I hope for your sake you don't get put in my dorm because you are no match for me, son." Vandeaga wasn't sure if it was the tone of his voice or the fact that he called him son, but he felt his face turn red. He didn't like to lose his temper as it showed a lack of control but, sometimes, he just had to let go.

"My names Vandeaga, not son, and we'll see about that." The lad's amber eyes glinted as he smiled, the colour matched his hair.

"My name's Taradin. You should remember this because one day it will mean something. I wasn't interested in knowing yours."

Vandeaga forced himself to grip his chair and remain seated. That primal part of his brain wanted to smash Taradin's face in and make him swallow his own teeth, but that wouldn't do him any good, not here anyway.

He looked away from Taradin in order not to show how he had affected him. It was at that point he noticed that there were girls in the hall. He had never seen one his age before and some of them looked quite similar.

He slowly looked behind him and for the first time in that hall he used his eyes and looked properly. In fact, there were six boys all of the same age all sat in different rows, but other than the hair cut they were identical. He glanced to his right and another six that looked different to the first but were still identical to each other.

This isn't right. His mind tried to figure out what could be in front of him. The more he stared the more people looked the same. Some of the opposite sex also looked far too similar. *Could there be someone that looks like me here too?*

He quickly scanned the people he could see but no one was like him. *There is something very wrong here.* There was something horribly wrong, but Vandeaga didn't know what it was and he felt sick. He wanted to leave and he almost did, but that was until the wall in front of him lit up and a face appeared.

"Welcome to our house." There was a roar as everyone present cheered, Vandeaga didn't join in. The face was a blend of female and male features, a computer-generated image to appeal to everyone.

Vandeaga checked the corners of the room as best as he could but he couldn't see where the image was coming from. "We have your names and numbers. You have been divided into test groups. You will face a series of tests that will tell us, and you, your future career path."

"I'm going to be an Officer. You'll see I've got the drive for it." Taradin looked straight at Vandeaga. Vandeaga didn't give a shit right now. His mind wasn't even in this hall any more. The face continued its speech.

"Whatever you are chosen to do, you will do your best at it," the emphasis on WILL was clear. The face flickered slightly as it said the word. It bared a mixture of pointed black and red teeth in a silent ear to ear scream for one tenth of a second.

There was another cheer, but this time Vandeaga noticed more people didn't join in. He once again forced himself to stay seated. Something compelled him to see this through. The face called out a series of numbers. As the numbers were read out the people concerned stood up and walked to the front.

It seemed like hours had passed as groups of twenty were called and lead away. When it was finally his turn to go, he almost ran. He couldn't help but see the same faces over and over again.

Later, he would describe them as those with dead eyes, or simpler than that, the Similars. That constant forward stare, like they would wait until they were ordered to blink. What amazed him more was that no one else seemed to notice, but if they did see it then each person hid their feelings better than he could.

His group were led out of the hall and down a corridor. Minders stood at every doorway as they were taken to their testing room. If 45 hadn't looked right at the Minder as he walked by, he would have missed it. It appeared that one of them nodded at him. He looked down and noticed the two bullet holes in its stomach. The open wounds still refused to bleed.

Can this not get any more fucking weird?

He wasn't sure who that was aimed at, maybe even the Creator himself, but he had hoped that something heard him. Whoever it was, wasn't listening as this was just the start of the first day.

They must have walked a mile before the group were seated in a small room. Each person had a desk and on that desk was laid a simple piece of paper with a pen attached. On this paper was a series of squares set in columns with letters on one side and six numbers after each letter. This repeated across the front and back of the sheet.

As each person sat down, they scanned the paper to see if there were any clues as to what they were about to do. A person in a white uniform was already stood at the front of the room. She waited as they took their seats. Bar one every seat was filled, yet she waited for confirmation that there was no one left to come.

She tapped the side of her head and listened before she nodded and took her hand away. The equipment from the empty desk was removed and disposed of. Apart from the silver eyes and the sidearm, she looked relatively normal. The woman had already scanned each person for hidden weapons as they walked in. There wasn't a need to but it was an old habit.

"You will be asked a multitude of questions." She started to talk so suddenly, Vandeaga almost jumped.

"Answer these questions honestly and you will receive an accurate score. If you try to mislead the test in any way you will be removed." Everyone knew that being 'removed' didn't just mean from the room.

There was no emotion in her voice like she had done this a thousand times, which to her credit, she had. She remained stood up as there was no desk or chair for her to use.

"I will read out the questions and you will listen to each one carefully. I will never repeat myself and I will read them only once. After each question, I will give four or six possible answers. Next to the corresponding letter you will mark your selected answer. There will be no talking or fidgeting, I don't even want you to look at each other. This test will determine your future so you will take it seriously. The test will start in sixty seconds, so centre yourselves and concentrate." Even though she said the word 'read' multiple times, the woman wasn't holding anything. Her hands held firmly behind her back.

Vandeaga looked down at his desk and to his horror realised he had nothing to write with. He shot his hand up to get her attention, this action was so quick he jarred his shoulder. She didn't look too impressed at being waved at. Both of her silver eyes rotated as she stared at him.

"What is it, Vandeaga?" It almost threw him when she said his name and he had to rethink what he was about to say.

"I have nothing to write with." He picked up the sheet of paper to prove that it wasn't underneath it.

"Then you have lost it and have failed this test before it has even begun." There never was a pen on that desk but this was a test within a test and Vandeaga was unfortunate to have picked that desk to sit at.

"You can be removed now or you can be removed later?" Mid-way through she couldn't be bothered to speak to him anymore and looked to the back wall.

"It's your choice and I don't care which you decide."

"I will stay for now, thank you." Vandeaga said as he scanned the desk for something, anything to get him out of this situation.

"The test will start in thirty seconds." The desk was perfect, no splinters or sharp edges, then Vandeaga had an idea. He slid out of his chair, took off his belt and dropped it to the floor. The woman was intrigued as he used the bottom of the chair leg to smash down onto the belt buckle until she heard the metal loop snap.

He pulled off his shirt and carefully folded the garment into a bowl shape. He then slashed his thumb with the broken metal loop. Blood pooled into the synthetic fabric. When he had enough to use, Vandeaga stuck his thumb in his mouth.

The fabric absorbed a little of the liquid but most remained inside the make shift inkwell. He bent down and yanked the lace out of his boot and dripped the tip into the blood. He looked straight at the woman and nodded.

She almost forgot herself and was about to clap because she had never seen that before. She was more used to test subjects having a slip but this was not over yet. Regardless of what just happened she had a test to run and began to speak.

"Question one."

A. You have been asked your number by someone that is unworthy, do you?

1. Give them your name and number.

2. Give them your name only.

3. Ignore them.

4. Ask why they need to know.

5. Strike them for asking.

6. Kill this person for speaking to you.

Vandeaga didn't need to think about it, he dabbed a dot of blood on number four. The questions kept coming and he dotted the answer best suited to the situation. Some questions he did not understand.

The basic medical training would have come in handy if he had bothered to remember half of it. The same could be said for the basic computer training that he only just scraped through. It wasn't that he didn't like computers or their functions, it's just that the information didn't stick.

The decision-making questions are where he excelled, but that was the whole point of the test, see what would be considered a foundation and build on top of it. A male who sat at the front hadn't moved since the test had started. His hands were clamped on to each side of the desk like he was scared to touch the pen or the piece of paper. He just stared at them with those unblinking eyes as his fingers turned white with the pressure.

Vandeaga thought he had seen him before, or someone who looked identical to him. Without warning or even a sound his grip tightened and he started to repeatedly slam his face into the hard-wooden top. There was a crunch as his nose shattered and blood flowed but he didn't stop.

"Stay seated all of you." The woman instructed the rest of the room with a wave of her hand.

No one moved? Vandeaga thought to himself as he watched the male rearrange his own face with repeated strikes. The woman placed a finger to her temple.

"Slip in room sixteen, we have a slip in room sixteen, send Minders in at once." The woman wasn't concerned about her safety because she had a hand attached to her sidearm. She just didn't want to clear up the mess after he was finished.

The door swung open and three Minders pushed their way into the room. The guy had pretty much already destroyed most of his own face. Hot blood sprayed over the two people who sat either side of him. Each of them closed their eyes and forced themselves not to react.

The last impact happened just before the Minders placed a hand on him. There was a loud crunch as the wooden desk snapped in two. He slumped forward onto the splintered wood. Between the three Minders they picked up the body and dragged him out the room. All that was left behind was a pool of blood, a broken desk and scattering of teeth.

The woman visibly sighed and without a second thought continued with the test. It must have been a regular Tuesday in the office for her. The rest of the test passed without incident. The last question threw Vandeaga a little.

"Question one hundred and ten."

6E. How long has this test been running?

1. 1 hour.
2. 1 hour 15 minutes.
3. 1 hour 45 minutes.
4. 2 hours.
5. Not sure.
6. Does not matter.

Vandeaga had already marked number six but before he'd thought about it. After, he would say a test is a test and will take as long as it needs. There was however a clock behind the door as they walked in, no one saw it, no one ever did.

"Mark your name and number at the top of the paper." She looked straight at Vandeaga as she knew he was going to have trouble with this little problem.

Now what do I do? There was no possible way he could accurately write his name or number with the end of a boot lace dipped in blood. He needed something thinner and looked down for the remains of his belt.

He never saw who moved it but it was gone and couldn't help him now. He was about to stand up and try and grab a piece of broken wood when a pen bounced onto his desk. He grabbed hold of it like it was made of pure gold.

"Who threw that?" She walked over and yanked the pen out of his hand, but it was too late, Vandeaga had already marked his paper. Everyone else sat ridged in their seats and not one of them dared to take their eyes off the front wall.

"I will find out who threw it, who else is missing a…" She had to stop because the pen wasn't one of hers and with one squeeze, crushed the plastic into fine splinters. "The Test is over, now you will be escorted back to the hall." The group stood in unison and left. Vandeaga thought about not making a mess with the fluid in his cloth bowl but the room was already a disaster zone and threw on his shirt.

Most of his blood spilled onto the table and floor. The blood that had stuck on his shirt just added to the rest that he already had. The woman didn't seem to care as it wasn't her job to clean up after an incident, or to clean up at all. In the corridor a taller male made sure he stepped in line behind Vandeaga as they walked.

"I thought that was a good throw, didn't you?" He spoke so low, you couldn't even call it a whisper.

"That was your own pen, wasn't it?" Vandeaga never turned his head in case the woman still had her eyes on them.

"Don't know what you're talking about mate, but Frankie said to say hi." The lad brushed past him and moved ahead. Vandeaga couldn't help but smile. On the way back to the hall the group passed several people being led away by Minders. They were the failures and they were to be 'removed'.

They took seats in the hall once more and waited. Vandeaga started to feel tired, not physically but mentally. He tried his best not to let it show but his eyes wouldn't cooperate with him.

They remained there for another five hours, the Minders in the hall poked a number of recruits with their batons to wake them up. The electric snap, followed by a scream woke the rest. The last group had been taken for their test but no one came back this time. The main wall lit up once more and that blend of features appeared.

"You have all done well. Your scores have been taken and checked. Each one of you has been assigned a career path and a new dorm. Depending on your speed of progression this may change. You will be called and you will follow your assigned Minders to your dormitories. Good luck."

The face flashed its teeth and there was a cheer. It started to call out numbers in rapid succession and the hall was emptied in less than an hour.

Chapter 5

Vandeaga stood at the end of a metal framed bed. The crisp white pillows and sheets looked almost too inviting. He wanted to turn and flop face first onto it. He didn't even care about taking off his bloodied clothes, all he could think about was sleep. The need to lay down almost blocked out the smell of bleach and cleaning chemicals, but not quite.

Every one of them stood to attention and waited, whether this was a test or not they didn't know but this seemed to be the trend lately. Their dormitory was the same as all the others he had been in. A long room lined with beds, each bed had a simple side table and a lockable metal chest at the foot end.

He didn't need to look to know he was part of a group of thirty. To his disbelief Jake was stood two beds down. Terry was one bed down from Jake and a couple others from his dorm were there too. That guy that threw him the pen in the test was up the far end, and the lad that got locked in the chair stood to his left.

The only problem he had was that he recognised Taradin and he had mixed feelings about the prick. Taradin had pushed past him as they entered the dorm and gave him a smug look. Vandeaga was torn about what to do about him.

He didn't want to cause trouble, he just wanted to do what he was meant to do.

On the other hand, this could be quite fun. A number of the recruits glanced at the door as raised voices echoed from the corridor. As they got closer, the dorm could make out a woman's voice and one other.

"Don't give me excuses just tell me where he is." Her voice was followed by something in a language they didn't understand. This woman sounded livid, and wasn't shy about letting her feelings known.

"I know they can understand me, but my point remains the same. Where the fuck is Greefash?"

The dorms heavy doors swung open like they weighed nothing. A woman in full battle armour walked into their dorm, the only piece that she didn't wear was the helmet. She walked a lap of the room and eyed each recruit. She stood just in front of each one and stared, when she got what she needed she moved onto the next.

It could have been her presence or just the stare but a couple recruits almost stepped away from her. If a pin was dropped three rooms down it would have been heard as she moved around the room.

Her jet-black hair stopped at her shoulders, and her eyes matched. It almost seemed like her pupils blended into her iris, this was a complete contrast to her pale skin. Even though her eyes were almost black, they seemed to shine in an almost unnatural way.

As she stood in front of Vandeaga, he made sure his eyes stayed on a fixed point and didn't wander, she towered over him as she was close to seven foot tall. He wasn't sure how much height the armour added but he guessed he would find out at sooner or later.

He tried to take his mind off the fact he was eye level with her chest. Layers of metal and compound covered her whole body but he still felt awkward. It was a split-second slip but somehow, she recognised Vandeaga, if anyone noticed what they saw, they never repeated it.

As she moved on Vandeaga tried to keep his eyes front. It was difficult not to look at her collection of scars. One of them was a deep silver ridge that ran from her chin up the right-hand side of her face and stopped in the middle of her forehead. The other was on the left and it looked like shrapnel or buckshot.

"You have blood on you." Vandeaga forced himself not to make eye contact.

"Yes, sir."

"Get yourself cleaned up," she turned to the rest, "your beds will remain clean at all times."

"Yes, Sir!" screamed the dorm, Vandeaga included.

She finished her walk and stood at the top end of the dorm. Her powered armour made a low clicking sound combined with a constant hum. If the recruits weren't paying attention, they would have missed it.

"I will keep this quick as I now have twice as many dorms as I should have and you're not the last dorm that I need to…" She turned her head towards the person that had been stood near the door the entire time, he looked beyond petrified of her. His uniform was white with a bright yellow thunderbolt on the lapel.

"You're not part of this dorm, go wait outside." Before she had even finished the sentence, he had already started to force himself backwards through the doors. She smiled to herself for his instinct reaction of her. Techs never got their hands dirty and they were so easy to scare.

"I am Officer Faleama. Your introducer should be Officer Greefash but the kank can't be found." Vandeaga and several others forced themselves not to laugh. Only Officers ever used that word in normal conversation.

"You will do your best or you will be removed. This time the dorms have been mixed. In here are possible leaders, medics, infantry and engineers. You all have your training schedules. You will be coming back here at different times but the point of this is, you are a team. You will be working together when it comes to the group assessments," she placed her hands together and clasped an invisible ball.

"This place is your hub. This place is your core. After the training is complete, you will be assigned to new squads or be created as a new one depending on who or what is left at the end. You will meet recruits from other dorms and you will give them your respect. That does not mean you can be pushovers as you are representing me, you will protect yourselves and each other if you have to. This should not have to be said but I will say it regardless as I feel great anger regarding this issue." The muscles in her face tightened; it looked as if she was about to lose her temper just from the thought of what she was about to say.

"The female dorms are in the same housing block as yours. You can and will speak to each other when in the food halls or in your training sessions in a civil manner. If you have urges, you will keep them to yourselves, all of that comes later. Do not feel like you are being treated differently as they are also told the same. If there are any incidents involving forced physical contact and I find out about it, and I guarantee you that I will find out. That person will have a really fucking bad day, I will take great pleasure in removing body parts from them. I will not use anything sharp either. Lastly, do what you are told and don't fuck with my instructors or me and we will get on like a house on fire."

She turned and walked out the dorm. No one moved, no one even blinked, they just waited like they were supposed to. Thirty seconds went by before she walked back in again.

"It's good to see they teach you something at that lab, at ease, get some sleep." She turned and shouted through the doors as she walked. "If you haven't found Greefash in the next ten minutes, I will kill him myself."

The doors swung behind her as she entered the corridor. Jake walked over and shook Vandeaga's hand with the firmness of friendship and respect.

"I wasn't expecting to see you again my friend. Did you find a name?"

"Same here my friend, yeah, it's Vandeaga." Jake thought about it for a moment.

"Good name, I like it, where did you get it from?" Vandeaga shook his head as Jake asked.

"I couldn't tell you, but I like it too. What career path did you get?" Vandeaga hadn't even checked himself so he ripped open his envelope that was on his bed and scanned across it until he found what he wanted. He gave himself a smile as he read the words 'Leader's Role'.

"That's a good point." As the others shook Vandeaga's hand, Jake walked to his bed and lifted a brown envelope off the bottom end. He peeled the top back. His name wasn't printed on the top just his number, he followed the details down.

Blond hair, blue eyes, he followed the list down until he got near the end.

Assigned Career: Combat Engineer.

Jake smiled to himself as that meant fixing stuff or blowing shit up. He turned to walk back to them but Taradin bumped into him.

"Watch where you're walking shithead." Taradin had hoped for a fight but the problem was Jake didn't take any notice at all.

"Yeah, sorry about that, my fault," without a second thought Jake walked past and showed Vandeaga his papers. "Combat engineer mate, this is gonna be fun. What did you get?"

"I got the Leader Role so I should be an Officer depending what I score over the next two years." The problem with having the leader role on your card was if you failed any part of the test, you got transferred straight to grunt squad or worse, removed.

"I hear that's hard work, I just got Infantry." Terry didn't look too happy about his selection as he double checked his paper work. The older looking lad that had thrown Vandeaga the pen joined in with the conversation.

"I got Combat Medic and to be honest I would rather be infantry but shit happens." Terry still wasn't convinced.

"Why would anyone want to be part of the front-line infantry?" Terry asked.

"They don't just throw you out the door with a gun in your hand. You are trained with every weapon and every vehicle. You're equipped with the best armour, other than Officers of course, but still better than most. Infantry can progress to the Ghosts or Dogs depending on your skill, same goes for Engineers as they also have options. I am a Combat Medic and that is what I will be till the end. I'm Mike, by the way." Mike held out his hand and Vandeaga shook it. Mike's eye colour was almost the same as Vandeaga's. Vandeaga had to make a mental note to stop staring into other people's eyes.

There was a bang as Taradin kicked open the footlocker at the end of his bed. He began to loudly rummage through its contents. Someone Vandeaga had never met walked up to him.

"That person is called Taradin," the guy let out a nervous laugh as he said it.

"The best way to describe him is an arsehole, but he's dangerous, so watch your backs when you're around him."

"Thanks for the information, what's your name?" asked Jake.

"Erm…it's Muncher," as he said his name the group tried their best not to laugh, but it was hard.

"Why did you pick that name?" Jake wouldn't be able to speak to him unless he asked that question.

"I couldn't think of one so the dickhead in the booth gave me this one. I swear he smiled as he typed it into his computer. Before any of you ask, I have checked. It's on the system and it cannot be changed unless I hit the rank of Officer."

"What's your path?"

"Possible Leader, but I'll end up in Grunt Squad." His whole body seemed to drop with those words like he already knew them to be the truth.

"Why's that?" Vandeaga asked.

"That's how my luck goes. Everything looks great and then I get shit on from up high every single time, so it's better for me to expect the worst." The guy from the chair incident had waited for his turn to shake Vandeaga's hand, it was a firm grip.

"I'm Broo. Thanks again for the help and sorry for having a panic attack. I honestly thought you guys were going to leave me behind for sure."

"Don't mention it, we just worked with what came into my head at the time." Vandeaga hadn't noticed at the time but Broo's eyes were a light orange colour.

As the introductions continued Vandeaga soon felt his eyes start to hurt and he knew he had to get some sleep. The group dispersed and they got ready for bed. As he lay there in the darkness, his mind couldn't help but wander as he got closer to the depths of sleep. He tried his best not to think of the worst bits of the last day but the images were there and would be for a long time. He sat bolt upright in his bed and looked towards Jakes bunk. He was still awake too and signalled to him. The boys sign language being put to good use once again.

"You alright 45?" Jake had already forgotten his new name.

"Did you hear Officer Faleama say lab too?" Jake thought about it for only a second before he shrugged.

Chapter 6

Their first day was spent with an escorted tour of the new facility. The dormitories were in one block. Males and females were separated but not confined. The food hall was huge and next door, fifty long tables with hundreds of chairs. The serving counter was quite small but the queue line was half of a mile long.

Each department had its own set of buildings. The largest was the engineering block, then the infantry and assigned training grounds. The medic training building came after that and the leader building was the smallest. They had only a number of learning segments more than the infantry. But the longer you looked into the segments the larger they got.

There were also several buildings that they were not allowed into. The same reason was always given and that it was 'not required'. The grounds covered more than fifty square miles, and each set of buildings had its own piece to work with.

Even though the training complex was located on the outskirts of their home city, it was surrounded by a metal wall and this was over eighty feet tall and thirty feet thick. The wall itself had aged well for being hundreds of years old.

Half the guns that were mounted on the walls also aimed into the vast compound. It was discussed between the recruits that the training complex was itself a fortress or a very secure prison, both were true. After the 'tour', each group was sent to the food hall and then back to their dorms. Nice and easy first day, it didn't last long before the complex had its first run of incidents.

In the first week alone, there were two misfires on the live fire range. One person had to have a slug removed from her collar bone. The other was not as lucky as a similar slug passed through his eye and turned his brain into scrambled eggs. The dead had their names struck from the data base and their bodies liquidated. The dead were not allowed to be spoken about, incidents happen in training and that's that. The dead faded into the void.

As the weeks turned to months there was always an incident to speak of. Jake watched another engineer lose a hand in the workings of a motor. The machine itself had no power and was isolated, so it was impossible to be switched on. It didn't change the fact he watched a guy scream as his digits were drawn into the mechanism.

No more than a couple days later another engineer lost a finger to the same motor. A decision was made and this particular piece of equipment was taken to the scrapyard at the back of the engineering block and used as target practice.

*

Vandeaga got to his dorm at the same time every single day. As he turned the corner, Mike was leaning against the wall by the doors. As Vandeaga got closer, Mike looked in his direction and gave a nod. He stepped away from the wall with a stretch.

"Afternoon, could you do me a favour?" asked Mike as he stepped in front of the doors and forced Vandeaga to stop.

"Sure, what is it?" Vandeaga had assumed it was bad and prepared himself for anything.

"Can you have a word with Jake?" Vandeaga opened his mouth but Mike continued. "He respects you and I can't hear about that guy losing his fingers one more fucking time. It's been over nine weeks and that's all he talks about." Vandeaga just nodded with a smile, out of every scenario he had thought of, he didn't think of that.

"I can try but he doesn't leave things alone. He will keep telling that story until he gets bored of it, and Jake doesn't get bored very easily. You know, he sometimes still calls me 45?" Mike looked him up and down as he tried to work out the name.

"Why 45?"

"That was what everyone called me back in our first dorm before we even thought about names. It's the first two digits of my number. I think someone said it as a throw away nickname but it stuck."

"That makes sense, and with Jake, it might be best to leave it alone then." They both laughed and pushed through the doors. Jake sat on the end of his bunk and told, anyone that would listen, his story again.

"Where have those two gone?" Vandeaga gestured to the empty bunks at the far end. He thought for a moment.

"I'm trying but I can't remember their names. My mind has gone blank."

"Those two got sent to grunt squad." Mike said with a shake of his head.

"This early!" Vandeaga shook his head too, "we've barely hit the three-month mark and they are gone already."

"No leniency mate, if you can't do what you're asked to do then you go." Terry walked and placed his hand on Vandeaga's shoulder but gave them both a nod.

"Hey guys, you alright Van?" He nodded, "I have a question," Terry paused longer than was necessary so Mike spoke first.

"What's grunt squad?" Terry nodded at him.

"I have heard the name a lot, but what are they?" Terry asked.

"They're just cannon fodder mate. You're transferred straight to the front line. Minimal training, you're given a gun and sent on your way. Some don't even get armour." Terry's face dropped as he shook his head.

"Look, infantry is the best path to be in, you can only fail if you literary shoot someone in the face while training."

"That's fucking great," Terry said. He didn't look any happier as he walked away. Mike turned to Vandeaga and whispered.

"Did I say something wrong?" Vandeaga leaned in so only Mike could hear him.

"It was Terry that had the accidental discharge, he shot that girl in the chest. I told him it will be fine as it wasn't fatal, but that's a big mark against him." They all knew mistakes could happen but the live fire range was the worst place for an accident.

"Wow, fuck, I didn't know that. Should be fine though, because if it was deemed that bad, he would have been moved already. At any rate, he should have checked the damn safety was on in the first place." Mike shrugged with a sideways glance, Vandeaga couldn't help but agree with him. As a group, they all headed towards the food hall.

Technically, the food hall was only open at certain times, but it was always busy. There was a food rota printed over the walls; to be fair none of the food ever looked any different no matter what it was called.

One-inch slab of what could be meat.

One portion of colourless vegetables.

One glass of silvery water with the option of one refill.

Two slices of leather; everyone was told this was bread but none of them believed it.

The servers had no emotion as they worked. They just stood behind the counters and loaded this shit onto plastic trays and handed it to the recruits. Vandeaga's dorm queued together and found a table. Taradin, on the other hand, had already eaten and was on the way out when they sat down.

"What's with that guy?" Terry still didn't understand what his problem was, none of them did.

"He's always been like that," Muncher said with a sigh. He had seen this behaviour too many times. Terry wasn't sure if his facial expression was for the dislike of Taradin or the food in front of him.

"He was the best shot in our old dorm and can take control in any situation. He has a bit of a temper though and can just snap at times. He believes that doing the whole social thing gets in the way of training and improving yourself. To be honest, I just think he's an arsehole."

"I heard that he has been getting extra training." Everyone turned to Mike. "It could just be a rumour, but where does he spend his free time and all of his breaks?" The group exchanged looks because, of all of the theories and rumours, this made the most sense.

Since they had been together, Vandeaga had only said a couple sentences to Taradin and both of them were to 'stop being a dick head'. They ate their food in semi-silence, each with their own thoughts to deal with.

*

By the end of the fifth month their training intensified. It didn't matter what role the recruits had, they had to produce results and they all knew the price if they didn't. Vandeaga started his day with a walk to the leader's block.

The sky was a tint of blue and orange, his breath hung in the air as he walked through it. As he breathed, the faint aftertaste of smog was still there. Vandeaga guessed he must be further away from the factories than before. He couldn't help but wonder what they could be making in those gigantic buildings.

His mind came back to this place and he thought about the rest of the complex. He wondered if he could walk into any of the buildings around here. One day, he would find out one way or another. The main entrance of the leader's block was a series of single glass doors set into the concrete wall. Each door had a scanner and a second door behind it.

Vandeaga placed his hand on the scanner and waited. As the screen flashed up his details, there was a loud buzz and the magnetic lock released for only a second. If he missed the release then he'd have to do the process again, and this would be recorded against him.

Every recruit knew they couldn't hold the doors open. Each person had to let themselves into the building. He glanced at the multiple 'you can be the best' posters as he walked into the entrance hall and away from the main doors.

He turned as he heard a crash and a scream emanating from behind him. A large guy had tried to get through the door and the scanner had flashed up someone else's information. The lights flashed red and the door refused to open. He had tried again with a different door but he got the same result.

With an instant blast of rage, he dropkicked the scanner into a sparking mess. Minders rushed past and almost knocked Vandeaga off his feet. It had been a good few weeks since the last time he saw someone snap. Another similar, that looked like the first, had stopped next to Vandeaga to watch the fight.

"He's going to have a bad day." With that, he turned and run his fingers down the wall. He hummed an unknown tune as Vandeaga watched him leave.

I need to find out what is wrong with these people. Vandeaga thought to himself while he fought to supress a yawn. The Minders had pretty much restrained the individual so there was little left to see. Vandeaga walked up the corridor and through the door to his training room.

He grabbed a sheet of paper off the stand next to the door. He fed this into a large machine and placed his hand on another scanner. The machine detected who he was and laser printed the paper with his name and the details of the next test. On the paper were reference points to the material he needed to read, and a second printout for yet another test.

Whenever the machine printed his paperwork, he always noticed the symbol on the screen flash. It looked like a cog but in bright yellow and next to that was a lightning symbol. He always wanted to press it but the silver chemicals that flowed through his blood stream always persuaded him not to.

The desks in the room curved around each seat in a half moon shape. On one side, you filled out your papers and on the other, was an interactive screen. He took a seat and tapped a button on the desk. A pen like object popped out the top, there was no ink inside as it burned the special paper, mistakes were not allowed.

Vandeaga, as always, just got on with what was instructed on the paper work. He didn't even notice the person who stood at the front of the room anymore. Whoever it was today, wouldn't speak and would just blend into the background like the rest of them. All they seemed to do was watch them work.

They only seemed to get involved if there was a problem with the equipment, this included the recruits. The room had fifty desks in it, but so far this morning, only four people sat in them. The incident at the main doors must have held up the rest of the session.

It wasn't too long before the remaining recruits flooded through the door. The usual group of faces walked in and queued at the machine for their papers. He tried his best not to look at the girls as they walked in but there was a part of his brain that couldn't help itself. He tried even harder not to stare at the Similars but that was even more difficult. They had been there about an hour when someone behind him started to speak loudly; this also wasn't allowed.

"Why are they asking this again? I've answered this question a dozen fucking times?" Vandeaga heard something heavy strike a desk so he turned in his seat to see what the problem was. A blond-haired female, that he had never heard

73

speak before had one hand on the desk and the other wrapped round her pen.

The force that she exerted made the pen crack and bend. The blood had drained from her face giving her complexion a deathly pale hue. The person at the front, a woman today, walked over with a glass of silvery water. Vandeaga never saw where the woman had retrieved this glass from.

"You need to calm down and follow the process, drink this if you need to." The girl scanned the paperwork with widened eyes. Saliva ran from the corner of her mouth and onto her chin.

"The same question again and again and again." She snatched the glass of water with such a swift movement it looked like it disappeared from the observer's hand and into hers. She crushed it between her fingers and a mixture of blood and silver splashed across the desk and floor. The observer stepped back and placed a finger to her temple.

"Minders required in room 18b. We have a snap on our hands." While the distress call went out the girl just repeated the words 'and again' over and over. She suddenly stopped as her bulging eyes darted towards the observer.

"I'll show you a fucking snap!" With an explosion of emotion and strength she lunged at the woman. The observer tried to draw her sidearm but the recruit was too quick. She effortlessly picked up the observer by her clothing and slammed her head first through the screen of a desk.

Before the fragments of glass and wood had hit the floor, the recruit was on top of the her. With a scream of anger and hatred, she began to pummel the woman's face with her fists. The impacts sounded like dropping heavy weights into sand.

Two of the closest recruits rushed forward to try and help. The first was knocked unconscious with a ferocious punch. The second had the remains of the pen lodged two inches into her chest. More joined in, just to try to get her to stop but she wasn't going to, the room turned into a one-person riot.

Four minders charged in then another six, they flipped the desks to make more space. From this point, the fight was ended abruptly with the flash of stun batons. She kicked and continued to scream as she was dragged by her arms and legs towards the door.

A Minder must have gotten a little too excited as it gave her a number of solid punches but this had no effect. On the way out she passed close to Vandeaga. Their eyes met and she smiled through bloodied teeth.

"Don't drink the water," she whispered just for him. "Their killing us, they're slowly killing all of us," she screamed at everyone else.

"And there goes another one." In the commotion, no one noticed another observer enter the room. The man took a moment to watch the female being dragged up the corridor. She had stopped struggling after the fifth zap from a stun baton.

This man was dressed like all the others that stood at the front of the rooms. He walked over to the woman's body and felt for a pulse, there wasn't one. This was more out of routine because most of her face had been caved in.

"Killed by a recruit, how pathetic," he touched his temple. "I'm going to take them to my room, this one needs to be maintained and a body to be cleared and," he glanced at the damage and the injured, "five for medical."

He paced the room and waited for a response. He nodded to himself before he turned and addressed the room for the first time.

"Every one of you will scan what paperwork you have and wait outside." One recruit picked up his paper and the words had become illegible through the coating of red smears.

"Mine's covered in blood, sir." The recruit said before he looked towards their new observer. The man just sighed to himself and rubbed his eyes. He wanted to be anywhere else, but instead, he was having to deal with this nonsense. A shot of black would make him feel better, and he was going to do just that after this.

"Scan it anyway what can't be recorded will need to be redone." It took time for the recruits to file past the machine and get what paperwork they could, scanned. When they had finished, he made them line up in the corridor.

Half of the Minders waited behind to see if there was going to be any more problems. When everyone was done, they were escorted under heavy guard to their new room. They repeated the process of getting new papers and sat down at a desk.

This wasn't like the other rooms Vandeaga had seen. It smelled sweet, like a fragrance was being pumped into the air. A large desk was positioned at the front with multiple screens and a nice comfy chair. When the last recruit was seated the man cleared his throat and gave them a slim smile.

"Before we begin," he removed his jacket with a stretch and hung it on a hook attached to the back wall. "This is my room; you do not fuck with my room is that understood? I will take your silence as a yes." He took the pistol out of his side holster and placed it on his desk. The second pistol that no one knew he had rested next to the first. He slipped two blades from his sleeves and placed them next to the pistols. None of the other observers were ever this armed.

"Right, let's get this out of the way first. I've had a pretty boring morning so if anyone would like to cause me any problems please do." Vandeaga couldn't help but see just how different this man was to the normal people that would stand at the front. His eyes were like that of an Officer, a deep rich green with that same shine about them. Physically, he was the same as the others in the leaders block but something about him just said more.

"Any work that is not completed on time because of," he gestured to the door with a flick of his hand, "the incident, you will come back here after training and complete it." One recruit had barely started to raise his hand when the man looked straight at him.

"That is not a request, that is an order." Instead of continuing to raise it, the recruit's hand landed flat on the desk.

"Good, now we can all get along. If your equipment fails, raise your hand. If you need to take a piss, raise your hand. Do not speak to me before I speak to you. Now begin."

The next three hours passed without incident. The signal was given and the recruits started to scan their papers back into the machine. Vandeaga was at the back as he always liked to check over his work before he scanned it in. As the papers were final it made no difference, but he still checked regardless.

"454376AHF a word when you're finished." Their new observer called with a slight glace in his direction. Vandeaga fed his papers into the machine and stood to attention in front of the large desk. The man turned to the other recruits that had decided to hang back in the corridor.

"I don't need to speak to any of you so I suggest you leave, and quickly." They left with such haste, one of them hit the door frame on the way past.

"I'm impressed with your scores and not just because your paperwork wasn't covered in blood."

"Thank you, Sir, and I will always improve." Vandeaga couldn't help the smile that spread across his face. These simple words seemed to fill him with a sense of pride and acknowledgment.

"Manners as well, this gets even better. I will tell you a little secret. The leader's role has a five percent pass rate, which means, across all classes roughly, eight to ten people will become Officers, that's if they can maintain their scores and not get themselves killed. The rest will be sent to grunt squad or transferred to infantry. You could easily be one of those passes if you don't screw up. If you help me when I need it, I will help you and you will pass. Nothing major, just the odd word to other recruits now and again. Do you have any questions?" Vandeaga spoke before he'd thought about it.

"Why do you seem so different to every other observer that I have seen?" The man smiled and relaxed back into his comfy chair.

"Good question. Well, you see I was an Officer, I'm sure you noticed my eyes?" The man placed a finger below his right eye and Vandeaga nodded. "It's a side effect of the Boosters they give us. Fuck knows what's in them, but extra speed, strength, healing is all good, but there are some things it can't heal. So, as you can see, I ended up here helping out with the leader's block. Does that answer your question?" Vandeaga nodded again.

"I'll give you another nugget of advice. I'm quite lenient, as you can see, but never ask another Officer private information until you're an Officer yourself. It just makes the day easier on you. Right, get out, I need time to prepare." He began to take pill bottles out of a draw and stack them neatly on the top of his desk. As Vandeaga turned to walk away the observer stopped him again. "Not sure if I mentioned it, but my name is Chrisa."

Vandeaga nodded one last time and headed out the door to join the rest of the room on the training field. He was already late as he entered the wall that surrounded the live fire area. He could see a couple people stood outside the inner compounds entrance.

Are they waiting for me? Shit I must be really late.

As he got closer, they stopped their conversation and waited with their arms held behind their backs. The two instructors stepped forwards in unison. Both of them brimmed with muscles and pride as they puffed their chests out.

"We started half an hour ago, where the fuck have you been?" The first instructor almost shouted. They took turns to speak and got louder each time, like it was some sort of game.

"Is that what you want, to be waited for? Would you like me to drag a bed over and give you a fucking blanket too?"

"I'm sorry, I—" Vandeaga knew he shouldn't have even tried to open his mouth.

"You're sorry? You're going to be fucking sorry when you get triple night sessions. Or, how about giving your whole dorm night sessions." No one had noticed Officer Faleama walk through the heavy doors and stand behind them.

"What's the problem and why have we not started yet?" Both instructors turned and saluted with a practiced snap.

"Sir! This one is the reason we haven't started as he decided he would be late. We needed to express our concerns about lateness before we began today's drills." She nodded and pointed towards the doors.

"Good, I will take over and he will catch up." She never shouted, she didn't raise her voice, it was almost too quiet.

Shit! I'm in trouble.

Vandeaga was already stood to attention but he saluted again when Faleama looked at him. The instructors exchanged a look and this look said, 'Oh shit, rather you than me, kid.'

"Yes Sir!" both instructors sprinted through the doors. Vandeaga heard them both scream instructions from the other side as they ran. Faleama sighed before she turned to him.

"At ease Vandeaga, why were you late?" He didn't want to but that was an order so he relaxed but only a little.

"I'm sorry, Sir. I was asked to confer with an Observer in the leader's block." Her normal pale complexion turned slightly crimson.

"Oh really, who would hold back one of my recruits for a conversation?" Faleama's voice remained calm but her face told a different story as her skin tightened.

"Observer Chrisa wanted to give me some advice," Vandeaga said. Faleama was motionless, he couldn't even hear her breath. Faleama didn't blink as her eyes drilled into his.

"And what was this important advice?" she asked after a small pause.

"He said only five percent of people pass the leader's block and I could be one of those. He said that if I help him that he would help me. Also, he mentioned his Boosters and the side effect that can happen to your eyes and that he was an Officer once."

It was at this point that he thought just maybe he should have kept some of that to himself. She swore in another tongue, drew her side arm and fired eight rounds into a target three hundred feet away. The noise from this large pistol boomed across the open space. The hits were perfectly spaced, all shots were within a half an inch of each other. This target was not meant to be used for live ammunition but no one was going to reprimand Faleama for this violation.

"Wasting my recruit's time, son of a bitch," she turned back to him.

"Do not trust Chrisa, he took risks and got himself placed there. If you have any more conversations with him, you come and speak to me directly. I don't care where you are supposed to be next. You speak to me immediately, understand?"

Vandeaga understood and was sent in to continue with his training. Faleama watched him pass by the doors and enter the compound. She reloaded her pistol, drew her second and unloaded at the target. Both thirty round magazines dried in a matter of seconds.

Just one bullet had not grouped with the others and was at least six inches out. She had wanted to subdue her anger but seeing that one tiny mistake seemed to have destroyed her entire day. Her jaw muscles tightened further as she jammed her guns back into her holsters and stormed towards the leader's block.

Faleama marched down the main corridor in full armour, the plating moved within itself seamlessly but it still made a low clicking noise. It had always been requested that all armour was removed before entering an administration building. Faleama had, however, chosen to ignore this rule at every opportunity she could.

As she walked, everyone else moved out of her way. She had that look in her eyes again, like someone was about to get hurt. Faleama stopped in front of a door and she checked herself.

With polite intent she gently tapped her knuckles on the surface. Her metal encased hand caused the door to vibrate in its frame. There was no answer but she waited a moment anyway she read the name plate on the door, 'CHRISA', she tapped again.

"Fuck off, I'm busy." Chrisa shouted from inside the room. It took Faleama a couple seconds to register what he had said. She clenched her fist and used that to tap against the door once more, this time it sounded like she had used a hammer.

"Are you stupid or something, I'm busy?" Chrisa's voice sounded a lot louder this time. Faleama looked up at the camera pointed at her face then glanced to her left, her gaze met that of a Tech's, he was just about to walk past. His mouth was wide open and his eyes matched the action, he knew what was about to happen.

Faleama attempted a smile but instead she just clenched her jaw. She tried to be polite, she had tried to use tact and respect, but some people just weren't worth the effort. She stepped back and with all her anger kicked the door. She used so much force that the doors lock shattered.

She strolled past the remains of the splintered wood and up to the desk. She was already in a bad mood when the smell hit her. The overwhelming aroma didn't help in the slightest. Chrisa calmly tapped at his computer and the two large screens went blank. He folded his arms across his chest and sat back in his big comfy chair, a thin smile spread across his face.

"I did say I was busy. How can I help you today?"

"You spoke to one of mine, didn't you?" Faleama said as she placed her hands on his desk with a resounding thud. One of Chrisa's pens was crushed between her hand and the wood.

"I presume you are talking about Vandeaga. He looks very promising; he could do well with the enhancements." Chrisa said with a grin.

"You will not turn any of my recruits into your fucking guinea pigs without getting it cleared with me first." Faleama emphasised, this with a point of her metal clad finger.

"Well it's not really your choice is it, that is what this whole place is after all." He sat up in his chair and pulled open one of the draws in his desk. He grabbed a slip of paper from the pile and handed it to Faleama.

"You need to read that, there will be posters going up for promising advancements for trash to take if they are failing their courses." Faleama flicked her eyes across the page and smirked.

"You must be running out of ideas for getting them to volunteer for the tests." She tossed the page back onto his desk, it didn't stay as it slid past a monitor and onto the floor.

"Someone like Vandeaga wouldn't need to take THAT offer, even with the shit you are putting in their water supply." Chrisa smiled again, he liked to know everything about everyone even if it wasn't his job anymore.

"You see I don't have any intention of Vandeaga going for the tests, but people like him will get others to go instead."

You cunning, weaselly bastard. Faleama tried to not let her feelings show.

"I can see by your face that you understand what I am talking about. You see that recruits like Vandeaga are going to be top of whatever they do. They get respect from their peers and they get asked for help when someone else fucks up, they give sound advice and bla bla bla. I don't care really. I just need subjects to test our new Boosters and serums on."

"You already have all the test subjects that you could get your hands on, what about the lows."

"Lows?" Chrisa had to think for a second. "Oh, right, you mean the people that we scrape off the floor after our armies have rolled past. Our research facilities go through hundreds of those animals a week. They are basically cattle and I don't test my best serums on those types. If the tests work then they could have real power, so I need proper subjects. The ones that we can bend to our will and fight our battles."

Faleama had gone past having emotions for the Lows as everyone of worth knew the world was like it was because of them.

"I'm telling you that my recruits aren't stupid enough to agree to partake and you know it."

"You would be surprised how the stresses of failing a course can make people do things they normally wouldn't. I still don't understand why you lot even bother calling them recruits, most of them will never leave here. Anyway, I have a lot of work to be getting on with so could you please take your leave." He thought about waving her to the door but better judgment stopped him.

"If I find out that you are targeting certain recruits because they are assigned to me. Then we are going to have another argument that you are not going to like." It was her eyes that made Chrisa look at his desk. He tried to fake a laugh but it came out as more of a cough.

"You seem to think that I still bear a grudge and you couldn't be further from the truth. I'm in charge of this block and I have access to the best failures to test on." Chrisa smiled like he spoke to a puppy. "I have no ill feelings towards you what so ever."

"I thought Tyler was in charge of all the tests?"

"He is, but Tyler always needs a helping hand and I am more than willing to get out of this shit hole when I can."

Faleama had nothing to say that would make the situation different. She couldn't even warn Vandeaga about what might happen as that would break her own rules. She stood to attention, threw up a half-arsed salute and walked out of the room. Chrisa watched her leave and when she was out of the room his face dropped. A look of purest disgust and hatred now etched onto his facial features.

"You fucking whore, I hope you die a painful death, you self-righteous bitch." He tapped at his temple and waited.

"Maintenance here, how can we help?" The sound of a hammer hitting metal rung off in the back ground, this was followed by the screech of a metal sealer.

"This is Chrisa from the leader's block, I need a new door, and this one will be reinforced and magnetically bolted on all sides."

"Yes sir, we will be with you in minutes." The line went dead with a click.

*

After the day's training, Vandeaga concentrated on his food and hardly spoke to anyone in the food hall. He had questions for anyone that would listen and certain people wanted to speak to him. However, there was one exception that he had to make. He made sure he stood next to Larooa in the queue for food, she glanced at him once but spoke forwards. It was enough time for him to gaze into her hazel eyes.

"I heard you got shot." Vandeaga stared into her black curly hair.

"Nope, not today, I'm not saying it won't happen just not this time. How are you feeling today?"

"Ok, there are some little things stressing me out, but I'm working on it." They continued to exchange pleasantries until they were given their food and separated to go off to their own dorm tables.

On the way back, he made sure that he was the last one to enter the dorm, he even waited for Taradin. Taradin looked like he was in no hurry and even seemed to slow down. As soon as the doors closed behind him, he couldn't keep it in any longer.

"What the fuck is going on!" He held his hands up to the ceiling. He needed any information the others had, even if it was bullshit. "You heard what happened at the leader's block?" A couple of the dorm nodded and glanced between each other.

"I was told there was an incident and some people required medical attention." That's all the information that Jake could get from the people he knew, or that would talk to him. Vandeaga pointed to himself before he paced the floor.

"I was fucking there. One person couldn't get in the building so he kicked the shit out of the door pass. He was dragged off kicking and screaming by the Minders. Then a recruit lost it in the middle of a session and beat an observer to death and wounded five others."

"I heard you had been shot outside the live fire grounds." Jacob piped up from the back.

"I should have been. I was late, I answered back without thinking, and an Officer was present as well."

"Which Officer was it?" Terry asked.

"Faleama," Vandeaga said.

"Even I think you're lucky. You're not her plaything, are you?" Taradin snorted from his bed. He didn't even bother to look up as he picked something from under his fingernail.

"Anyone else noticed weird stuff from the people that look similar? I'm not joking either, there is something seriously wrong with those people."

"I heard they're clones," everyone turned to Mike, "they put clones in with the general populace, it's a way of bulking up the army numbers but they're prone to snaps."

"Where did you hear that?" Peter showed what he thought of Mikes opinion with a shake of his head.

"I have my sources and I'm told they are conditioned to not talk or remember anything about clones."

"Well, I think that's stupid if I'm being honest. Where do people come up with this shit?" Peter shook his head again and walked back to his bed. Terry was about to ask a question when Mike held up his hand. With his fingers he counted down from five to one.

"Peter, do you know anything about clones?" Peter turned from his bed, that same blank expression on his face.

"Of course not, clones don't exist," Peter smiled and with no more to say, turned his attention to his footlocker. Mick gestured to the rest of the room; some of them had forgotten to close their mouths at Peter's reaction.

"There you go, what did I say? As I said before, they're prone to snaps so try not to get in their way." He tapped his temple with his finger. "Not all switches are on if you know what I mean. I have also been told this is the worst year for snaps and removals. That's including everyone not just the clones."

"Why's it happening then, the snaps I mean?" Vandeaga asked, but Mike just shrugged.

"Don't know, I will ask the question when I get a chance."

"Frankie said to me that some of the people that have had a snap were fine one minute then they go completely off the rails the next. Something must set them off?" asked Broo.

The group nodded. Could it be something they did every day and any one of them could be the next person to go. They would have to wait and see.

"This is getting more and more strange and I need to sleep." Vandeaga didn't even take off his clothes as he slumped onto his bed. He tried to recall what the girl said about the water but he couldn't remember the words. All his mind could remember was red and the broken table.

Chapter 7

The incident was forgotten as more strange occurrences happened over the next few months, but the strangest was only around the corner. Every recruit, in one way or another, was told there was something special planned for the next day. It seemed that every so many weeks a surprise was planned, and like most surprises Vandeaga had quickly realised they were not enjoyable.

Every dorm was still woken up at the same time, but there was no signal to go to their normal sessions. Vandeaga's dorm had been ready to go for the last thirty minutes and waited in front of their beds. Jake fidgeted with his hands and started to make clicking sounds with his fingers.

"Can you stop doing that? you're giving me a headache" Taradin gave Jake a dirty look and held it into a stare.

"So, no one knows what is going on then?" Jake asked the room.

"Don't know, let's ask someone. Big V, do you know what's going on?" asked Taradin, but no one answered him. He raised his voice as he directed it at Vandeaga.

"I'm talking to you Big V, don't ignore me. It's rude." As the rest of the dorm looked at Vandeaga, he glanced over to Taradin just before he shook his head.

"No, I don't know what is going on." He said with a sigh.

"Oh, so you don't know everything then?" Taradin smiled to himself.

"Can one day go by where you are not being a dickhead, just one day, that's all I'm asking for?" Vandeaga asked with a smirk. There were more than a number of sniggers from across the room. This seemed to affect Taradin more than the words themselves.

"Come over here and say that. I'll break your fucking hands. What do you say to that, son?" Taradin's skin had already gone red as sweat formed on his brow. He glared at Vandeaga so hard his eyes began to hurt, but he did know how to push Vandeaga's buttons.

"If I come over there then I've already wasted too much energy on you, so why don't we meet in the middle." Vandeaga had had enough of the shitty remarks for one day and they hadn't even had breakfast yet.

The room fell silent for a second but a low cheer rolled as both of them stepped forward with their fists raised. The fight between them had been anticipated for months. They were mere feet from each other, and Taradin raised his hand to swing, but they froze.

Low voices crept through the cracks in the door frame and with practised ease the dorm slid back to their positions. Three instructors pushed through the doors in mid-conversation. The dialect used was not one the recruits could understand.

Vandeaga recognised two of them from the firing range but the other one, he had never seen before. As the instructors formed a line, the recruits stood to attention. The instructor that Vandeaga didn't recognise stepped forward. He cleared his throat and began to read from the script in his head.

"Today we will be holding a different type of training session, it's a possible one off but we will see how well it is received. Everyone in this academy will be taking this session but you will be working with your dorm as a team. There will be no support given." Vandeaga and Taradin managed to glare at each other without anyone else noticing.

"You, as a team, will be assessed and scored on the time you take to finish and how you cooperate during it. You will follow your instructors to the area you will be using. Are there any questions?" He looked round the room. No one put their hand up or stepped forward. He let out a subtle sigh of relief.

"Good, you know the drill by now, so move out."

"Yes Sir!" the dorm screamed back at him. He smiled as they filed out of the doors. As a group, they were taken back to the main entrance hall. None of them had been back there since their first day at the facility.

The huge hall had been segregated into many smaller rooms complete with walls and a ceiling. They looked like they had been made out of welded metal and wooden frames. There were no windows that any of them could see. They were led into a room of their own and the door sealed behind them with a loud metallic snap.

The recruits lined the walls, just in case the person closest to the middle was picked as a volunteer. Jake was about to ask a question, but he saw Vandeaga shake his head at him.

In the centre of the room were three wooden boxes and each of these were about the size of a vending machine. The wooden slats were nailed tightly shut so no one could see inside them. They must have waited in silence for about sixty seconds before the speaker system kicked in with a crackle.

"In front of you are four boxes." Vandeaga counted them again and only saw three.

"These boxes contain equipment that when you leave this facility you will use every single day. All of you will work out what each piece is used for, and how to maintain them. Drinkable fluids may be available after the third day and please use the facilities provided."

Two enclosed chairs were built into the corner of the room. One was marked for urine and the other was marked for excrement, "Good luck."

The group glanced between each other.

"Do not take the piss!" Taradin was closest to the door and gave it a try. It didn't open, the handle didn't even flex as he gave it more of a pull.

"Great, we are stuck in here together," he looked around the room, "Get the boxes open!"

There was a mad rush as two thirds of the dorm charged the wooden boxes and began to tear them apart. People started to shove each other as they tried to get to whatever was inside.

"Guys, get a grip, for fuck sake, there's too many of us to crowd three boxes," Vandeaga shouted from the wall.

"What do you expect?" said Taradin "You want us to take turns and hold hands?" Taradin raised his arms above his head. A number of the dorm stopped to watch what was about to unfold.

"That's actually a good plan," Vandeaga said with a grin.

"Don't take the piss out of me!" Taradin pointed at him and took a couple steps forward. "We still have something we need to finish, son." Vandeaga clenched his jaw, he had no idea why that word triggered his temper but he tried to breathe through it.

"This isn't about you or me, this is about us as a group, look." Vandeaga pointed at the two cameras.

"They are watching us, to see if we will work together or not. We divide down the middle and one group will rest while the other works. If we are not getting any food or water, then we have to conserve as much energy as we can."

"So, you're giving the orders now, is that it? Is no one else worthy of making a decision?" Taradin gestured to the whole room.

"I am not in charge here as I'm not the only person in the leader's role. It's a suggestion and if no one wants to, then we will carry on as we are. Right now, we look like thirty people trying to force our way through the same door. We look stupid." There were numerous nods of agreement as it seemed more of the room wanted to side with Vandeaga.

"We should split the paths as well so there is a balanced chance that we will get more done," Muncher said. He seemed to be getting into his leader's role a little later than the rest.

"Fine, but I'm not working with you. It's pointless having two strong-headed people in the same group anyway." Taradin gave Vandeaga a forceful point. Vandeaga never did admit it, but he had to agree with him. They separated into two groups and got to work.

*

The first crate contained one object and a digital screen. The screen itself was almost like a plain sheet of glass until it was touched. When it flickered to life, there was an interactive list that had to be filled out. They needed the name of the object and as much information about it as possible.

Taradin's team made good progress as the first object was a medical injector and fluids for said device. The medics on his team named all the vials that came in the box and the engineers knew how it worked. When the digital screen was filled out and completed, it flashed a green smiley face at them and then went blank with a da ding.

The second crate contained a battle rifle. The frontliners were up as they had been trained with this weapon, be it only recently. They named the gun and took it apart. The group crowded round as Terry explained how the internals worked.

The engineers were the most interested as they hadn't had the opportunity to take this type of weapon apart yet. The progress was fast until they reached the ammunition that went along with the rifle. They named all but two rounds, Taradin tried to guess on the readout but it flashed red and the counter ticked down from three to two.

"None of us knows what this is?" Taradin asked his group, but all he got back was a mixture of head shakes and shrugs. "Fuck's sake," Taradin growled to himself.

Both of the rounds were longer than his middle finger and palm combined. One had a green and orange tip and the other had a green, orange and blue tip. Broo was sat against the wall and smiled to himself as Taradin's group started to argue. Vandeaga walked over and sat next to him.

"What's so funny?" He asked as Broo stretched his back up the wall.

"I know what they are but I'm deciding how long to make them wait for me to tell them." Broo couldn't help himself as he had almost come to blows with Taradin over the last month.

"The longer you wait, the longer we all have to sit in the room."

"That's fair," Broo got to his feet and walked over to Taradin.

"The green and orange one is armour piecing and explosive. The other one is the same but it has a tracer attached." Taradin didn't say anything as he tapped it into the screen. It flashed green and he dropped the glass onto the floor with a thud. Vandeaga stood up and stretched.

"I guess that is a shift change then. You guys have been at it for roughly six hours." Vandeaga was given a few nods of agreement.

"I should have already known that." Taradin swore under his breath as he leant against the wall, he was joined by the rest of his team. The last box was, by far, the largest and was untouched. That didn't last long as the wooden slats were pulled apart. Inside was a skeletonised set of armour; alongside this, was a smaller box and a printed note.

This armour set needs to be named.

This set will need to be assembled.

This set will need to be worn by someone that is capable.

All loose items that are not part of the armour set will need to be stored or used.

When you are finished, you will be given the green light.

Good Luck.

Vandeaga read the note aloud so everyone understood what they had to do. It didn't seem that difficult until Jake popped open the smaller box. It seemed to burst as dozens and dozens of items fell out. Even though it was smaller than the first it was still a two-person lift.

"That's a lot of stuff." Mike said while he knelt down and started to sift through the mess.

There were empty magazines for at least three different weapons, medical supplies, tools of several different types and shapes. There were also armour plates that needed to be fitted, a number of fusion batteries and a complete wiring set. These had been stored in such a way that it looked like a tangled mass of decorative lights.

"Jake, get someone to give you a hand and see what you can do with that wiring set and batteries. The rest of us see what we can do with that lot." Vandeaga looked round at Muncher. "Unless you want to do it a different way?" Muncher looked at the assortment of parts and read the note again.

"That sounds good to me, let's get to work."

*

It was a replica Warrior armour set, these had built-in air conditioning, exterior lights on the shoulders and targeting systems in the helmet. Jake and Makka had made a school boy error whilst assembling the torso, they left out the internal armour plating.

They had to strip it down again which took another two hours. The shifts changed multiple times as the Warrior set took shape. They found more hidden compartments the further along they got. They filled each one with as much equipment as that could fit.

"This is taking too long and I really need a drink." Mike said to Vandeaga as they sat against the wall again. "How long have we been here now?" Vandeaga rubbed at his eyes, he must have been one of the few that hadn't tried to sleep yet. He thought for a moment and counted the shift changes.

"We have changed shifts eight times, so that's like two days."

"Fuck me, it's just an armour set. When would we ever need to do this in the field?" Mike shook his head as this had gotten dull far too quickly.

"I don't think they care, but we need to do this, what the hell is that?" Vandeaga stood back up and tried to listen. Anyone that was awake did the same.

They could hear muffled shouts and screams but this was suddenly cut off by a huge bang. Whatever caused the noise was very close and two of their walls seemed to flex a little. It must have been from one of the rooms next to theirs.

"What the fuck is going on out there?" Taradin shouted. There were a few more noises and a body sized impact thumped into the door from the outside. The group scattered and grabbed anything to arm themselves with. They waited for something to happen, every single one of them watched the door as more shouts followed.

The eruption of noise soon died down to the silence it was before. They jumped when the speaker that was bolted into the corner of the room crackled into life for the first time.

"There is no need for alarm. The incident has been resolved. Do continue with your assignments as they still need to be completed." Several of them looked at each other and shrugged before Taradin dropped the lump of wood that was in his hand.

"Come on you dickheads, stop staring, we need to get this done." Taradin said and turned back to the armour. There were a few mumbles as they continued with their work.

Chapter 8

They had completed the armour set and Terry had the honour to wear it, but they didn't get the green light. They had been in that room nearly three days and tempers had really started to flare in the confined space.

There were a number of incidents where punches were thrown, but the leaders had calmed it down each time, but only to a point. It didn't help that Vandeaga and Taradin had to be separated on more than one occasion, but now they reluctantly sat next to each other.

"Have you tried the lights yet?" Taradin asked as he tried to think of something they missed.

"Yes, I have, multiple times but I will test them once again." Terry's voice sounded robotic as he pressed the buttons on his forearm. The shoulder lights flashed on then off.

"The internal fan is working the heads-up display in the helmet is working. All the wiring is fine and the power is stable. The compartments are filled with stuff and we have checked this thing a hundred times to find any more compartments and there isn't any." Terry looked around the floor at the broken boxes and packaging.

"Is there anything left to put in this? I don't think there's any room we could use but did anyone check the floor?" Both teams cleared the floor and after they had tidied up almost the entire room, a vial of white fluid dropped to the ground. Broo handed it to Mike. Mike held it up to his face with a puzzled look.

"I have no idea what this is. Are you sure we couldn't squeeze anymore in that thing?" Mike asked but the Robotic looking Terry shook his head with a low hum.

"No chance, I think we broke some stuff as it is to make it all fit."

"What did the note say about the extras again?" Muncher asked.

"The items need to be stored or used." Vandeaga said as he glanced at Taradin, they both had the same idea. Taradin picked up the injector and held out his hand for the vial.

"Hold on we have no idea what this is, it could be a suicide shot for all we know." Mike protested as he stepped back. Taradin lowered his hand, but from his point of view, he didn't really care anymore.

"What other vials were there?" Vandeaga asked as he popped open the compartment on Terry's leg. A dozen different colours fell to the floor. Mike sifted through them and found a light blue one.

"This is a stimulant," Mike said. With ease, he slotted the vial into the injector and armed it. There was a low pop as the seal was broken.

"How strong is it?" Vandeaga stared at the vial. He remembered getting shots of something like that when he was younger.

"It's meant to get someone back into battle or to offset major fatigue, so it's very powerful. We will need five people to drain the vial. Don't expect to sleep for a day or two and as we have had no food or water. We will most likely blackout at times until we get something inside of us".

"Why do you say we?" Taradin asked.

"I'm taking a hit, anyone else?" Vandeaga, Taradin and Muncher stepped forward.

"I will go last who's first?" Mike said to his volunteers. Taradin held out his arm as Vandeaga turned to the rest of the room.

"Everyone else put that shit back in the armour, let's get out of here. We still need one more person!"

There was a mass scramble to put the items back and this almost knocked Terry off his feet. Jake stood next to Mike.

"This isn't going to feel good is it?" Jake slapped his right arm twice and held it out.

"It's going to feel great but I'm not sure for how long. You ready?"

"I'm always ready, just stick me with it for fuck sake," Taradin said. Mike stuck the needle in his in arm and pulled the trigger. They all heard a low hiss and a small portion of the vial disappeared.

Taradin felt nothing at first and was about to tell Mike that he got it wrong when an unbelievable surge of energy charged through his body like electricity. All feelings of hunger, thirst and tiredness left him in an instant. His heart rate doubled and felt like it was trying to break through his ribcage. The others stared at him and waited for any ill effects.

"How do you feel?" Vandeaga asked. In the blink of an eye Taradin's head snapped in his direction.

"This is amazing, I feel like I've had twenty-four hours sleep and I can take on the whole world." As he said those words, he never took his eyes off Vandeaga. Mike gave everyone else their jab and finally stuck himself.

They all stood there and stared at each other for a full minute as the light above the door turned green. Muncher stayed completely straight as he toppled backwards and landed square on his back.

"We need to burn off energy as quickly as possible." Mike said as he dropped to the floor and started to perform push ups. The group watched him power through a full set before they had thought of anything to say.

"That's a waste we could…" Taradin started but didn't get to finish as his vision started to swim and his legs almost buckled.

"Everyone drop," Vandeaga shouted and as they did, he called to the rest of the group. "Is the door open?" Terry walked over and pulled it open. In-between each mouth full of air Mike shouted at any of the dorm that was still within ear shot.

"We need fluids and food or we are going to do our selves some serious damage." Mike didn't have the time to look up.

As the room emptied a number of their team grabbed food and fluid from the dispensers outside and handed it to them. They devoured it even though they did not feel the need. Muncher sat up in one swift movement and without much thought he joined in with the push-ups.

It was a shame Mike never knew what was contained within the white vial. It was called a Body Clean Shot or B.C.S. It was used to remove simulants and other contaminates from the body. This would have prevented them from the hardship of another twelve hours of push-ups, but it gave the researchers a good laugh none the less.

Chapter 9

The warfare portion of the training had ramped up dramatically. The drills continued as normal but more was added and each recruit had to be tested to their limits. The recruits had been shown weapons, that fired rubber bullets. It was explained to them that these were mostly used for training, or crowd control.

Once they were made familiar with these. The following day, the recruits were moved by transport to an exterior location from the academy. At first, they were told that they would be transported by the Slab, but after one failed pickup, smaller vehicles were ordered for them.

It was rumoured that the Slab had a major malfunction and a number of people died but no one knew the real truth. Shortly after this, they were told the last Slab in service was decommissioned and dismantled. The dorms waited in lines to be picked up, the Selirus sun hadn't even started to rise yet.

The pickup point was a huge disused carpark next to a set of gates. These 'gates' led to the outside and were fifty feet tall with a set of guard towers built at the top of each side. It looked like they were unmanned but the large mounted guns moved and rotated at will.

It unsettled some of the recruits to see the guns were aimed into this part of the compound and not towards the outside. The recruits turned as sets of lights seemed to appear in the distance, but they heard no noise. The shuttles drove round the facility and pulled up at the pickup point.

Where did they come from? Vandeaga asked himself. The shuttles moved in a perfect line, nose to tail with no less than an inch gap between them. If the first one moved even slightly to avoid a dip or bump in the tarmac, the rest followed like a wave. The shuttles looked like bullets from the front. Four small wheels on each side with a smooth silver surface that didn't allow for windows.

When it was Vandeaga's turn, he clambered aboard and picked a seat. It consisted of a single aisle with ten seats each side, so a fleet of them were needed to move all the recruits. There was no driver as it was controlled completely by the city's computer intelligence. Jake sat behind him.

"I've been told the front-line guys have been doing this for over a month. Could be even before the group assignment," Jake said.

"I heard that too, Terry has been itching to tell everyone but he said he couldn't," Vandeaga replied and turned in his seat to face his friend.

"I'm really trying to forget that even happened." Jake didn't seem to notice what he said.

"Yeah, none of them will talk about the training facility we are going to." Jake shrugged at his own comment.

"It's going to be some kind of shock and awe thing. I think everyone will be here today." As Vandeaga spoke Taradin slumped into a seat just across from him.

"The groups will need to be led, so it makes sense if I take that honour for one of them," Vandeaga smiled to himself as Taradin spoke.

"Sure, if that's what you want to do then go for it." Vandeaga had something far more interesting to focus his time on. He was trying to work out if the lump stuck to the seat in front of him came from someone's nose.

"That wasn't a request, I'm just better than you, unless you want to compare scores," Taradin said as his hand moved towards his front pocket.

"I don't keep my scores with me." Vandeaga said with a sideways glance, he wanted to see if Taradin was bullshitting him or not. It seemed that Taradin was getting more competitive lately.

They should be working together within their dorm but Taradin always seemed to make it about himself and Vandeaga. Taradin lifted a slip of paper so it was at eye-level between them.

"I always have mine. I assumed you wouldn't think of doing that." Taradin put the paper back and buckled his seat belt. Once the belt was secure, he leant back and closed his eyes, he seemed more agitated than normal. Vandeaga leant round his seat and pulled a face at Jake. Jake just rolled his eyes and shook his head.

What a prick! Even after everything we have done together. Jake stared at the side of Taradin's head. He tried his best to not dislike Taradin, but this was turning into borderline hate.

When the twenty seats were full, the doors closed and the safety belts locked into place. It took no more than thirty minutes to get to their destination. Vandeaga wished the vehicles had windows as he would have loved to have seen what the surrounding area was like.

The arena was still within the compound's furthest walls, but because of the danger the building possessed it was as far away from the main complex as possible. The closest operational building was 'The Shell'. This held the recruits that were deemed too dangerous to house in general population.

Unless you were transferred there, you were not allowed within five miles of it. The recruits poured out of the vehicles and into a huge parking area in front of a colossal warehouse. There were only four regular vehicles parked along the main wall of the building.

Vandeaga looked down the road that they had come from and then up the other. The six-lane road stretched beyond the distance he could see. There was a scattering of street lights but there was no one else around.

The area looked abandoned with countless blacked out buildings stretching into the distance across the road. Wooden boxes and pallets lined metal racking that disappeared into the darkness. Vandeaga stared down the road and he counted the street lamps.

I could just go and see where that takes me.

For no other reason that Vandeaga could think of, he just wanted to go for a walk.

There were no Officers watching them and with this many people in one area, the Minders wouldn't notice if he walked away, but something stopped him. Jake nudged him with his elbow.

"You still counting everything?" Jake kept his voice low.

"It's the one habit that I cannot break, don't tell anyone about it, will you?"

"Don't worry, you can trust me," Jake said with a smile.

There were several dozen Minders stood in the parking area directing the hundreds of recruits into the building with silent waves and points.

After a short walk they arrived at the waiting area, they knew this because of the painted floors and signage. As was normal to them, they sorted themselves into dorms and formed lines as they waited for instructions.

"Right you lot, I'm battle simulation coordinator, Dean." The voice's owner would have seemed more at home as a game show host. It seemed to resonate from everywhere at once, several of the recruits looked round for the source of the voice but couldn't find it.

"You will follow the blue line to my excellent scanners, wonderful machines they are. You will remove all of your clothing before you enter as this could cause a drastic impact on your health and state of mind. Once scanned please remember to put your clothes back on before you meet me at the ready area, move out soldiers!"

Several of the recruits puffed out their chests as they had never been called soldiers before. They followed the blue line and ignored the others. The scanners formed a black wall of metal which blocked their path.

On the far right of the row of scanners was a chain link gate. It was twelve feet wide, ten feet tall and covered in red and white markings. From the look of it, it was only possible to open from the other side. This wall consisted of a dozen scanners and each one had a small conveyor belt on its right-hand side for clothing to be put through.

They did what they were instructed and removed their clothes and placed them on the conveyor. Just like the doors, these disappeared into darkness. Vandeaga was more interested in his surroundings than the guys and girls getting undressed. He had never seen a member of the opposite sex in their birthday suit before, but the machinery in front of him pulled all of his attention.

As their clothing was placed onto the conveyor, each piece was sucked into the machine with a substantial amount of force. When their garments had gone, they stepped into the scanner and were bathed in blue light before they disappeared from view.

Vandeaga's turn couldn't come quick enough as he threw his cloths on the conveyor. He didn't notice a female recruit mutter something to her friend. With a large grin she cocked her head to one side and nodded.

As he stepped into the scanner, the increase of temperature surprised him, but when the blue lights clicked on, he felt the heat intensify all over his body.

"You are about to use the Tissue Scanner Mark 4, please remain calm and face forwards at all times." Vandeaga had to force himself not to look for the origin of the voice. It sounded oddly metallic but slightly gritty.

The floor shifted under his feet and he was moved forwards and rotated. The blue light seemed to get thicker and turned into a haze, he caught a glimpse of something over his shoulder. It looked like it gave him a glance from head to toe before it disappeared behind his back.

"This scanner is mapping your body for future repairs and other requirements. Step off the belt and have a nice day." As the floor stopped dead, Vandeaga half stumbled and was ejected into natural light. He grabbed his clothes and started to redress himself.

This half of the hall was the same as the first but with more metal racking and coloured lines. The sunlight bleeding through the roof windows cast lines through the dust in the air.

"That was odd and rather humiliating." Jake said and Vandeaga turned to him.

"Yeah, just makes you wonder what could happen in here." They continued to follow their line deeper into the building. The ready area looked just like the waiting area but with more metal mesh and glass. Every surface that they could see was taken up by large black holdalls. Vandeaga tried to count what he could see but there were too many. The Deans voice echoed across the building once more.

"You will be split into two groups. Once you are in your group you will be given one bag off the racking. Group one will follow the purple line and the other will follow the yellow line. Ignore the rest and make it quick. I have a grand day of games planned, chop, chop!"

A number of helpers who had been stood there the entire time appeared from the shadows. They smiled at the shocked looks they were given from some of the recruits. The Shades began to hand bags to each person and sent them down the opposing corridors.

A 'Shade' is a member of a select part of the standing army. All of them are enhanced in many different ways. These specialists in covert operations would be used in anything from blowing up targets in enemy territory to assassinations.

You didn't need to be enhanced or modified to be a Shade but you lived a lot longer if you were. As the war became more about numbers and brutal force, the Shades were given other duties. Many of them liked working at the arenas as it gave the recruits drive. Even still, some of them were regularly called back into combat.

"Take this bag and do not open it until instructed to and follow that line." They said this to each recruit and the words never changed. If they were asked a question, it was ignored with a flick of their hand.

Without any information or a screen to look at, the Shades kept all the dorms together perfectly. Vandeaga took his bag and threw it over his shoulder and waited for the Shade to finish her lines. This Shade looked like she was made up of many different parts. Her left hand was dark-skin coloured with silver tips whereas her right hand was jet black and made of metal. Her face was covered in scars and her bottom jaw was a different colour to the rest. One eye shone bright green whereas the other looked like it came from the inside of a computer. It was amber but Vandeaga could clearly see the wires inside of it as it rotated inside her skull.

"Thank you," Vandeaga said. It wasn't that the Shade was shocked but it was just uncommon to be thanked by anyone.

"Faceguards are optional but I recommend you wear it and have fun." The Shade tapped her index finger on her jaw and gave a plastic stretched grin.

"You want to protect these unless you want what I got." The Shade's smile widened to show numerous rows of serrated metal blades.

Vandeaga nodded his thanks and headed for the door. It dawned on him as he followed the yellow line that this is all they ever did, follow this line and do this in this order. A second thought made him realise he was here to do a job and to follow orders, the sick feeling in his stomach dissipated as quickly as it started.

He followed the corridor and it was long; he must have walked for a full two minutes before he saw the first door. In that time, he counted two hundred and seven ceiling lights. He pushed it open and walked into the preparation area. The fact that they were about to train alongside the female recruits went clear over his head.

The males were outnumbered two to one, yet it was still not observed. Officer Faleama, Officer Josef, Officer Jenna and Officer Lysa stood at the front of the hall. Each of them was stood in their formal uniforms instead of armour. When the last recruit entered, Officer Faleama stepped forward and addressed the room with half of a salute. None of them had earned even that much respect, but today she was being nice.

"Good morning and welcome to the Arena." Her voice boomed, no one in that hall could say they did not hear her.

"Thank you, sir!" the response was one.

"There are a lot more of you here than normal so you do not need to stay in your dorms. This is a team exercise." She stepped back and Josef took her place. Josef was tall and well built, he wasn't the biggest, but he still had a dangerous air about him.

"You will make your own squads, Leaders lead, Medics look after your team and Engineers use the environment to aide your side." Lysa was curvier than the other female Officers that Vandeaga had seen. To be honest, he'd really only been instructed by one, the others faded into the background.

"Front line, you are the most experienced in this type of simulation, use this to help bring your team to victory," and finally Jenna took her place.

"If you have a question, you do not need to speak to your Officer. We are all here to help you. We will now pass you over to Coordinator Dean or as he prefers to be called The Dean."

As she returned to the line of Officers, a number of projectors in the hall spun round and lit up. A green figure made of see-through wires appeared and bowed with a flash. As seconds passed, the green lines filled in and he was flushed with colour. The bright red jacket and matching trousers where a sight to behold.

The Dean's long blonde hair was pulled back into a pony tail. He raised his hands up to the ceiling and a football stadiums worth of people started to cheer.

"Ladies and gentlemen, I welcome you to my arena." The Dean's voice was perfectly boarded by screaming support. "It's good to see that you have all found a place to stand. In your bags, you will find a rifle type weapon and a side arm. A select few have been given the opportunity to use the sniper version of this weapon."

Taradin held up the weapon, it was a third bigger than the rifles. The Dean spun on the spot, his head turned first, followed by his torso and finally his legs.

"Yes, that's the one, good on you." The Dean pointed and this was followed by another over the top cheer.

"The weapons entrusted to you are live and fire rubber bullets at very high speed. They have been known to open skin and break bones. Depending on your style, armour is not compulsory but I would recommend it. You take the chance at your own risk so don't blame me if you swallow some teeth."

The Dean's laugh stretched out at least ten seconds longer than it should have. He gestured towards the four sets of doors with an exaggerated flurry of his arm, that led out into the arena itself.

"Beyond these gates is your battleground, but in here, this is my safe space. No one and I repeat, no one, will put a magazine into a weapon in my safe space, it that understood?" The Dean's voice changed just enough so there was a simmer of a threatening undertone.

"Yes Sir!"

"Good, you are a wonderful lot." The Dean's image crackled and sputtered, the image drove its fingers into its own head and screamed. Within the blink of an eye The Dean had vanished from sight and was back to normal on his return.

"The battlefield will be different every time you are here, and it may even change during play, so beware of this. Any questions so far?" There was a moment's silence when a hand went up at the back of the hall.

"Ask away," Dean said with a smile, his face flickered the larger it got.

"How are we removed from the field? One hit and we're out or is it something different?" The recruit asked as some others nodded with him, it was a good question.

"I would have come back to this later but as you have asked, I will cover it now. You go as long as you can. Being hit without armour will hurt a lot, so if you can't go on then you are out. If your weapon is knocked out of your hands by an enemy round, then you must switch to your sidearm, simple, yes?"

"Yes sir!"

"Good, I will be back in five minutes to give you your briefing so be ready. Bye for now!" The Dean saluted them all and vanished with another cheer, the large room went oddly quiet. This didn't last long as a mad surge flowed across the hall as everyone emptied their bags across the tables.

Each bag contained the following.

One primary weapon,

One smaller sidearm which was similar to a pistol. It only held two shots.

One tactical rig complete, with arm and leg armour with their own team stripe. There was enough space to hold all of your magazines and more.

One light marker; the light marker can write on anything in any bright colour depending on the person's choice.

One flash light,

One radio head-set,

Six unloaded magazines with a full box of rubber projectiles, and finally, a mask.

The mask was a simple oblong shape with hardened plastic inserts behind the eye slits. The only problem with it was that the narrow eye slits made visibility difficult. The wearer wouldn't be able to look down at their chest rig and see where their spare magazines were.

Before anything else Vandeaga tried on the mask for size and strangely, it was a perfect fit. He would have to make do as he wasn't about to ignore the advice of the Shade. No more than four minutes had passed before everyone had put on what armour they wanted and fully loaded their magazines.

The groups had been picked and Vandeaga was voted to lead a small squad. There were more leaders than squads but they were told that everyone would get a chance, but not given a reason why.

Taradin had forfeited his chance to lead a squad. He was more interested in getting up high and taking out his own targets. They stood in their squads and waited for The Dean to reappear.

"Are you loaded and ready for war!" The Dean roared at them as he appeared. His jaw opened wider than it should have and just before it reset, he threw his arms wide in a display of power. If an artificial intelligence could have a crazy look in its eye, then this was it.

"Yes sir!" The recruits jostled each other in anticipation. Vandeaga, on the other hand, just wanted to hear the brief.

"In this simulation you need to capture the arming codes in the centre of the play area and bring it back to your compound. These arming codes are in a briefcase which must be brought back as well. When the support weapon is activated with the arming codes, it is game over and we start again. One last thing, if someone is unconscious on the floor, don't keep shooting them it's an arsehole thing to do. We go live in 3, 2, 1, GO!"

The four fifteen-foot doors dropped into the floor, the squads piled into the arena with battle cries and roars of excitement.

Chapter 10

The arena was a square mile of memory foam, metal and plastic. It was designed to replicate any known terrain or environment. At any given time, the land scape could change to become anything that The Dean wanted. This ranged from simple things like dirt and sand to fully furnished buildings and even simple machines. The arena could even replicate rivers and water with the added effect of holograms and directed sound.

The battleground for today was an urban city scape complete with derelict structures and burning cars. Remains of people that looked a little too life-like were scattered across the floor. The payload was located in the middle of a decimated city square. Only a small portion of the arena was being used today so the rest was blocked-off by conveniently collapsed buildings and debris.

The teams on each side had split their people into smaller squads. Some rushed towards the centre and some slowly followed to guard their possible exit route. There were lots of places to take cover but a lot of open ground too.

Vandeaga led one of the squads that had rushed for the centre and the briefcase. He wanted to be seen to lead, to be the best. As he had not met some of his squad before, they decided to give each other numbers as this would be easier to remember.

Mike had the idea to write their numbers on the front and back of their chest rigs. Vandeaga looked round the last corner and spotted the pay load. It was a silver brief case with a black hazard warning symbol sprayed onto the front surface. It was laid on a car bonnet, but it was still attached by a chain to a body that was on fire. Vandeaga glanced round at the rest of the square in awe.

This simulation is amazing. He thought as he sent two of his squad to get into cover. He saw the flash a little too late as the rubber slug smashed off the side of his mask. It wasn't a direct hit but the force shoved his head backwards as he fell behind a wall. His team mate dived behind the same piece of cover.

"Number one, you alright?" Vandeaga shook his head. He knew his neck was going to be sore tomorrow.

"Yeah, I'm alright but fuck me that hurt," he squeezed the button on his radio. "Who's not wearing face masks?"

"Number six."

"Number three," they answered him in unison and he almost missed their numbers.

"Right, you guys stay in cover and don't take risks or you are going to get hurt. Everyone else move forward and return fire. We will keep them occupied and wait for the other squads to go around." Vandeaga changed frequency.

"Squad Delta is at the payload. We are exchanging rubber with!" As his squad opened fire, he ran and slid into better cover. The exotic movement wasn't required but he had always wanted to try it.

"At least two squads directly ahead of us, over." The car he hid behind took a dozen strikes.

What a waste of ammo. He looked down as one of the rubber bullets rolled past his foot.

"Received Delta leader, Alpha is far right and taking hits. Enemy is dug in so this side is boarded, over."

"Beta is coming up to reinforce you, CONTACT! Delta on your left!" Vandeaga turned and fired at the opposing squad that were about to advance on him. He shot one of them in the chest and skimmed a rubber slug off the forearm of another.

They quickly threw themselves behind anything they could. The members of his squad that weren't wearing masks had hidden themselves within a side building. The enemy squad had taken cover across the street but had not seen them yet.

To shoot fish in a barrel would have been harder for them. Vandeaga had been so preoccupied with their left, he hadn't seen the movement on his right. He couldn't have guessed how much it would have hurt until his was shot in the ribs.

Unlucky for him the rubber missed all of his armour and mesh. He felt something crunch within his chest and couldn't stop the sound he made. Mike opened the car door and used it as a shield and placed his hand on Vandeaga's side.

"Shit, it feels like two of your ribs are broken!"

"How bad?" Vandeaga said through his teeth.

"They are in place but," a bullet smashed into Mikes leg armour from under the car and knocked him off balance. He was forced to grab hold of the car to keep himself up right.

"Fuck me where did that come from? You will be ok but don't move around a lot or you will make it worse."

"Where the hell is Taradin?" Vandeaga could feel that anger building up inside of him again. This only seemed to happen when Taradin was involved.

"Radio him, number three has gone down." Mike stared at the slumped body of his team mate. It never seemed strange to any of them that no matter the rivalry, Taradin wanted to be in Vandeaga's squad. At the end of the day, they had more important things to worry about.

"Go, I'll be alright. Number two, we are in need of some serious support here." There was no response as Vandeaga took another hit in the exact same place. He collapsed against the car in pain. He could leave the field but he had only been out here ten minutes. Taradin's voice crackled over the radio.

"That looked painful, that's really shit cover you are resting against kid. Give me a second, this thing's having feed issues. Right, all good now, time to smack some people."

"Fuck you!" Vandeaga hadn't used the radio, no matter how much he had wanted to.

Taradin laughed from his end, it seemed he was having a great time. Vandeaga looked past the car and Taradin appeared in a top window. Every shot he fired he got a hit. He forced the enemy squads to fall back and made the squad below him take a full-on retreat.

"It's alright, I will keep you babies safe. Anyone of you idiots want to grab the payload? I'm starving." Vandeaga almost said something he would have regretted down the radio. He took a breath and centred himself before he tried to carry on.

"Five, four and seven on me and press forward and secure the payload."

Charlie Squad quite literally appeared from nowhere. They charged forward under full fire and didn't even stop to take cover. They grabbed the briefcase and rushed past Vandeaga and his squad.

"Everyone, keep Charlie covered, escort them back to base." Vandeaga said as he forced himself to his feet.

They hurried back to their starting point, and kept the enemy at bay as dozens of rubber slugs were fired between the opposing squads. Mike had to support Vandeaga the last twenty feet as he had started to find it difficult to breath. As a member of Charlie squad jammed the briefcase sized item into the box a siren blasted across the simulation.

"Well done teams, back to your ready areas and wait for round two. You will remember to not take live weapons into my safe area! All magazines must be removed and that includes any rubber left in the chamber!"

The Dean's voice made their ears ring. The enemy team had to walk back through the entire Arena. It wasn't too far but this did give them a chance to have a better look at the simulation on the way back. They thought up plans with their knowledge of the arena's layout, until the break where it changed.

Mike helped Vandeaga into the ready area and sat him down on one of the tables as Faleama walked over.

"You performed well but there is much to improve. Get yourself into the medical cube and follow all of its instructions. Taradin, come here, I said come here, I need a word with you!" Mike pushed Vandeaga into one of the booths and pressed his hand onto the door sensor and it started to close. Just before the door shut, he heard Faleama's voice.

"What the fuck do you think you are…" and then Vandeaga was in silence. Inside the cube he was bathed in the same blue light that was in the Tissue Scanner. It was only four feet by four feet and just tall enough for him to stand in.

"Please remove any clothing from the affected area and place your hands, if possible, on the yellow area." It was difficult for him to move his arms but still managed what he was requested.

Vandeaga waited there with his hands on the yellow parts of the wall. He didn't know what to expect but just after the humming started it felt like someone had started to rummage around the inside of his rib cage.

He almost dropped to a knee but a force held him upright. With his eyes clamped shut, he didn't see where the device came from. The immense pain soon stopped as a fluid was injected into his arm and something else started to massage his neck.

He could still feel his ribs yanked back into place and the intense heat from a bone welder. It only took a minute and the door slid open. He picked up his armour and walked back to his bag.

"How was it?" asked Mike as he continued to load rubber into his magazines. Vandeaga looked back to the cube and then to Mike.

"That was one of the weirdest sensations I have ever had, but I'm good now," he patted his own rib cage, "you see, it's all good." He felt no aches or pains, if he hadn't been in the cube, he'd have said it didn't happen.

Officer Faleama strolled over like she had done this too many times. All recruits present stood to attention.

"At ease, are you good to go for round two?"

"Yes Sir, if you don't mind me asking but where's he gone?" Vandeaga nodded towards Taradin's empty space.

"It was he who shot you in the ribs, twice. The Dean sees everything that happens in there." The Dean appeared with a flash of green and gave them all a big thumbs up before he vanished again.

"Son of a bitch," Vandeaga muttered and quickly remembered he was in the presence of an Officer, "Sorry Sir, it just slipped out."

"It's understandable, but just remember that you getting hurt had nothing to do with it. It's part of the game and you deal with it, but shooting a member of your own squad is serious. Do you have any questions?"

"Yes sir, do the frontlines use those?" Vandeaga pointed at the Medical Cube.

"No, those draw so much power you would need several reactors to power the mobile units. We tried them before and there were too many problems. Also, they have to work with a body scan, so if you don't have one or if it gets corrupted then the AI tends to put stuff back in the wrong place. Anyway, get ready and load your magazines as round two will begin shortly." Mike patted Vandeaga on the shoulder.

"You good?" He said and continued to rummage through his gear for more rounds. The sudden appearance of The Dean made him jump.

"If you run out of ammunition, there are dispensers on every available wall." The volume of The Dean's voice didn't change and the room turned in his direction.

"Erm, thank you," Mike said.

"That's fantastic, I'd forgotten to mention it before." The Dean turned, bowed and disappeared with an electrical sizzle.

When everyone had turned back to their own tables Vandeaga shook his head as he'd almost forgot what he was going to say.

"I can't believe that bastard shot me, why would he do that?" Vandeaga knew Taradin didn't like him for some reason that he couldn't work out, but this was over the top.

"It's because he is mental. You know when I got shot from under the car?" Vandeaga nodded, "that was him too."

"That's what I mean. He's so good at what he does, why feel the need to be a shithead about everything?" Vandeaga asked with a shake of his head.

"Your guess is as good as mine on that one." Mike just shrugged as he finished inserting rubber into his last mag with a smile.

"I just had a thought," Vandeaga said as he started to load his magazines.

"What's that then? Or am I supposed to guess?"

"Taradin is part of the leader's block but I have never seen him there."

"As I said before, the rumour is that he is getting one on one training but no one really knows," Mike said with a shrug.

"That was fun," Broo said with a forced laugh. The side of his face was red and swollen.

"Didn't you were a mask?" Asked Vandeaga

"I thought I would have better vision," Broo touched the side of his face. "It was a bad idea but we live and learn don't we. Did you guys ever hear about what happened at the group session?" There was a mixture of head shakes and confused looks.

"Someone used a battery to blow the door and several others tried to force their way out."

"I guess that ended badly for them," Mike said.

"They were all removed," Broo said.

"How did you find that out?" Vandeaga asked. At the time, he had spoken to everyone that he knew but no one could tell him anything.

"Frankie told me, he seems to know everything or at least where to find out."

"Right, you wonderful lot, are you ready for War!" The Dean screamed at them.

"Shit!" Broo shouted as he ran back to his table, he'd forgotten to load his magazines.

Chapter 11

Vandeaga had been sat in the canteen pretty much on his own. The Leader's block had sustained a power cut. The complex's artificial intelligence had refused to turn the power back on due to nonorganic life forms in the air ducts. There wasn't any, but the AI wasn't going to change its mind any time soon.

He grabbed a sandwich from the counter and pressed his thumb onto the contact next to the computer. At first, it flashed up someone else's information, then the screen reset and his appeared. The computer then warned him that he should be consuming more calories so he walked back and grabbed another sandwich.

Once again, the screen flashed the same message, he thought it must be faulty and walked away. Vandeaga sat down at an empty table and breathed in the peace and quiet. With a smile, he began to unwrap the first sandwich and it smelt good. It contained strips of meat and salad with a slightly bitter sauce.

It was strange as this stuff was never on the counter when it was normal meal time. Then he remembered he hadn't got a glass of water, and that sick feeling started to build up in his stomach again. He rushed back to the counter and filled a pint glass with the silver fluid.

The recruits had a choice in what they could drink. They were requested to drink the silver water but they were not stopped from drinking the clear. The clear still had chemicals in it but not the new silver persuader.

The sick feeling only stopped when he took his first sip but he continued to drain half of the glass. He topped the glass back up to the top and strolled back to his table. He glanced up and read the poster stuck to a support next to his table.

Do you require a challenge?
Do you require a change?
Do you want to help us with the most advanced technology our people can offer?
If the answer to any of these questions is yes, then you should apply.
Send your information to .6734tcejbushcraeser.

Vandeaga could apply for it as he loved a challenge. He could get others to apply for it too, they might even give him a medal. He winced with pain but it wasn't too bad and the feeling came from his stomach so he put it down to hunger.

So, he turned his attention back to the sandwich, as he picked it up, he glanced to the entrance doors and Jake rushed in. Jake stopped and glanced round the hall until he spotted Vandeaga.

This is going to be bad. He thought and with great regret put the sandwich down, but it was alright as he had his water. Jake walked over with a sense of urgency and slumped into a chair on the other side of the table.

"Van, I've fucked up," Jake felt he had to say this in a whisper even though he didn't need to.

"Aren't you supposed to be in your block?" Vandeaga asked. He felt really good for some reason, even the paintwork looked better today. The walls had a certain shine about them that he couldn't quite describe.

"No, there was a power failure and the whole place has been shut down for the day. I heard the same happened to the leader's block." Vandeaga nodded with agreement.

"So, what's the problem then?" Vandeaga asked but couldn't take his eyes off his sandwich. It was there waiting for him. He felt his mouth water and just wanted to jam the entire thing into his face.

"I can't do it," Jake placed his head in his hands, "It's all too much to learn and I'm falling behind." He hit the table with a clenched fist. "Why can't I do it Van?" Jake tapped the side of his head. "Why doesn't this work like everyone else's?" Vandeaga looked up at the poster, something at the back of his mind screamed at him to be quiet, to ignore everything in the room and not talk to Jake. He took a sip of his water; the voice and that rational part of his brain fell silent.

"You could keep doing your best and hope the information sticks or you could apply for that?" Vandeaga pointed at the poster and took a large bite out of his sandwich, and it was beyond amazing. It was all he had waited for as his taste buds exploded in joy. He let out a joyful moan as his vision flickered.

"I could do," Jake thought for a few moments, "I will see what happens. Thank you for the advice as always. I'm going to get some food. Did you want anything else?" Jake looked at Vandeaga's 'sandwich'. "You really should put something between those."

As Jake walked away Vandeaga looked down at his plate. What he thought he saw, wasn't real. He stared at the two slices of brown bread and those colours that he enjoyed before began to bleed into each other.

Within seconds, he fought the urge to empty his stomach over the table and reached for his water, and that is when he realised what he was doing. As he looked round the hall everything turned grey and dull, like he was drained of happiness.

Someone told me not to drink the silver, but who was it?

He couldn't remember, his memories seemed to have acid poured over them as they swam together into a blur.

I swore I wouldn't drink this stuff, when did I start?

He couldn't remember.

Jake sat next to him with a full plate and no drink. Jake nodded towards the glass and whispered.

"I thought you said not to drink that." Jake gestured towards the pint glass.

I did tell everyone not to drink it didn't I, but when?

He couldn't remember.

Jakes expression changed from worry for himself to concern for his friend.

"Are you ok?" Jake asked as Vandeaga pushed back his chair and stood up. The colour drained from his face.

"I need to take a piss. I'll be back in a minute." He briskly walked towards the toilets. As he passed a random table, he picked up a salt shaker. He pushed the door open and jogged past the two dozen cubicles and turned a tap on one of the many sinks.

The water was clear so he knocked the top off the shaker and poured the contents into his mouth. He bent down and drank straight from the tap, after the tenth mouthful he retched and ran to the closest cubicle and slammed the door. He almost missed the toilet as he threw up.

When he was finished, he looked into the pan and it was coated in a silver sludge. He opened the door and went back to the tap and did it again. He couldn't throw up this time so he jammed his fingers down his throat and made it happen.

More silver gunk landed with the rest. He flushed the toilet so he didn't have to look down into it. Vandeaga had to steady himself against the wall as his head started to float, his knees buckled and he collapsed to the floor. He heard someone enter the toilets but he couldn't do anything about it. The only noise he could make was a gurgling sound as his limbs started to feel numb.

"Van? You alright?" Jake called from the doorway. What little energy Vandeaga had left, he pulled off one of his boots and kicked it out of the cubicle. Jake watched it slide across the floor and knew there was a problem. He ran up and grabbed Vandeaga's boot and banged on the cubicle's door. "Van! Mate, you ok?" he heard nothing,

"Sorry if this hits you!" With as much force as he could muster, Jake kicked the door and the simple slide bolt snapped. Vandeaga was in a crumpled mess in the corner. He tried to stand but couldn't find his legs. Jake picked him up and dragged him outside.

Scores of people had started to enter the hall so Jake dropped him into a chair. "I will find Mike and be back, don't try and go anywhere." With that, Jake left the hall. Vandeaga's hands clamped onto the table in an effort to stop himself from being back on the floor. The food hall started to blend together, people, tables and food seemed to become each other in fluid movements. This didn't last long as the hall and everything in it began to fade into darkness.

His body started to ache and his head throbbed. He tried to open his eyes but to his shock they already were. Vandeaga realised he couldn't see anymore. He was filled with panic but couldn't do anything about it. He had no recollection of how long he had been sat there. He pulled back with a start when he felt a hand grab his shoulder.

"Vandeaga, it's ok, it's Mike, what the hell happened to you?" Mike placed two fingers onto his neck and looked into his eyes.

'Why have his eyes gone that colour'. Vandeaga's eyes were a mixture of blood shot and grey.

"He was acting odd, I found him like that, but on the floor in the toilets." Jakes voice crackled a little.

"This looks like withdrawal symptoms but from what I don't know. Vandeaga, can you speak to me?" Mike got no response other than a drunken slur of breath.

"He was drinking a lot of silver." Jake had lowered his voice so the other people that had taken seats nearby couldn't hear them.

"I mean, he drained a pint glass of the stuff."

"His pulse is through the roof. We need to get him to medical, right now!"

"Why?" Jake didn't quite pick up on the urgency of the situation.

"Because it looks like he's had a reaction and I think it is getting worse. We need to get him to medical immediately, because I have no idea what to do."

Vandeaga tried to ask what was happening but all that came out was a garbled mess. He felt himself picked up by his arms and was dragged out of the hall.

*

Faleama had been requested to attend a meeting; all that she knew was that it was for 'urgent' business. Urgent business, normal business, it didn't matter either way as she had no choice in the matter and had to go. Faleama donned her Officer uniform and made sure it was perfect; she would have preferred to wear her armour.

When two Officers go toe to toe it's always a sight but when a room full of them strike off, it often turns to chaos. It was rare that a fight broke out during these meetings, but it was always interesting when it did. She placed her hand on the scanner that led into the Officer's block and pushed through the door, four minders stood to attention as she walked past.

She gave them a single nod as any more than that was a waste of her time. She could only guess as of the reason for the meeting. Her first thought was that she was going to be recalled back to the frontlines, and that news couldn't come any sooner. Her wounds, mental and physical, had healed and she was ready for something more than this.

It wasn't that she didn't like the routine of training the recruits but she felt bored with it all. To be honest with herself, she was still here for only one reason anyway. Her second thought was that another one of her selection had snapped. Everyone knew this batch had been the worst they had ever seen. If the secret tests had been stopped when they were supposed to, then they wouldn't be in this mess in the first place, but who would listen to her anyway.

Faleama walked up to a solid set of wooden doors and tapped on them. Within seconds they swung inwards and she walked towards the rectangular table that dominated the centre of the room. It appeared that she was the last of the Officers to arrive, but there was one chair at the head of the table that needed to be filled. The Officers all stood and saluted her arrival, she stopped and did the same.

"Good afternoon Officer Faleama, and how are you today?" Officer Nash called across the table; he always liked Faleama, it was a pity she detested him for being a pervert.

"I'm well, I take it that you are the same?" She pulled out a chair and sat down. Nash made no attempt to hide the fact that he eyed her body as she sat down.

You wait until I catch you on your own, you slimy little bastard.

"Very good, I would be better if we knew why we were here." This was met with general chatter. A second door opened and a dark-skinned man and woman walked in. Her uniform was a pristine mix of black and red layers of cloth, only the best would sit on her shoulders. The man was dressed similarly but wore an ankle length leather jacket.

There was an eruption of sound as all the chairs slid back, everyone stood, everyone saluted with no exceptions. Each person placed one hand over their heart and the other on their forehead before they bowed. This salute was reserved for the highest of ranks. The man walked over to the head of the table and pulled out the woman's chair. She sat down and pulled herself towards the table.

"Thank you," she said. The man bowed and stood just to her left. He folded his arms behind his back and stared at the opposite wall. He didn't look that different from an Officer but this man was beyond anything the Officers could comprehend.

He was the direct protector of the chancellor herself, and would do anything within his power to keep her safe. The long jacket wasn't just for looks as it kept all of his weapons out of plain sight. He was always armed and always ready to take a life.

She cleared her throat twice, the man walked to a machine that was in the corner of the room. "Is anyone missing?" she asked, this was followed by silence. The man turned back to his chancellor and presented her with a glass of clear water.

"Thank you," she took the glass of water and the man went back to his position.

"At ease, you may sit." There was another clatter of chairs as the Officers sat down. Officer Nash made a conscious effort not to look at the woman.

"You have been called here to be informed that the dorms are to be merged." The woman gave them a moment for this to sink in.

"This means that there will be too many Officers so some of you will be sent back out to support the front lines. They are ever expanding and we need as many Officers out there as we can get." The man seemed to hand her a pile of papers that he wasn't holding before and she flicked through them on the table.

"As you all know, this is the worst cycle for snaps, so a new type of Silver was added to the food and water to calm the recruits and increase their focus. The findings conclude that many, take to the substance with no issues, but others have a drastic reaction to the chemicals over a period of time. I have been informed that it is due to a collection in the brain, which is normally followed by mass rejection and organ failure due to the brain's miscommunication with the rest of the body. This part of the research department, have concluded their tests and the Silver has now been removed. The colour will remain in the water and food to offset the mental change due to the reduced amount of the product. The deaths due to this have been buried so as not to cause any more problems."

Each Officer looked at the others, they knew about the silver of course, but not about the deaths. A female Officer further down the table raised her hand. Scars ran up her face like she had been slashed by an animal. She was also the only Officer that wore gloves to this meeting. The woman at the head of the table looked in her general direction, "Yes, Officer Katrina?"

"Why the need to cover up the deaths?" Officer Katrina lowered her hand. There was a moments silence before the woman smiled at the question.

"It's because some of you get a little too attached to your recruits." The Chancellor turned her gaze to Faleama.

"We didn't want any more incidents between Officers and Command, so the information was withheld. Anyone else with a question?" Faleama was in the process of raising her hand when Nash shot his hand up first.

Prick! Faleama thought with a shake of her head.

"Yes?" The Chancellors jaw tightened as she turned her gaze towards Nash, but he kept his eyes on the table.

"I do feel that a death or even a removal that are due to circumstances that are out of my control should not go against me. So, will we receive a list of the deceased, as I would like to know for my personal records?" The Chancellor gave this question a thoughtful nod before she answered.

"That is a valid point Officer Nash. Makes a change, does it not?" His eyes remained on the table, but he did grant himself a small grin. The woman turned to the man behind her and he lent forward.

"Bring me a list of the silver deaths for each dorm." she glanced down at her watch, "you have four and a half minutes." He turned his head a little to the right and waited, "I will be fine." She said and tapped the firearm on her hip, he nodded, bowed and left the room. She glanced down at her papers and gave them a shuffle.

"Right, this brings me to the merging of the dorms. Male and female dorms will be merged as some of them now have less than fifteen recruits in them." Nash raised his hand again, the woman glared at him for a full minute, the room was silent.

"Yes, what is it now?"

"Is it wise to mix the sexes as there could be, how I can say, problems?" The woman put her papers down and lent back into her chair.

"Officers, Faleama, Katrina, Jenna, Cartright and Lysa. Please stand and take a bow." In one swift movement the five female Officers stood and bowed.

"Let me ask you a few questions. Katrina, do you feel your female recruits would have a problem being merged into a male dorm?"

"No Chancellor Torn," Katrina said with a cold voice.

"Why?"

"Because if need be, they can and will defend themselves. I'm sure the males will believe they can do the same if the situation arises."

Torn asked each Officer in turn the same question, and each gave the same answer until she reached Faleama.

"Officer Faleama, as the only Officer that deals with a male and a female dorms. Do you feel there will be a problem?"

"No Chancellor Torn."

"Why?"

"Because they know better and I will see to the punishments personally, if there is an incident of any kind, and this will go for both sides."

"Good, that is what I like to hear. However, I am not concerned about the females. I know how they are trained and I know what each one of them is capable of. I only have one thought and that is for weak-minded males." She glanced at Nash. This time it was Faleama that allowed herself a small grin.

"Some of the females will be very forward and stupid, and so will some of the males. The Officers that are left will need to keep a very close eye on what is happening in your dorms. Is that understood?"

"Yes Chancellor." A door opened and the man walked in with more paperwork; he handed it to the Chancellor. She glanced at her watch and gave him an agreeable nod.

"At ease, thank you," Torn checked the sheets and handed them back, "Give them out please." He nodded and began to walk the long table and give each Officer their figure's, and they were bad. After a quick read, Cartwright raised a hand.

"Yes?"

"Going by this, all of the recruits that I thought were transferred to G Squad are all dead. That's over half of my dorm." At first, she looked concerned.

"Yes, your dorm was hit the worst." Cartwright nodded and her look of concern changed into a smile. It seemed her scores weren't that bad after all. If they died of silver then it wasn't her problem anymore.

Officer Faleama glanced down at her paperwork and there was one number '454376AHF' and her heart sank into her stomach. It took everything she had not to react to that set of numbers and letters. She raised a hand and was convinced there must be a mistake.

"Yes?"

"How accurate are these lists, I have not been informed of 454376AHF being transferred, so how is he on this list?"

"That would be the one that was bought into medical roughly an hour ago, organ failure followed by zero brain activity like the rest." Faleama just nodded and rested the sheet of paper on the desk.

"Now back to the merging of the dorms, as stated there will be too many Officers. Do we have any volunteers to go support the front lines before we have to bring up success records?"

To the surprise of everyone present, Officer Faleama raised her hand. It was time for her to leave, she had only stayed for him anyway.

Chapter 12

Vandeaga woke up and immediately wished he hadn't bothered. Pain, like he had never felt before in his life, flowed from his head down to his toes. This was before he had opened his eyes. When he finally managed to prise them open, the dim lighting made them hurt.

He was laid on a metal medical bed with a sheet pulled up to his neck. He scanned the rest of the beds that were in the large room. He couldn't move his head too far for the discomfort, his neck muscles felt like lead mixed with barbed wire. He grimaced as pain ran up his spine and punched into the top of his head.

Only a few of the beds were occupied but most had the sheets pulled over their heads. His arms were not covered by the sheet so he could see the numerous drip feeds plugged into each one of them. To his right, he saw the mass of machinery he was hooked up to.

It was more than a slight shock when he realised, he wasn't able to breathe on his own. He could barely feel the pipe down his throat like the sensation was being numbed. He watched the air pump raise and lower with a hum as it kept him alive. He must have only been awake minutes but that was enough, his eye lids refused to stay open any longer.

A woman walked past his bed, it could have been minutes or hours later before she made another pass, but he didn't know. The covered bodies on the other hand had been removed and their tables were clear. She stopped and glanced towards him. He blinked at her, she starred at him for a second before she moved towards his bed. She checked his feeds and looked into his eyes to make sure he was conscious and that this wasn't an after effect.

"Blink twice if you can understand me?" Vandeaga did what he was asked.

"You're lucky, we were going to turn you off tomorrow." She pressed a finger to her temple and changed dialect.

"454367AHF is awake, yes he responded, yes I understand, it will be done." She pressed several buttons on his machine and the noise changed, the clear fluid in the drip feeds changed to a dull orange colour.

"You will be up and walking about in a few hours, but you may feel a strange sensation for a little while." As she walked away, he never took his eyes of the feeds. He could see the orange fluid getting closer and closer to his arms.

A mere second after the fluid touched him, his heart rate triple. All the colours in the room became so bright he couldn't see past the flood of rainbows. The air pump vibrated with the increased amount of oxygen that was required and Vandeaga blacked out.

*

Vandeaga sat bolt upright in his bed. He was no longer plugged into any machinery and he felt like a new weapon.

He had never felt this healthy in his life, he could feel his heart beat and it was strong.

He looked down at his arms. Where the tubes had been his skin had gone a light orange colour. He rubbed at them and looked round the hall. He was the only person awake. The same woman was about to walk past when she noticed him sat upright. She smiled and walked over to him.

"How are you feeling 454367AHF?" He had a quick look around before he answered her.

"I feel amazing thank you, but that is not my number." He spoke so fast she almost missed what he said. The woman reached for the screen at the bottom end of his bed and gave it a puzzled look. She pulled it free and tapped the thin glass. It flashed up figures and charts, she handed it to Vandeaga.

"So that is not you?" As he read the text, he shook his head.

"My number is 454376AHF, the last two digits are backwards." Still confused she tapped the screen again.

"Place your hand on this please." The thin glass showed a picture of a hand print. With his first attempt he almost slapped the screen out of his own hand. It took every fibre of his being to move his hand just enough to get it correctly on the glass.

After a couple seconds it flashed green and she pulled it away. Another brief wait and a couple impatient taps from the woman, his information loaded up. She looked at the glass then at him, then back to the glass.

"This is going to be a problem. How does someone mess that up?" Vandeaga just shrugged, he had no idea what this could mean.

"Your number has been confirmed deceased, but that can be reversed, I will send your information away now. Please remain here until we can get this little problem sorted out."

"Ok, I will," she smiled at him and walked away. Vandeaga's mind processed information far quicker than it normally would have.

"Can I ask a question?" his speech came across as a blur. Her hand almost touched the door when she turned.

"What's the question?" She asked and Vandeaga forced his eyes closed as they started to burn. He would have to make a conscious effort to blink.

"Why am I talking so fast?" Without really thinking he pointed to his own mouth.

"The process to heal you will leave certain side effects. You will run out of steam at some point and need to sleep. So, you need to remain here, understand?" Vandeaga just nodded and waited for her to leave.

As soon as she had, he flipped off the sheets and rushed to the door. He looked down at the thin gown he was in. It barely covered his crotch and didn't even attempt to cover his arse. He tried to pull it down but the fabric didn't stretch. With a shrug he pushed through the door.

*

It didn't take him long to get out of the medical block, the only problem was that his hand print didn't work. He had to wait for someone else to let him out. Every time, he expertly persuaded each person that it was an AI malfunction or he had been mugged and even other bizarre reasons.

It was his reasoning and ability to answer any question he was given that got him all the way to the dorm. He did however get more than a few strange looks as he ran bare arsed up the corridors to his dorm.

The Minder that had taken the two shots to the gut for him watched him run past and started to slowly follow. Vandeaga pushed open the dorm's double doors and with open arms shouted.

"HI GUYS!" He was met with a number of different reactions as his thin gown slipped fell off his shoulders and onto the floor. A number of girls giggled and turned away, a few of the guys did the same. He didn't recognise half of the people that were stood in his old dorm room.

Mike dropped the paper work he had been holding onto. He left his mouth open a little longer than he had initially wanted too.

"What the fuck are you doing here?" Muncher yelled, who was also in a mild state of shock.

"I'm alright, I'm here now. Who the hell are all you people?" Vandeaga's speech was so fast no one understood a word that came out of his mouth.

"You were reported dead, we had words and everything, you were dead." Mike said with a number of slow steps towards his friend.

"That was yesterday and I'm ok today." Vandeaga took a huge breath, he felt so good right now.

"No, that was a week ago. The dorms have been merged and Faleama has been transferred to the front lines. Why are you talking so fast?"

"A week? Shit, that's not good and Faleama is gone so that means I'm screwed," Vandeaga glanced round the dorm "Where's Jake?"

"He sent his information away on that poster," Mike pointed to the one on the wall, "he hasn't been seen in four days." Vandeaga stood ridged then his legs almost gave way, Mike steadied him, "We need to get you some clothes."

"No, wait a minute this is going to wear off soon and I need to say something. How old am I?"

"What?" Everyone thought it, but Mike was the only one that said it out loud.

"Think about it, I was in dorm thirteen, I was told I was thirteen and you were dorm sixteen, right?"

"Yes, that's right, so I was sixteen." Mike said with conviction, that was what he was told, so that was the truth.

"We are the same height! Most of us are all the same height!" Mike had never thought about it, he just agreed with what he was told, they all did.

"If I'm thirteen and I do this training which should last two years at the minimum. Do you really think they would let a fifteen-year-old boy, lead as a squad leader or as an Officer?" Vandeaga had raised his arms towards the ceiling.

"Fuck no!" A guy he had never met before was stood next to him. Vandeaga reached over and shook his hand with a firm grip.

"I'm Vandeaga," Vandeaga smiled and gave a nod.

"I'm Karl," Karl repaid the gesture.

"Do you see what I mean," Vandeaga threw his arms back up to the ceiling. As he spoke, he didn't stop or take a breath.

"This whole place makes no sense what so ever. Oh, and on the day I collapsed I drank way too much silver and

143

remember about an hour of that whole day I need to speak to Jake and why does the bottom of that poster say research subject backwards and I'm really tired and I think I need to sleep."

Vandeaga took a huge breath and dropped to his knees before he toppled face first onto the floor with a slap. Everyone looked at each other as Vandeaga began to snore. Mike knelt next to him and checked his pulse.

The double doors slowly opened as the Minder that had followed Vandeaga pushed them open with its head. Everyone stepped back as this Minder had gotten the reputation of being unpredictable. He walked over to the nearest bed and pulled the sheet from it.

This Minder had been repaired for the damage it had sustained, but not its armour. For a reason that none of the Techs could understand, it kept intercepting signals. It would take routes and tasks so that it could be as close to Vandeaga as it could be at any given time.

"Hay! that's my bedding." A girl at the back of the group shouted at him with the added menace of a pointed finger. The Minder turned and looked through the group for the speaker.

"Never mind take it," and all the venom dropped from her voice. The Minder wrapped Vandeaga up in the bed sheet and threw him over his shoulder. With the unconscious Vandeaga, it looked to the group and placed its index finger on its mask where its lips would be. It made a hiss sound as if it was telling them to be quiet and walked out the dorm.

"What the fuck was all that about?" Taradin had only just woken up and watched the Minder leave before he looked at Mike.

"Well, Vandeaga is not dead anymore and a Minder just took him wrapped in a bed sheet. I'm hoping he is taking him back to medical and not to be recycled." Mike looked over his shoulder as Taradin just shrugged at the announcement.

"We could try and stop him?" someone said from the back. Terry looked round to see who it was. He had a black and swollen jaw.

"Great idea, one of them freaks fucked me up because I didn't get out its way in time and you want to try and force one to stop?"

"Great, now I have another score to beat. Keep the noise down, I'm trying to sleep." Taradin rolled over and pulled the pillow over his head.

*

Vandeaga once more woke up in the medical block and this time he was strapped to the bed. He didn't mind this as he felt like death and just wanted to sleep anyway. The same woman walked into the room.

"I said don't leave, didn't I?" Vandeaga wasn't sure if she was angry or not, he just mouthed the word 'sorry'. "Your treatment wasn't finished, you idiot. You could have had a relapse and that would have ended badly for you. You're lucky that Minder found you and brought you here. We can't, however, retrieve the information as to where he found you, and now he won't leave."

She turned to the double doors and the Minder was stood with its mask pressed up against the glass.

"Leave, that is an order," the Minder took a step back and turned a full circle and went back to the window.

"There is something very wrong with that Minder, it needs to be fixed. Like everything else in this place. Why did we have to be stuck with the 3rd generation models? Anyway, I have sent a report away to have it removed from service."

Vandeaga wasn't sure if she was talking to him or herself. Behind the door, the Minder twitched its head from one side then the other. That report was somehow suspended in the system, along with dozens of other reports relating to it. 3rd generation were pretty much the same as the gen ones and twos, but not as well-tested.

"The building's computer flooded room sixteen because of a fire that wasn't there. One day the A.I. will all work again," she turned back to Vandeaga.

"Your information has been corrected and you will be out of here later, today or tomorrow. Do you have any questions?" Vandeaga could only think of one.

"How old am I?" he whispered and fought the urge to throw up. The woman smiled at him like a mother would smile at a small child that asked her if the moon was made of cheese. She had no reason to answer that question and left him to rest.

Chapter 13

It didn't take long for Vandeaga to get back into the routine. It did, however, get tedious having to explain to people that he wasn't dead and it was a mistake. Several weeks had passed and he still saw no sign of Jake, he wanted to see him even if just to explain that he wasn't in his right frame of mind.

He had so much work to catch up with, within the leader's block, and Taradin seemed even more resentful than ever before. Vandeaga tried to talk to him on more than one occasion, but Taradin just looked through him and walked away. Vandeaga kept telling himself that it didn't matter, but on the inside every time he saw Taradin's face he wanted to punch it.

The food hall was busy as normal for the evening meals. Vandeaga's dorm sat round one table like they always did. He got used to the new guys and girls pretty quickly as it didn't make much difference whom he shared space with. He ate his food with one hand and read paperwork with the other. Vandeaga was however very happy to see one particular new face in his dorm. As always, he kept that information to himself.

"Will you put that down!" Terry waved his arms around before he pointed to Vandeaga's hands. He had a forkful of forgotten food in one hand, a set of paper work a quarter of an inch thick in the other.

"I have to keep ahead. It is not normal to be allowed time off sick." Vandeaga gave him a toothy smile and continued to read his papers.

"Yes, you said this before." Terry picked up a lump of something off his plate and popped it into his mouth, and immediately regretted it. "What is this shit they are feeding to us now?"

"I don't know but it tastes rancid, and I'm not eating it anymore." Larooa held onto the table with one hand and tried to crush her fork with the other. She didn't manage to crush the utensil but did turn it into a u-shape, with added pressure from her thumb.

The closest members of their group slid their chairs away from her. She was due a snap quite a while ago, but Vandeaga seemed to be able to calm her down each time. He put down his papers and looked straight at her from across the table.

"Do you like pepper?" Larooa and everyone else turned towards him. Karl had a fork full of something suspended next to his mouth.

"What has that got to do with anything?" The force in her hands had turned her dark skin pale.

"I'm interested in your opinion, do you like pepper?" There was no emotion in Vandeaga's voice as he tapped his fingers on his paperwork.

"Yes, I think so, I don't know," Larooa shook her head as none of this mattered, this conversation was pointless.

"Grab a couple packets and dump it on top, that's what I do. Also, it doesn't come under the food ration so you can use any many packets as you like."

She seemed to stare at him for a moment, her jaw tightened. Vandeaga never let his eyes move from her glare. A full minute passed before she released the table and walked over to the service counter.

"How the hell do you do that?" Muncher asked. He made sure his voice was low enough so Larooa didn't hear him. He wasn't scared of her, he was petrified.

"Not sure really, everything seems clearer since I was ill. I'm not sure I want to do this anymore. None of it makes sense." Vandeaga gestured towards his own papers.

"Don't say that out loud for fuck sake. You know people have been disappearing!" Mike leaned across the table and almost went as far as to slap him. He stopped when they heard someone scream and the shattering of glass.

"Where's Taradin?" Vandeaga asked and he stood up to scan the hall, and there he was in the middle of the commotion. Taradin punched another recruit in the face, and then disappeared under a mass of bodies.

"He's getting his arse handed to him, come on!" Vandeaga shoved his chair out of the way and stepped from the table.

"Fuck him, he's an arrogant prick." Karl continued to shovel food into his mouth. Broo gave him a nod of agreement.

"He's part of our dorm and we look after our own, don't we?" Vandeaga turned and rushed across the hall, the rest of his group got up and followed suit. He charged into the fray, but only to get to the centre of it. He blocked a blow with his arm and shoved the girl onto her arse.

When he got to the centre Taradin and this group's leader were trading vicious blows. Taradin had a swollen eye and a busted lip, blood running down his chin and neck. The other guy was missing some front teeth and had a gash above his eye.

Something hard connected with the side of Vandeaga's head. He turned to see a large guy with the remains of a glass bottle. Vandeaga's right hook knocked him backwards and through a table with a splintering of wood.

Vandeaga's group cannoned into the fight, no one held back and everyone got stuck in. This was until Vandeaga screamed for it to stop. He shoved Taradin and the other guy away from each other.

"If you don't stop, we are all going to get screwed for this." Vandeaga could feel something wet run down the side of his head. It was only then he felt the pain and knew he was bleeding.

"This piece of shit started all this!" The other guy screamed at Taradin.

"Fuck you, did I?" Taradin screamed back and tried to get another punch to connect.

"You think the Officers will give a shit when they get here, we have only seconds before the shit hits the fan." With that Minders flooded into the hall followed by several Officers.

Minders don't have great decision-making skills at the best of times. So, when they were ordered into the Food Hall to break up a fight that had already stopped, it threw them a little.

A couple pushed their way to the middle of the group with their stun batons ready, but they soon strolled away again, but not before a random recruit got the full taste of a baton. Officer Josef was the first at the scene.

"So, would anybody like to tell me what is going on?" Officer Josef never raised his voice and he never swore. As this was met with silence, Vandeaga had to lead the way again. He stepped forward and saluted in the most formal style that he could.

"Sir, I can only speak for myself but I violently fell over. I will also apologise for the damage as I broke that table on the way down." He pointed to the table he knocked the guy through.

Josef took a closer look at the glass fragments in his hair and tried not to laugh.

"That's really strange, because it looks to me like you have been glassed, and those tables are capable of taking far more than your body weight," he pointed to Vandeaga's hair.

"No sir, my head struck a glass as I fell. Believe it or not but it was on the exact same table." Vandeaga looked round and the guy that hit him with it still clutched the broken remains. Josef followed his line of sight and smiled before he folded his arms.

Fucking idiot.

Vandeaga caught his eye and spoke clearly. "Sorry I didn't catch your name." The big guy's eyes seemed to widen when he realised, he was the centre of everyone's attention. Or, it could have been concussion, as his face had started to swell.

"Erm, it's Braker," Vandeaga nodded and continued the tale.

151

"When I broke the glass with my head, Braker here picked it up so no one else could hurt themselves on it." A second Officer stepped forward.

This was Officer Jason, and Officer Jason was a top contender for the biggest arsehole of the year award. He looked slightly thinner but was a little taller than Josef. Jason always had an expression on his face like he had stepped in something vile.

"So, if you were picking up said glass, how did you take a punch to the face, Braker? Don't be a fucking prick and tell me you fell over, because," Jason pointed at the red marks on his face.

"They are knuckle imprints under your right eye." Vandeaga remained silent as Officer Jason had not spoken directly to him. Braker thought for a moment before he turned to Vandeaga.

Please play along Braker or I'm screwed.

"Sorry I didn't catch your name either." Braker held out his free hand and Vandeaga shook it.

"It's Vandeaga," Braker nodded and started his tale.

"You see Vandeaga was still on the floor. I picked up the glass with one hand and lent over to give him assistance. He must have been dazed because as he went to place his hand on my shoulder he misjudged where I was. This is how his hand connected with my face, purely by accident." Josef just smiled and shook his head. Jason on the other hand hadn't finished.

"So, you both admit you were involved, with you." He pointed at Vandeaga "punching you," he pointed at Braker "in the face?"

"I slipped," Vandeaga said.

"By accident," Braker agreed.

"And the glass that's still in your head and his hand?"

"I fell," Vandeaga said with a nod.

"He fell," Braker agreed once more.

"Fuck sake, someone is going to get done for this and I will find someone."

Jason had no cause to reprimand either of them and he knew it. The only things that would need to be looked into was the damaged furniture in the Food Hall. The third Officer, Officer Jenna, knew this was going nowhere and left the male Officers to deal with it. She waved at Josef and left the hall.

He smiled at her and took a moment to watch her walk away. Her off-white hair was tied into a plate that ran down her back. She was slightly shorter than Josef but trained nearly every spare minute she could. She'd given Josef a few injuries in her time. Josef realised that everyone else had been staring at him for maybe a few seconds longer than he would have liked.

"Right you lot, you do know we can just check the cameras and find out who was at fault." Josef gestured at the two dozen small boxes positioned around the room.

"I will not file a complaint for an accident." Vandeaga gestured towards Braker.

"I will also not file a complaint." Braker agreed and Officer Josef couldn't help but smile again. When he passed his training, he was considered the smartest, and he had done the same when his dorm almost caused a riot. Though, back then he didn't think he sounded quite as comical.

"You two go to medical," He sent Vandeaga and Braker on their way with a wave of his hand.

"I guess that all of you have as good reasons as to why you are injured or bleeding?"

"Yes sir," They said in unison. Vandeaga and Braker only spoke when they left the Food Hall, and only when they knew no one else was about. They spoke like old friends as they walked to medical.

"Sorry about your face Braker." Braker's eye was almost swollen shut and had turned a very odd shade of purple.

"No problem, I'm sorry about your head. This was the only thing I had in my hand at the time. Should I get rid of it?"

"No, keep it on you just in case anyone asks questions when we get to medical." Braker nodded and kept hold of the remains of the bottle.

"I have to ask what started all that off?" Braker gave him a grin.

"To be honest it was our man that sort of started it."

"How do you mean?" Vandeaga would have put money on it that Taradin was at fault.

"Your guy bumped into one of our girls, and showed no sign of saying sorry. Personally, I would have let it go and just thought he was a prick but Sean is very protective of us. So, he demanded an apology which is when your guy…"

"Taradin," Vandeaga said his name to ease the confusion.

"Which is when Taradin told him quite bluntly to fuck off. Then Sean told him he would speak to you to sort him out. Fuck me, he flipped like nothing I have ever seen, he grabbed a chair and smashed it into Sean's face. You saw what was happening. I thought you were coming over to get stuck in. Do you and Taradin not get on or something?"

"Why would Sean want to speak to me about the issue?"

154

"You are your group's leader, aren't you?" Braker thought that this was common knowledge.

"It's never really come up, most of them look to me for advice but that's about it." Vandeaga shrugged.

"Most of the other dorms think that is the case, so yeah, everyone else has brought it up. So, do you and Taradin have a problem then?"

"We don't really talk. I've tried but I just get ignored or he walks off."

"He sounds like a prick to me, but Sean won't let this go. You saw what Taradin did to his teeth."

"I did and I will see if I can sort this out somehow."

They had gotten some very strange looks as they passed through numerous sets of doors. Vandeaga checked behind him and saw more of the two dorms had been allowed to follow them to medical. As they pushed open the medical block doors the same receptionist from before was stood in the entrance room.

"This is becoming a habit. What the hell happened to you two?"

"He slipped and fell on this glass bottle," Braker said and nodded towards Vandeaga.

"I went to place my hand on his shoulder for support and clipped his face." She gave them a quick once over.

"Ok, that is going to need to be sealed and you seem to have a broken cheek bone, go through that door." She pointed to the closest one and turned back to her screens. It was at this point she realised just how many people were about to walk into medical. She tapped her temple twice.

"Support required at the front desk."

Chapter 14

Vandeaga was the first back to their dorm. The gash on his head had been cleaned and glued. He was only a little disappointed when he was told it wouldn't leave a scar. He sat down on his bed as his head started to throb. He only opened his eyes and turned when he heard the doors open. Larooa and Mike walked in.

"You are one crafty bastard." Mike clapped his hands together but Vandeaga could only look at his bruised face. He also had a thin line of glue up the side of his cheek that would have been a deep cut, and his left hand had started to change colour.

"It was like magic, each person followed your plan and each one had a story that worked, it was amazing to see. I will say it's a very odd way to introduce our selves to another dorm as everyone knows each other's names now." Larooa stood next to Mike, her jaw line was bruised. The knuckles on both of her hands were red and swollen.

"I'm glad you enjoyed yourself Mike. How are you doing Larooa?" She looked down at her knuckles and touched her eye.

"Yeah, I feel ok, actually I'm better than ok. I haven't felt this good for months, and I'm not stressed at all." She strolled over to her bed and laid down with a grin. It didn't take longer than an hour for most of their dorm to return.

They stood around and laughed about what happened, each person showed off their injuries with pride. Broo walked in and he looked like he had needed stitches across his lip and forehead. Both areas were red raw, he had blood smears across his eye brow and nose.

"What happened to you?" Mike asked with a point of his finger.

"Mate, you wouldn't believe it. Of all the things in that hall, I got hit with a fucking chair," he raised a hand to his swollen face. "On a different note has anyone seen Frankie?" There was a number of strange looks and head shakes.

"I'm just asking as I haven't seen him in almost a week."

Muncher burst into the dorm and the double doors struck the door jams with a loud bang. He was already talking before anyone could ask what was wrong.

"Vandeaga! Taradin has screwed everything up!" Several of Muncher's fingers were tapped together on one hand and his little finger was splinted on the other.

"What do you mean?" Vandeaga moved past the others so he was at the front of the room.

"It was myself, one person from the other dorm, Taradin and the guy he was fighting with." Muncher counted the people off on his non-injured fingers.

"He's called Sean. I will need to speak to him about all this, what has Taradin done now?"

"Well, he told the Officers that you said they would be too stupid to see what you had started."

"When the fuck, did I say that?" Vandeaga turned to the rest of his group.

"You didn't, I was next to you in the hall the whole time," Jenny said. Vandeaga looked round to her, she also had the starting of a black eye. Muncher continued with a wave of his hands.

"He then started arguing and swung for Officer Josef."

"That's him transferred then!" Terry couldn't hide the fact that he was relieved about it.

"You should have seen Josef, damn that guy is fast. Before Taradin's punch was even half way through, Josef slapped it out of the way, picked him up and threw him through a table."

"That doesn't sound that impressive," Karl puffed out his barrel chest.

"One arm Karl, he used his left arm and didn't even move his feet. Officer Jason dragged him out of the hall by his shirt." Muncher was in awe, if he could be anyone, it would be Josef.

The doors crashed open as a Minder fell backwards through them. A long piece of metal stuck out of its eye socket. It convulsed and twitched but stayed on its back. Taradin stepped over the body and into the dorm.

His face and torso were splashed with blood, he held a make shift knife in his right hand. A set of handcuffs hung from his wrist. The other loop was still closed with chunks of skin stuck to the metal. The fingers on his left were twisted and broken. As Taradin stepped forward everyone but Vandeaga stepped back. Vandeaga readied himself and took his stance.

"This is how you wish to settle this?" Vandeaga clenched his fists but kept them at his sides.

"This is all because of you, you know that!" Taradin shouted as blood ran from his fingers and trailed across the floor. He pointed the knife at Vandeaga and took a step closer with each word.

"Fuck you it is. You take things too far. This is all down to you. Don't force your mess onto me." Vandeaga couldn't see how any of this should be on him.

"It's people like you that race ahead and do all that you're told that raise the bar for every other fucker. It's because of you I'm screwed no matter what I do, no matter how hard I try, you get there first."

"Don't try and…" Vandeaga didn't have time to finish as Taradin rushed at him with his blade. Vandeaga had just enough time to side step the lunge. Muncher hadn't backed away enough and took the full length of the blade to the chest, he screamed and fell backwards.

Taradin took this moment of hesitation from Vandeaga. He pulled out the blade and slashed sideways. Vandeaga felt the metal run up his ribs. He jumped back and placed a hand on his side, blood ran between his fingers and soaked his shirt.

This wasn't training, this wasn't an act, Taradin was going to try to kill him. Something snapped deep within him, this was the moment Vandeaga changed, every pissed off feeling every hate-filled moment, he just let go.

Mike dragged Muncher out of immediate danger and started to treat his wound with anything at hand, another medic from the dorm joined in. Mike tried to calm Muncher down as he began to cough up blood. Karl saw a chance and stepped forward, but Taradin heard the movement, he turned and slashed the side of Karl's face with an upward swing.

Karl couldn't do anything else except clutch at his face. He'd felt the metal blade run across his teeth. He never realised how lucky he was as Taradin had aimed for his eyes. Mike looked towards the double doors.

Where the hell are the Minders, this shouldn't be happening.

"Stay back this is between us!" Vandeaga screamed and charged. Taradin threw the blade, Vandeaga caught it mid-flight and dropped it to the floor as they connected. They traded a volley of blows, only a quarter of each connected as each one of them defended what they could.

Taradin was doing remarkably well but in the heat of the moment he punched Vandeaga in the ribs with his broken fingers and pulled back in pain. Vandeaga capitalised with six good hits to his face. Neither of them heard the doors open, or notice Josef move across the room.

He sent Vandeaga flying over ten feet and onto a bed. He wasn't as gentle with Taradin as he picked him up by his throat and slammed him into the floor. Taradin remained still, as Vandeaga rolled off the bed, he stood up straight and tried to salute. The crisp white sheets were peppered with red.

"Sir, I…" Josef waved his hand as he wasn't interested in what Vandeaga had to say. Josef pointed at him.

"You get back to medical and Mike take him as well," Josef said as he looked around the room. He pointed at Karl,

"Medical, where are the Minders?" He was greeted with a number of confused looks before he tapped his temple.

"I need Minders on my location now. They will be taking a prisoner off site. Yes, he is, yes, he's still breathing, just get the Minders here!"

Vandeaga helped Mike pick up Muncher, Karl followed them as he held his face to slow the flow of blood. Josef walked over to a bed and in one movement ripped the bed sheet in two. Clara would once more need to find a new bed sheet. He used one half to tie Taradin's legs together and the other for his arms. He tapped his temple again

"Do we have an update on Jason?" He could speak frankly in the Officer's tongue.

"Yes, I need that information, so he will be fine? Might scar, and no loss of function? Thank you." Josef wasn't sure if Taradin was conscious but he got close to his ear.

"You're lucky because if you had killed him. I would have taken great pleasure in breaking your fucking spine." As Josef stood up four Minders rushed the room. Josef welcomed them with open arms.

"Well, it's nice to see you have turned up at last, but the action is over. Take that one to the Shell and that one." He pointed at the Minders body that was still on the floor. Dark red gunk had started to pool around its head.

"That one needs to be recycled."

The Minders did their tasks and left the room. On the way out, they smeared the spilled blood across most of the floor and quite the distance up the corridor. The other members of the dorm hadn't moved and neither had Josef.

"Right, you lot, stand at your beds and let's do this properly." The recruits stood at the ends of their beds and waited. Josef paced the room end to end and tapped his finger on his chin. He reached the double doors and looked like he was about to leave when he turned and saluted them.

"At ease," everyone breathed out at once, "there is going to be a lot of questions asked. You will answer them honestly and accurately. Now, does anyone have anything they want to ask me?" Larooa stepped forward "Yes?"

"Will Taradin be coming back?" Larooa kept her eyes forward, her fist visibly clenched when she said his name.

"I don't think he will but would there be a problem if he did?"

"I can only speak for myself but as he has harmed a fellow dorm member that I like." She stopped for only a second but Josef saw the anger burn on her face. "He will not be safe if he were to stay within these walls." Larooa couldn't contain the amount of venom that flowed with her voice.

"You do understand how that could go against you to say that?" Larooa nodded and remained where she was, she wouldn't back down, she wasn't going to fade away. She would face Taradin if given the chance, she now longed for it.

"Who else here feels the same?" without a second thought everyone stepped forward. Even the guys and girls that hadn't been part of the dorm that long felt the same.

"Unanimous it is then? I suggest this is not to be spoken of again, and I will make sure Taradin will not come back to this dorm. I will promise you that, and if I must say I doubt he will be training here anymore. If it was my decision, he wouldn't be breathing, but it is not."

Josef walked over and picked up the shiv. *This is nice work, very well made.* He twirled it across his fingers. He pulled a black plastic bag out of his back pocket and dropped the shiv into it. "Who is on cleaning duty today?"

"It was Muncher then Mike, Sir!" Terry said and tried not to think about who's blood he was stood in.

"Ok, well they are both not here so I suggest straws are pulled or you all get this cleaned up. Take whatever you need

162

from the supply cupboard and it will be replaced with no penalties. Does anyone else have anything they need to ask me?" There was silence.

"Good, I have to go and make sure that idiot gets the proper treatment." Josef turned with a slim smile and left the dorm. The group raided the supply cupboard down the hall and began to their clean their dorm. They talked amongst themselves as they got to work.

"Do you think they will be alright?"

"I'm sure they will both be fine."

"Muncher looked pretty bad."

"Mike was with him."

"Did anyone else notice Officer Josef knew Mike by name? I thought he mostly used numbers." There were a number of nods and hums of agreement.

"I think that's a bit odd, I'll ask him about it later." Clara said. Broo nodded and dunked a mop into a bucket of water and bleach.

*

The injured party burst into the medical block once more.

"Can you lot go a day without coming in here? What's happened?" The woman called at them as they hurried towards her. She quickly realised how bad this was as Muncher coughed blood down his front and onto the clean white floor.

"He has been stabbed in the chest and his left lung is filling up with blood, he has a deep cut on his face that most likely will cause facial problems. He has been slashed up the ribs and has lost quite a bit of fluid." Mike shouted as the

163

group got to the desk, several assistants entered the room and prepped each person for their treatment.

Mike followed Muncher's gurney all the way to the operating theatre, when they passed the doors, he stopped. The surgeon that was in the room walked towards Mike and pushed open the door.

"Why are you waiting out here?" The Surgeon asked and Mike stood to attention, he wasn't sure why but he did it anyway.

"I'm no longer required to be here so I will head back to my dorm sir."

"I have been told you seem quite knowledgeable. You are being trained as a combat medic, is that correct?"

"Yes sir," Mike gave the statement a nod.

"Then come in, this will be a great experience for you."

"I'm not ready for this type of procedure sir." Mike knew he wasn't going to get away from here without getting his hands dirty but he had to try. Being made to use Muncher as his guinea pig wasn't how he pictured his first time.

He listened to Muncher cough and cry with pain through the half-closed door. He would swear that he also heard the faint splash of blood.

"I will tell you what to do but the longer we stand here and talk, the longer it takes for him to get better, that's if he does." Mike gritted his teeth, took a deep breath and followed the surgeon into the room.

*

Vandeaga had been glued back together once again and sent back to his dorm. Karl received similar treatment and was also sent on his way. They entered their dorm together and most of them were still active.

The floor had been cleaned and the bedding that had blood on it had been changed. Larooa gave Vandeaga a hug, he tried not to show the pain but it was hard. He also didn't know which part of him hurt more. He had a full collection of injuries from the fight.

"How do you feel?" She asked with a warm smile.

"It's healing well but it will hurt for a while." Vandeaga answered with a grimace as she touched his wounded flesh.

"Why don't you take some pain killers, you'll feel better?"

"They didn't give me any," Vandeaga shook his head.

"Why would they do that?"

"Not sure, they just didn't give me any and I didn't want to ask." As Vandeaga finished his sentence Terry laughed at the situation.

"You twat, you always ask for pain killers, you have to or they don't bother." Terry popped two pills into his mouth and swallowed. Vandeaga sat down onto his bed, he had to bare his teeth as the flesh around his ribs stretched.

"Wow, that hurts," Vandeaga placed a hand to his side and tried to breathe through the pain.

"How's Muncher doing?" Jenner asked, she looked between them both. Karl just shook his head and placed a hand to his face, he also forgot to ask for painkillers. He shrugged and looked at Vandeaga.

"I'm not sure, have you asked Mike?" Vandeaga said.

"No, he's not back yet," Jenner scrunched her eyes at him. They left as a group and it was odd that they didn't come back as one.

"Where is he then?" As if on cue, Mike pushed his way into the dorm. His complexion was almost white, he strolled between the beds and towards the gathering.

"What the hell happened to you?" Karl said.

"I think I did alright," This was met with silence so he continued, "Muncher should be ok, I think he should be." Jenner put her arm round him.

"You ok?" she asked.

"Not really, I was told to perform the surgery on Muncher." Mike's brain hadn't quite caught up yet. It was like everything that had happened, did so to someone else.

"Please tell me you are taking the piss," Terry couldn't believe it. Mike didn't look up, his eyes remained fixed on his bed.

"No, they erm, told me I was going to do it. I was under supervision but still I'm not supposed to be doing stuff like that yet." He half-looked at Jenner and let out a heavy sigh.

"But you have been gone hours," Karl looked between the others.

"The surgeon had a number of other appointments he wanted help with, so yeah I did them too." Mike tried not to think about all the blood and the screaming.

"But you are not qualified," Jenner said.

"I don't think they gave a shit if I'm honest, I'm going to have a shower and go to bed. The rest period is over and it's back to normal tomorrow."

Vandeaga wanted to ask Mike about Officer Josef but stopped himself. He too had spotted their less than formal relationship

How can anything go back to normal after today? What if Taradin was right about me, people like me cause the problems in the ranks? I don't understand anymore.

The group dispersed and got ready for bed. Vandeaga took a moment to scan all the bruises his group had, he'd never considered these people as his group before, but it felt good, he was proud. He let himself smile at the thought and rolled over. His lips pulled back over his teeth again as pain flashed across his torso.

This is going to keep me awake.

Chapter 15

Everything seemed to have calmed down after the flash point in the food hall. As the weeks passed, Muncher was back and training as normal. No one saw or heard from Taradin, officially, no information was given about him. Vandeaga had found the leader of the other dorm and smoothed everything over. It helped that Taradin was no longer part of their dorm.

Strangely this made a lot of people react to them differently. Their new Officer was Josef and being the least hated of the ones remaining was a welcomed decision. Broo had asked everyone he saw but Frankie never reappeared. It was rumoured he had been transferred but as he was the best in that dorm, it was unlikely.

Vandeaga was on his way out of the leaders block when he was passed a message by a member of staff. He unfolded the paper and scanned the text.

Please come to my office, regards Chrisa.

Vandeaga assumed this would not be good, but he had no choice either way. He left the exit behind and walked back up the long corridors until he found the right door. This one was newer than the others and a lot heavier too with its reinforced lock and frame. Vandeaga knocked twice and waited.

"Come in," Vandeaga pushed down on the door handle and walked into the room.

"How are you doing Vandeaga?" Chrisa placed his hands together.

"I'm fine, getting back to normal," Vandeaga replied, but thought to himself *'what is normal here?'*

"That's good to hear. Jake speaks very highly of you." Chrisa's face slowly crept into a smile as Vandeaga tried his hardest not to react, and failed.

"Where is he, have you spoken to him?"

"He is helping Tyler with our research problems. He may not have been much use as an engineer but he's doing great work in the labs."

Vandeaga didn't see it at the time but Chrisa's smile had turned into one of those that people learned to hate.

"Why is he not in the dorm?"

"It's different down in the labs so they have their own dorms there and even a really nice canteen. It's not that we want them cut off from everyone else but it just makes things easier for the people involved." Vandeaga didn't understand any of it.

"Can I speak to him?" Vandeaga asked. Chrisa seemed to think about the question like he hadn't already made up his mind before the question was asked.

"I'm sure you can, but I will have to move a few things around and it will have to be out of hours. I can get that arranged too if you want?"

"It would be good to talk to him, thank you." Everything that made Vandeaga who he was, told him that this was a very bad idea.

"Good, then I will see what I can do," Vandeaga saluted and headed for the door, "You owe me a favour though." Vandeaga knew this was coming. He saluted again and left the room. As soon as the door shut Chrisa's face turned to a hate filled snarl, and tapped at the intercom.

"Get me lab twenty-six, yes I can wait." He touched his left screen, it flashed up pages and pages data and charts alongside Jakes picture.

"Yes, I have a subject for a stress test. No, this test will be involving someone that's not strictly volunteered, do not record names," Chrisa laughed to himself

"Well at least it will be fun to watch."

*

It was almost a week later when Vandeaga received the message that Jake wanted to speak to him. Chrisa was very specific that it was an afterhours meet and not to pass the information on. The first time he read the message he wasn't sure it was even real. He knew something was going to happen but he had to speak to Jake, and more for himself to make sure he was ok.

The day had been the same so far. Get up, get washed, head to the canteen and have breakfast. Walk to the leaders block and do more paperwork and answer questions. Head to the training ground and practice drills and weapon skills, then back to the food hall for evening meal time.

Instead of going back to get fed, he was met by an assistant and a Minder. He was escorted through the medical block and down into the sub levels. Vandeaga was convinced that none of the other recruits had even seen this place, as the assistant had to punch in several different codes just to get to a waiting room.

"Make yourself comfortable and you will be called soon." The assistant said on the way to the exit. Vandeaga looked around the room, it was hard to see as half the lighting was off.

"Why is it so dark in here?" Vandeaga asked as the assistant had one hand on the door, he stopped and turned.

"It's out of hours and the lighting is controlled by the local artificial intelligence, as normal, it is having issues. Do you know what an artificial intelligence is?" Vandeaga gave him a very confused nod.

"Good, it most likely doesn't register that we are the only people here so it's stuck on emergency mode." With that the assistant rushed through the door and was gone from sight.

This is so wrong. Vandeaga thought as the only present Minder left through the same door. He knew that he needed to leave, he could just go and no one would be the wiser, but what if Jake had waited for him. What if he had needed this as much as he did and he had left him alone again.

Vandeaga pushed himself out of the chair and began to pace the room. It wasn't much of a waiting room as there were only four chairs. The door he came in from had no visible locks. However, the door on the opposite side of the room looked very secure. He could see it was twice as thick and the glass alone would have weighed more than the first door.

Above it, there were many panels with numbers on them and bright red strips ran down either side of the door frame. He must have waited over an hour, and more than once he almost let himself out. If he had followed his gut feeling he would never have agreed to come, but that was too late.

The secure door beeped and the side lights turned green. Vandeaga spun as the sudden noise made him jump, the number 16 flashed green and the door opened on its own. Vandeaga edged towards it and stuck his head through the opening.

Corridors led away in three directions, as he moved sensors detected him and turned on half the lights. He squinted and tried to see any numbers or lines for him to follow but there was nothing. He stepped back into the waiting room and looked at the flashing panel again.

He must have missed the luminous green arrow that pointed to the right corridor. With gritted teeth and clenched fists, he followed the direction of the arrow. He walked down the darkened corridor and froze in place. He heard something and the hairs on the back of his neck stood up. He snapped round to check behind him. That noise sounded liked someone had taken a deep breath somewhere in the shadows.

Vandeaga was starting to question if he was alone down here. With a heavy breath he started to edge his way forward. It wasn't long before he saw a green light flash above a door fifty feet in front of him. He turned when he heard two loud clicks somewhere nearby. It was either the secure door had sealed itself or another door had opened but it was too dark to see.

His mind screamed at him to run as the hairs stood up on the back of his neck again and a tingling feeling ran up his spine. He knew he was being watched by some hidden cameras but he had to see this through. He approached the open door with the green lights and walked through the frame.

The smell of something burnt hit his nostrils. The room itself was pitch black but it felt big, it could have been bigger than his dorm room. He took a couple more steps and the door slid shut behind him with a click. Half the lighting clicked on and past the many chairs someone was sat on a table. All he could see was an outline through the poor light. He tried to focus as he stepped forward.

"Hello, anyone there?" the person spoke, but it wasn't a voice he recognised. The voice was deep and slow, like they had smoked eighty a day for a century. The sentence ended with a fluid-based growl.

"Yes, I'm here, who is that?" Vandeaga took a few more steps. It felt like the person laughed but it sounded like a garbled exhale of liquid.

"Hello 45 and how are you today?" Vandeaga froze as his skin began to itch and turned cold. He had a feeling something horrible was about to happen, and he was right.

"Jake is that you?"

"Yeah, what's left of me anyway. I trusted you, you know that?"

"I came to see if you were ok and I needed to explain some things."

"Other than the constant fucking pain I'm fine, don't come any closer." Vandeaga had edged forward a few more steps before he stopped.

"I was told this would benefit me but I couldn't work out why they would arrange this, and now I know. You see I'm not that cooperative with them and well they want to see if I lose my temper with you." Jake was sat on a table with his feet on a chair. Vandeaga could just see his heavy boots and combat trousers.

"Why would you?" Vandeaga moved his head forward to see if he could get a better look at his friend.

"Oh, I don't know maybe because," Jake jumped off the table with a very heavy thud and took a step towards him, "I took your fucking advice!"

His voice echoed around the room like a fog horn. Jake held his hands at his sides and with a snap there was a flash of colour. Liquid blue fire emanated from his finger tips and palms. The flames rippled up his forearms and seemed to dissipate just past his elbows.

Jake took another step forward so he was under one of the dim lights. Vandeaga recoiled with horror at the sight of his friend. He realised that the burning smell was actually him. His skin was so burnt it had turned black, and in some places the damage was so bad that muscle was visible.

A harness had been welded through his skin and onto his bones. The harness itself held two grey tanks connected to his back. Silver flexi pipes lead from these tanks and connected into plugs on Jake's body in numerous places, at least four of them connected straight into the back of his head.

"Fuck me, what did they do?" Jake just grinned as bluish fluid ran from his eyes and down his pale cheeks. As each droplet of fluid hit the floor it ignited with a flash.

"It's called signing my life away as a test subject, that's what happened. This is pretty tame compared to some of the shit they have done down here. I should never have listened to your shit." As Jake growled a couple of the burn holes on his chest oozed and sealed over with enhanced healing.

"I didn't know what was happening that day, I was messed up on silver and other stuff, I don't really know why, I can't explain it all." Vandeaga held his arms wide in protest.

"You always have an excuse, always got a way out. You were dead, and I needed to get out before I failed the course and you said 'go for it', didn't you?"

"That wasn't what I wanted to say, I wasn't me." Vandeaga pleaded with him, but Jake turned and smiled. He had already convinced himself otherwise.

"You want to see something cool?" Before Vandeaga could think of something to say, flames exploded from Jakes hands and ran all the way up to his neck. With a scream of pain, his threw his arms forward and the liquid blue fire flowed across the tables.

Vandeaga jumped back but the fabric of his arm ignited. He yanked off his jacket and threw it to the ground as the material melted into a puddle of blue. The fire sensors kicked in and sprinklers sprayed a mixture of water and foam across the room. Neither of these touched Jake as the heat evaporated the moisture before it got a chance to touch his flesh.

"It was your choice!" Vandeaga screamed at him. Jake dropped his arms and all of the flames in the room ceased, like someone had turned off an oven.

"You told me to do it!" Jake slammed his fist into his own chest with each word. Flames erupted from each impact and hung in the air for a couple seconds.

"You made that decision not me. You asked my opinion and I gave it to you, but you didn't think even once about how fucked up I was and that my advice was shit because of it!"

"I always did what you said without question." Jake's voice lowered but the anger did not leave his eyes.

"Your choice!" Vandeaga had always taken the lead, not necessarily because he wanted to but because no one else did. Jake screamed as his hands burst into flames again, the small pumps on top of the tanks rumbled as they forced fluid into his body. This time the blue flames turned purple and ran up him like water, wave upon wave of heat destroyed his flesh. The wet floor was quickly dried from the shear amount of generated heat.

"So, this is it, you want to kill me for what they did to you?"

Jake laughed at Vandeaga, it sounded like gravel rolling down corrugated metal. As Jake spoke, he sucked in the flames and blew them out of his nose.

"No 45, I just wanted you to see what you forced me to become and to show you this." As his flames roared, Jake reached up and grabbed hold of the pipes that sunk into his head and pulled. There was a snap and the sound of his flesh tear as the pipes were yanked loose. Jakes skull was visible under the heat and the pipe pumped fluid over him and the floor. He ripped out the other two pipes and the fluid ignited which caused a blast of fire. Vandeaga threw himself over an upturned table. He watched the wood start to blister as he rolled away and stood up.

"Stop it Jake! Why are you doing this?"

"It's simple 45, I don't want to feel this pain anymore." As the fluid burned, Jakes flesh did the same, whatever chemicals were in those tanks no longer made his body regenerate. The secure door opened and four Minders rushed the room. Two of them carried what looked like flame throwers strapped to their backs.

"You are not taking this away from me." Jake screamed as one of the unarmed Minders ran towards him. With a burst of force Jake raised his arms and brought forth a torrent of purple flames that turned the Minder into boiled slush. What was left of the Minders arms snapped away from the boiled torso and dropped onto the floor.

The flesh on Jakes hands had gone way beyond his regenerative capabilities. His skin blackened and peeled away. Several of his fingers turned brittle and shattered, but he forced himself not to stop. The two Minders with the back packs opened fire and sprayed black foam towards him.

Jake tried to ignite it but nothing happened, he ramped up his power from purple to white, but the foam only just started to smoulder. The fire on the ceiling had already spread across the room, all the tables closest to Jake had been reduced to ash with the heat. The other unarmed minder grabbed Vandeaga by the neck and threw him out the room. As he landed the door sealed itself again. He scrambled to his feet and banged on the glass.

"Jake!" Vandeaga watched his friend collapse as his legs burned to nothing and snap beneath him. A Minder that Vandeaga never saw coming, picked him up by the waist and dragged him back down the corridor.

At first, Vandeaga tried to struggle but stopped as the Minder punched him twice in the ribs and he felt something crunch. He gave up and let himself be taken where ever the Minder had been ordered to take him. When they reached the waiting room it dropped Vandeaga into a chair, Chrisa and Research Head Tyler were already there.

"Hello Vandeaga, so how was Jake?" Chrisa said with a smirk, he said it the same way you would ask a child how their day was. Vandeaga said nothing, he just stared into his eyes. He'd only ever truly hated one person and now there were two.

"Oh, that stare won't work on me, because you in the grand scheme of things are meaningless."

"I think that went pretty well." Tyler glanced down at what first looked like a sheet of paper. This was actually flexi glass and as he touched his finger to it more data appeared. What happened in that room must have been a normal day in the office for him.

"We got some good readings here, very good, only minimal damage to the room too. Are we done as I want to get on with this data?" Tyler asked with a sigh, he wasn't asking permission, he was just making it clear to everyone present that he was about to take his leave.

"You should have accepted my offer Vandeaga, instead of running to Faleama. I think we will keep this between us won't we."

Like fuck we will, I'm going to tell everyone! Vandeaga wanted to scream it but he didn't.

"Let me help you to understand what will happen if you open your mouth." Chrisa stood up with a stretch before he paced the room, he tapped his chin with each step.

"We see and hear everything so if you mention this to anyone, other members of your dorm might end up in here. Larooa seems nice, maybe she could be used to test some new Boosters that the research team have cooked up. It might liquidate her organs but fuck it. It would be funny to watch her scream."

"I understand," Vandeaga said.

"What about the new Brain Director," Tyler seemed to brighten up with the chance to test his projects.

"It increases movement speed but does have a tendency to snap the patients arms back the wrong way. There are only a few minor kinks that I need to get worked out."

"I understand," Vandeaga repeated.

"Sorry I didn't catch that, try not to be so pathetic and speak up."

"I understand," Vandeaga spoke louder but was careful not to shout.

"You lot are a failed project. This farce has gone on too long already. You are already inferior before you even started formal training. The sheer amount of wasted time is insurmountable. You may leave now."

Chrisa gave a flick of his wrist towards the door. Vandeaga saluted before he was escorted out of the room by the Minder. Tyler's image flickered and crackled as he stood up.

"Are you hungry, because I'm starving?" Chrisa asked.

"I think I could manage to eat something. I will meet you in the lab in twenty minutes," Tyler nodded and his image vanished. Chrisa looked round the empty room and clapped his hands together for a job well done. He flicked a piece of lint off his shoulder with a smile.

"It's been a good day today," he said as his image also disappeared.

Chapter 16

As the passing weeks turned into months, Vandeaga hadn't spoken to anyone and in turn they left him alone. Everyone thought it was strange for such a change in personality but Vandeaga had to protect them anyway he could. He concentrated on the leader's training and aimed for high scores in the combat section.

He didn't really care for the scores any more. He just wanted to be as good as he could be, before he was made to leave. He knew he was going to be transferred out as Chrisa had made that very clear to him, he just didn't know when.

No one had seen Taradin since the incident and this was a plus for Vandeaga because he knew he would do something stupid to him if he could. Now and again, he saw the Minder with the gunshot wounds making its rounds. The wound itself hadn't changed over the last year.

Vandeaga thought that maybe they weren't even truly alive under all that armour, but he'd never know. Whenever they made eye contact, they exchanged a nod. Vandeaga didn't know if it meant anything but it helped him nonetheless.

Once again, he let himself into the leader's block and on the way in ran his hand up the door frame. There were two chips in the paint work and as he ran his finger over them, he counted both. It was a habit that only started in the last weeks but he felt he couldn't move forward if he didn't.

This time, however, a splayed piece of metal nicked the tip of his index finger. He had nowhere to wipe the trickle of blood so he jammed the finger into his mouth. He walked into the training room and followed the same process as he grabbed a sheet of paper and then watched the machine laser his details onto it. This was then followed by the day's instructions and the end of learning test.

He hadn't noticed at the time but he had smeared the smallest amount of blood onto his paperwork. This affected the print in such a way that his name wasn't all there. While the first 'A' in his name was there, it had been burned incorrectly. The horizontal line of that letter was missing. This meant nothing to him and he didn't even notice until the end of the session.

He had also got back into the habit of getting out last rather than first so he didn't have to talk to anyone. He waited for the rest of the room to leave. The Watcher normally couldn't be arsed to wait around and left before the test was finished and today was no exception.

Vandeaga placed his test sheet onto the computer with a sigh and then fed the paper into the machine, it spat it back out just like normal. He glanced at the screen and his score was 95.5%. The 95 was fine but as far as he was aware, you couldn't get half of a percent on anything. That's when he saw how his name had been misprinted.

Normally, if a name is misprinted you lost 1% due to lack of observation because the person concerned didn't notice the error. The system didn't know what to do with the missing line and just knocked off half a point. Even the final test score didn't take into consideration you could get a half mark.

He glanced over to the yellow cog at the bottom right of the screen and stared at it for a couple of seconds. His finger hovered as he decided what to do. This was also a habit he had formed. This time, it was different because he would have usually walked away by now. The longer he stood there, the greater the urge grew to press the cog and see what it did.

What can I lose?

Vandeaga tapped it with his index finger and everyone's information flashed onto the screen. He could check anything he wanted with all this data. He was certain that he wasn't supposed to see any of this but had already come this far, so he tapped on the department symbol.

He took a step back when the deceased marker flashed up on dozens and dozens of names. He scrolled the screen and the list just kept going, even people he had been told were sent to grunt squad were listed under the red marker. He also saw that many names had been marked for further testing.

He found Frankie's name and it was declared as an extreme testing pass. He could tell Broo but what would that accomplish? Jake's name was marked as a pass, deceased, and unknown. He punched the screen twice, each time the image flickered under his fist, all the lies and bullshit seemed to never end.

For the first time since Taradin left, he clenched his jaw and felt his face burn. He heard movement from the corridor, without thought he flung his pen down the room and tapped at the screen. As the display reset to the menu, the observer strolled into the room.

"Haven't you got somewhere more important to be? Why are you still here?" She asked but instinctively stepped back and placed a hand on her sidearm when she saw how red his face was.

"Are you ok? Are you stable?" She asked this in the same way she would have told Vandeaga that he had something stuck to his face.

"Yes, thank you, I have merely misplaced my pen. I keep losing it and I'm slightly agitated about the situation," Her left eye rotated in its socket as she looked past him. Her pupil expanded and then narrowed to a pinpoint. The other eye never took its sight off him.

"It's under the table, far left corner." Vandeaga turned and walked up the room to pick it up. He also folded up his paper and placed it into his pocket.

"Thank you for your help." Vandeaga said and walked past her then into the corridor.

"You're welcome," her eyes were fixed on him, even as he walked down the corridor.

*

Chrisa stared at the screens on his desk. He giggled to himself as he skimmed the research data Tyler had sent him. The red flash on his second screen grabbed his attention.

"Well, what have we got here then? Someone has broken their conditioning. So far, this day had been slightly boring." He flicked through the necessary log in screens and Vandeaga's picture and number appeared before him. He sat back in his chair and pumped his arms to the ceiling. "Got you, you little bastard, I knew you would give me another laugh." He tapped his temple and Tyler answered.

"I'm busy can this wait?" Busy was an understatement at the moment and Tyler didn't need Chrisa moaning at him for an hour.

"No, Vandeaga has broken conditioning, he touched the yellow cog."

"So? lots of them have, at this late stage of the trial it doesn't matter anymore. You need to let this feud with Faleama go. It's been ten years, you know that?"

"I don't care, anything she likes I will ruin." Tyler sighed and Chrisa heard him pick up some paperwork with a rustle.

"Let's break it down. You made sure Faleama had four dorms to look after to start with just to give her extra work. You've prodded and poked literary everywhere you could. Taradin was, by far, the best marksman being trained here and you caused him to snap. He snapped in such a spectacular way that he tried to murder a subject, and almost killed an Officer. I would add the Minder to his score but they are almost useless. You made sure Jake was selected for research, and you almost killed Vandeaga more than a couple times. You somehow managed to give everyone in the facility the access to get into the back ground data. Not to mention the countless other little things you have done over the last year alone. Also, no one thinks anything is amiss, you are going to raise suspicions if you continue to use the facility in this way."

"I never understood her thing for Vandeaga. Anyway, what's your point?" Chrisa squeezed his pen and felt the plastic crack.

"You know she believes him to be dead, right?"

"Yes, I know this," Chrisa could feel his tempter start to boil. Of course, he knew that, he knew everything.

"She is now at the front lines supporting the troops because of this. Am I correct?"

"Yes, you are correct."

"So why are you wasting your time on this. I have to go, there has been an incident." Shattering glass erupted from Tyler's end which was quickly followed by multiple screams and a fiery explosion.

"I could come by to support?" Chrisa needed to do anything other than sit in that office.

"No, we are more than capable, thank you," The audio feed went dead.

"Fucking Tech bastard, what does he know?" Chrisa stared at the screen for only a moment before a scheme had formed inside his head. He held his finger to his temple and selected a specific frequency. It was only seconds before someone answered.

"It's been a long time Chrisa," said the voice.

"Yeah, it's me, is Taradin still confined in the shell?" Chrisa tapped his pen on the edge of his desk as he spoke.

"He is, problematic little bastard won't stay down."

"Can you get a message to him but don't mention that it came from me."

"Stirring more shit, are you?" The voice seemed to lighten, because knowing Chrisa, this was going to be entertaining.

"Can you or not?" Chrisa threw the pen across the room.

"Yeah why not, I'm sure this will be a laugh. What do you want this message to say?" Chrisa just grinned to himself.

"You might want to get a pen."

Chapter 17

The dorms had been up before dawn and were meant to be at the simulator for a full day of training, but the vehicles were late again. Vandeaga had been awake an hour before he had to be. While everyone else in his dorm was asleep, he stretched and hydrated himself. He paced the dorm in silence and planned for whatever they would throw at them. He didn't want to lead a squad but he knew he would be voted in anyway.

As they waited in the brisk morning air, Larooa tapped Vandeaga on the shoulder.

"You ok?" Vandeaga asked as he turned to her.

"I think so, I just take one day at a time and try and stay grounded. Why does everything seem darker lately?" Vandeaga looked into her hazel eyes, and for whatever reason they looked brighter today. This made him feel better knowing that she was doing ok.

"I'm not sure what you mean?" Whatever Larooa was saying went straight over his head.

"Over half the people we knew are gone in one way or another. The final tests are coming up and no one is talking to each other," She went as far as to give him a nod.

"Yeah sorry about that, I've got a lot on my mind." Vandeaga didn't shrug but he wanted to.

"We all have, we need to stick together," she squeezed his arm a little too hard.

"That's not our choice though, is it?" She squinted her eyes at his answer.

"We could do everything they want and they could still split us up or move us on. We have no choice in the matter, but I do agree with you," Vandeaga said.

"That didn't sound like a contradiction at all." They laughed between themselves as Muncher walked over and joined the group. He looked like he had been in a fight with his crazy hair and flushed cheeks.

"Hi guys, I'm glad they're late, the AI wouldn't let me out the dorm block."

"Really, how does that happen?" Larooa shook her head.

"I wish I knew." Muncher laughed. "It let everyone else go but me. I had to wait for someone from administration to let me out." Larooa pointed to Muncher's chest.

"Feeling better, or is it still giving you problems?" she asked as Mike side-stepped into their conversation.

"Yeah, it still feels tight but my breathing is good," Muncher glanced round Larooa's shoulder.

"Thanks to your skill," Muncher said as Mike gave him a feint grin.

"I don't really want to think about it but thanks. They're here, get ready people." Mike said as a flood of people stepped towards the pickup point.

The vehicles were boarded and everyone enjoyed the ride in silence. They followed the same process of going through the scanners before being segregated and sent to different ready areas. The Dean appeared with a flash and showed his broken happy image once again.

"Hello everybody, today's session will be different so no team-on-team shenanigans or the like. We will be looking at live grenades. Which colours make what types of explosions and the best way to use them effectively. You will be provided with simple armour because you never know what might happen. I will be back in five minutes." There was a flash as The Dean disappeared, one of his projectors fizzled and let out a plume of yellow smoke.

There was the usual rush to get ready and then the tedious ten-minute wait for anything to happen. The groups were led out to the simulation and this time it was a throwing range. There was a red line that stretched over a mile. Beyond this there were targets set at different distances. Everyone lined themselves up and waited.

It seemed the dorms were mostly kept together, but each area was separated by a wall as an extra precaution. The Officers that were left walked past the recruits and into the range. Each carried a large two-handed metal case, and where each one of them stopped, a table rose out of the floor to assist them. They placed these cases down and unclicked the latches.

"Good morning recruits," Officer Josef saluted the group in his section.

"Sir!" all the recruits saluted back.

"Today we will be looking at these." He picked up a dark green ball the size of an apple.

"This is a grenade and this has a kill range of fifteen feet. I know that you have seen these before but today you get to use them." He passed it between his hands like it was a toy.

"Right now, it is harmless," he pulled out the pin, "and now it is deadly."

He tossed it ten feet down range and took a step back. A metallic ping noise echoed across the range as the release bar ejected from the grenade. When it was within an inch from the ground a two-foot hole opened up and swallowed it whole. There was a faint rumble beneath their feet as the grenade detonated.

"This does not mean that you are in no danger when using grenades on this range. Three seasons ago a recruit dropped a live one at his feet. You need to remember that this person was surrounded by his peers. The Dean, who controls this building made a decision and this was to take the grenade and him into the floor. It was the right thing to do because The Dean saved eight people, but the recruit and two more got swallowed. They were all compressed to about the size of this". He held up his hand and pointed to its palm.

"This is why, you are spaced out from each other, if you do something stupid it's all on you."

Josef began the long-winded talk on grenades and proper use. First there were the colours and what they mean.

Green: Standard grenade with a kill range of fifteen feet, and the damage is based on force and shrapnel.

Red: High explosive, same as the green but five times more powerful.

Blue: Flash and concussion, disorientation and knock out potential.

"There are many others but these are the only ones we will use in this range as we do not want to cause any major damage." The Dean appeared next to Josef with a flash.

"That's right soldiers, don't break my things," and in an instant he was gone again. Josef shook his head and continued.

"From this point I will refer to them by colour only. When instructed, you will firmly grasp a grenade in your dominant hand, with the other hand you will pull the pin. When the pin is pulled, throw it straight away. Do not be tempted to hold the grenade for any length of time. If you let the release bar eject and continue to hold it, this is known as cooking it. When you are on the front lines it can be a benefit but do not do that here. The Dean will remove you and the green. Is that clear?"

While Officer Josef had made his speech, several Shades walked the line and placed a metal box next to each person. When they were finished, they vanished back into the shadows.

"The last thing I'm going to say and you could say the most important. If I scream 'arms down' you will place anything in your hand back in the box and close the lid. You will remain where you are until instructed. If you have already pulled the pin don't put it back in the box. Yes, that does sound stupid, and yes it has happened before. Do you all understand me?"

"YES SIR!" The recruits shouted at him. Josef walked past the line and stood behind them. Even with what he had done before, the sights he had seen, this first part always made him nervous. No matter how much training or information was given there was always a possibility that someone could, and would, do something mind-numbingly stupid.

"Recruits! Pick up a green with your dominant hand. Pull the pin with your other and immediately throw it at the number twenty marker."

There was a cascade of greens thrown up the range and each one was sucked into the ground before it detonated. Josef repeated the process with each colour and moved onto aiming techniques.

Overall, the recruits he was dealing with followed instructions well and performed how he would expect at this stage of training. It was strange that the rumble of grenades under his feet made him relax. He came alert when he heard a scream from somewhere within the arena.

"Arms Down! Everyone, stay on your line!" Each person rushed to empty their hands and close the lid, only a few that had already been armed were thrown up the range. As the last lid was closed there was a second scream from the opposite direction. Josef touched his temple twice and changed dialect. "Officers, what is happening?" there was a rush of information as everyone spoke at once.

"Max here and we are clear."

"The Dean is…!" Josef recognised Officer Jenna's voice even through her scream.

"Repeat, we lost you," Officer Max's voice sounded like he was running.

"Get off the floor now, The Dean is…!" Jenna was stopped by a loud crunch then her audio went silent. Josef looked up and down his row. Vandeaga and some others picked up on the tension but waited for their Officer to instruct them.

"What, what is it?" Josef shouted and signalled to his group to move back to the ready room, this was followed by a scream a lot closer to their position. Vandeaga walked next to Josef but noticed the floor beneath his feet change colour.

"Run, The Dean is eating people!" Officer Nash screamed over the radio. Josef turned to shout orders as the floor opened up. Vandeaga cannoned into Josef's side and they both cleared the void below. The floor seemed to moan with disappointment as the hole closed with a snap. They skidded across the rough floor but before Josef had stopped, he flipped onto his feet and yanked Vandeaga up by his arm.

"Link arms with a neighbour and do not let them fall, Ready room NOW!" It seemed that The Dean had recognised the rush and ramped up his murderous efforts. The female that Muncher had linked arms with dropped down to one knee as her foot sunk into the floor.

It could have pulled her whole body down in one go but chose to pull her down inch by painful inch. The floor's flexible surface turned into a vice and squeezed the bones in the girl's foot and with unimaginable force they were slowly crushed under its pressure. She screamed as Muncher called for help and pulled at her arm.

Without much thought for himself Josef turned and rushed towards them. He pulled out a Shimmer Blade from his waist, it hummed with a purple energy as it passed through the air. In the seconds it took him to get to her, the floor had compressed her ankle to the thickness of a finger. "You will thank me later."

The Shimmer Blade passed through the bottom of her shin like it was paper. The stump burst into flame as he picked her up and threw her over his shoulder, her scream seemed to blend in with the rest of the noise. The arena started to play birdsong and ocean wave noises over the sound system.

"Keep moving!" Josef sprinted for the ready room and was mere feet away when he tripped and fell forwards. He threw the girl through the doorway but his right hand was swallowed.

"Sir!" Vandeaga wanted to help and almost stopped.

"Just go!" Josef felt the metal fibres in his fingers snap and twist as he sunk down past his wrist. He jammed his thumb into the inside of his elbow. There was a loud crunch as he rotated his shoulder and pulled, the joint detached as the rest of his arm was sucked into the floor. He rolled into safety as the floor tried to grab his legs.

Vandeaga turned and went back out when he saw Larooa in trouble. The recruit she was linked with had been sucked down to his chest. The floor rotated and dragged him through a hole that was only big enough for a can of soda. Blood and guts sprayed from his mouth as he turned, but the death grip of his hand wouldn't release her forearm.

Seeing he was already gone Vandeaga took the chance and planted a running kick into the dead guy's arm. It snapped under the force and Vandeaga pulled Larooa away from him. This was another face he knew lost to the madness of the complex. He would remember Jax for as long as he could.

As they threw themselves through the doors, Officer Josef made a quick head count, he was missing four people. He hit the door release and it slid shut with a clatter and a bang.

"Medics do your duty and take care of your team; I'm counting on you." He attempted to touch his temple, but he had already forgotten he was missing his right arm, and tapped it with his left.

"Officer Josef here, I and my group are clear, please respond."

He checked the room and made another count and he was still missing four. Two Recruits dragged a third, his legs were

193

twisted the wrong way. They had been wrenched by the floor, but he was lucky not to have been taken. Between them they took him to the Medi-Cube.

"Officer Cartwright responding, we are missing two and several injured. Command have been notified and we have support inbound." Josef nodded to himself and thought of what to do next.

"Officer Nash reporting, several dead and a number maimed, what a fucking mess."

"Officer Max, we are clear, no losses or injures, but that's only thanks to Jenna."

"Jenna, are you there?" Josef asked but there was no response.

"Max, Nash, one of you check on Jenna. It's unlike her to not respond, but you start to send your recruits out first."

"Rodger."

"On it," both of them replied.

Josef waited as it would take them a minute to work their way through the back corridors to Jenna's position.

Max sprinted down the corridor as Nash joined him. They reached Jenna's position at the same time and both froze in the door way.

"Fuck me this…is…just," Max had seen a lot but nothing like this. The floor had started to spit what was left of the recruits back into their ready room, the bits it liked stayed within its embrace. The jet-black floor rippled as bits of arm and leg rose to the surface. A crushed cube of meat and bone rolled through the shutter, Jenna's head protruded from one side of the mangled lump of flesh.

"What's happening?" Josef needed answer.

"Everyone on Jenna's side is dead," Nash said.

"What about Jenna?" Josef asked as he paced the ready room. Something struck the shutter from the arena side which made him stop. A long-forgotten feeling of dread filled him, as he looked towards it.

"I said everyone is dead, the arena is dumping what's left of them back into the ready room." Nash said as he stepped backwards towards the door. Max was already in the corridor. Josef closed his eyes and shook his head. He liked Jenna more than he ever told her.

"The shutter isn't down then?" Josef asked when another thump buckled the metal shutter that was in front of him.

"No, it's still…" Josef didn't wait for Nash to finish as he signalled everyone to leave with a wave of his arm.

"It's going to try and come in! Go! Go! Go! Get everyone out." There was an almighty roar as the jet-black floor formed hands and thrust them through the open shutter. Nash was almost crushed against the door frame but he threw himself sideways into the corridor.

Max aimed with his arm, his hand flipped back and with a scream of power a solid slug of pure energy struck one of the rippling hands. The arm rail was a powerful weapon but this had the same effect on the arena as throwing a marble at a train, his hand flipped back and he ran.

Both of them sprinted back to their ready rooms to quicken the evacuation. Most of Josef's recruits were already out of the door when a set of four-foot fingers prised open the shutter.

"Move, get out of the building!" As the last recruit ran past him, he sealed the ready room door. When he got to the scanner hall, he waited to see who was coming up behind him. Cartwright leading her group through a side door at a full sprint. She carried one recruit across her shoulders and dragged a second one by his clothing behind her. "Are you good?" Josef shouted.

"Those fingers smashed past the shutter and took two more." She handed him the unconscious one and followed him to the exit. The building shook as the entire arena floor began to move as it either tried to get out or get to them before they left.

The Dean appeared with a crackled flash, but his image was twisted around on itself. His torso faced them but his legs were a hundred and eighty degrees the wrong way. Recruits poured past him and forced their way out the small fire exit next to the scanners. It would have been quicker to go through the scanners but The Dean had sealed them off. Loud blasts of electrical discharge shook each one from the inside.

"What the hell is going on here, Dean?" Josef screamed at The Dean's image. The Dean had a frozen expression of horror, but this changed with a rigid snap. His eyes opened so wide they looked like they were going to pop right out of his head. His bottom jaw touched his chest as he tilted his head back and screamed.

It wasn't a noise that could come out of a person's mouth, this was a high-pitched electrical screech. Other than the Officers everyone else covered their ears. Josef just stared at the twisted image. Nash and Max sprinted into the hall with a wave of recruits.

"Run! It's coming!" Nash roared over the noise. Josef stared no longer and ran for the exit. Most of the recruits were outside when the entrance doors sealed themselves.

"Cartwright, make us a way out!" Josef knew that she was most likely the only person that could get it done without taking out half the wall with it.

He turned so he could see the doors at the other end of the hall. Huge hands made of plastic and metal smashed themselves through it and into the hall. The metal door frames gave no resistance as the concrete wall burst inwards.

Cartwright dropped the injured and removed her gloves. Her hands were made of hundreds of dull silver disks, each one slotted behind the first. She had the same number of digits as everyone else but they locked together and sealed themselves, they now looked like flippers.

Cartwright slapped them together and they started to glow white with a crackle of energy. She started with the tips of her fingers and slowly pushed them into the solid doors. She moved left then right as her hands passed through the metal like it was water.

A large lump of the door fell away and exposed the outside world. She stood back as her hands began to cool from white to silver. The building shook again as more of the arena tried to force its way down the long hall. Recruits and Officers piled out of the opening until only Josef was left.

"This is Officer Josef at the arena, Command please respond."

"This is Command, we are aware of the situation and are sending support." The voice of Command was a blend of many. At first it was given a choice but couldn't decide what it wanted, so it decided to use all of them.

"The arena floor has left confinement and is heading for the front entrance."

"We are not aware of this. The destabilising barriers should have stopped its ability to form."

"I'm telling you the floor has formed hands and is dragging itself towards me." The roof buckled as the hands grabbed onto the buildings support beams for purchase.

"What do you require Josef?" The voice sounded uncertain as Command processed all the available information. With all the problems, this was the first Arena that had gone haywire.

"We need the power to the arena shut down."

"That will shut down the entire region and will cause issues at the nearest facilities."

"It will cause untold damage and endanger more lives unless it is shut down immediately."

As it moved beyond the scanners the mass crushed the wall of metal flat as it forced its way over them. Blasts of radiation and electricity lit up the hall with cracks and booms. Josef, for a moment thought it had calmed as the fingers remained still, but it was just drawing more of its form into the hall so it could lunge.

"Hold on Officer Josef, let us process."

Josef shook his head and for a split second took his eyes off the moving mass. It charged with full force as most of the structure was dragged with it. Support beams bent and the roof windows shattered as the side walls caved inwards.

Nash wrenched Josef out of the damaged door by his jacket. The hands were mere inches away from them as they fell to the floor and froze. The hands tried to move that last inch as all of the remaining lights on the building went out. This was followed by all of the street lights and Officer Max dropped to his knees.

Vandeaga was stood next to him and tried to support his weight but couldn't hold him up. It was like he was made of lead. Mike was closet and got to Max first, he checked for vitals but couldn't find any.

"What happened?" Cartwright said.

"I don't know he just collapsed," Vandeaga said. Max landed square on his back. His unblinking eyes counted the stars in the clear night sky.

"What's going on!" Josef shouted over the recruits, he sent out a loud whistle and all the talking stopped.

"The power has gone so his heart has stopped, we have about two minutes to get it powered again or he's not getting up." Cartwright could have felt for a pulse but it was pointless to even try with Max.

Fuck, forgot about Max. Josef thought as he and Nash pushed pass the recruits to get to him. Nash knelt by his side. The odd Minder was still trying to get anyone other than the Officers to form lines.

"Cartwright, what's the plan?" Nash called as Cartwright pulled two recruits that she knew towards her.

"We need all the best engineers from each dorm. I'll need those two vehicles stripped and the batteries that are in them over here."

She pointed at the only two working Vehicles in the car park. These were the Officers cars which had been for them to drive back, but this need was greater.

"Minute and a half," Nash said. He hadn't moved from Max's side. Nash didn't understand the tech as he had no major implants of his own. Between them they tore through the vehicles and dragged the heavy batteries over to Max.

"Thirty seconds," Nash shook his head, "this is taking too long." He would never show it but he was seconds away from losing his best friend.

"Get his shirt off!" Cartwright screamed as she dumped one of the batteries near his arm. Nash pulled off the jacket and exposed his metal plated torso.

"Link them together quickly, I'm sorry but I'm going to have to fuck up your chest Max." The recruits stripped cables and wired the batteries in parallel as she cracked two of her fingers. As they glowed, she pushed them into his chest and pulled apart the layers to expose the flexi bags he used for lungs and a large metal heart.

"Five seconds," Nash hadn't taken his eyes off him. Cartwright pulled out two connectors and was about to wire them to the batteries when she stopped.

"Hold him down, he's going to feel this." Nash pushed his weight on his arms as she jammed the ends together. Max sat bolt upright and almost made Nash perform a full back flip.

"What the fuck happened?" Max's eyes were wide open as he looked down at his chest and moved his hand towards the wires but Cartwright and Josef grabbed his arms.

"Slow down, the local power went out and we had to power you up." Cartwright pointed to his temporary power supply.

"With a fucking car battery?" Max said as Nash walked over and slapped him on the shoulder.

"Four car batteries and a shit lot of tape. Now will you listen to me and have a power unit fitted?" Nash asked but Max shook his head.

"But the added weight would slow me down or I could have my leg enhancements upgraded?" Max replied.

"Also, we haven't had a power outage this bad since I was a recruit so it could still be worth the risk."

Josef realised all the recruits were staring at Max as they understood nothing of what was being said. Being able to see all of Max's internal workings would give them all something to talk about when they got back.

"Attention!" All the recruits turned to Josef and saluted.

"Today's tragic event will forever be on your minds. No matter what you are told, our people will be remembered. Never forget their names, they did not die in battle, they died in that mess, which is unforgivable."

Josef turned to the remains of the building. He had assumed it was just the entrance that the hands had tried to force their way out of. Every door or side window had some form of expenditure pushed through it. Most of the roof had collapsed onto itself but the arena floor was frozen in place. Josef saluted the carnage that was once the arena. He wanted to give respect for the fallen, but mostly his friend. Apart from Max, the other Officers stood and joined the salute.

I will miss you Jenna, rest well. Josef turned to the recruits and issued orders for them to form lines and wait for the transport to arrive.

Chapter 18

Any one of the recruits would have said they had been sat outside the arena all night, but it had only been an hour. It didn't help that it was cold and always seemed like it was about to rain. Their twin moons passed in front of millions of stars. Nash was still trying to convince Max that a power unit would be better than frequency feed. Nash turned to Josef with an odd look as he'd only just noticed that something was amiss.

"How did you manage to lose that?" Nash nodded at Josef's missing arm.

"The Arena took hold of my hand and began to pull me down. I'm glad the quick release worked, but that was the second time it got me. The first time was when the floor opened up and tried to take my legs but Van saved my arse."

Vandeaga thought he heard his name and turned slightly. He caught Josef's eye, Josef nodded and touched his forehead just above his eyebrow with two fingers. Vandeaga repaid the nod. He turned back to the floor and smiled to himself. That gesture was a mark of respect that Officers normally gave each other, but even then, that was rare. The first set of transports announced their arrival with a series of headlights coming into view.

"Command have sent the unmanned mobiles, haven't they?" Cartwright asked with a shake of her head.

"Yes, they have, why are they so stupid?" Max replied.

"Are we agreed that injured get taken home first?" The other Officers nodded.

"We will go from there but this does include you Max. I don't know how quickly you will drain those batteries completely." Josef said as he looked down at his arm. He still counted himself lucky the floor grabbed the metal one. Max had to agree with him.

"I'm going to need a hand getting my batteries on board. I've turned off some minor systems but I can feel the charge is starting to slow." The first two vehicles were promptly loaded with injured recruits and Max. The next two got filled with a mixture, but volunteers were asked to wait.

Vandeaga knew he was ok and took the initiative to stay back. He also wanted to speak to Josef, and as Josef was known for always being the last to go, he didn't mind. Vandeaga had managed to work his way round and stand next to Josef as each vehicle was loaded.

"Sir, may I ask you a question?" Vandeaga asked and Josef gave him a sideways glance.

"Sure, but depending on the question you may not get the answer you want."

"I didn't realise Officers were so different to everyone else." Josef smiled as he looked down at the place where his arm should be.

"We're each unique but normally not by choice. I lost my hand and most of my forearm to a mortar strike. I was persuaded to have the whole arm replaced and a power unit fitted. It was a shame to lose it as all my medical supplies were in that forearm. Have you heard of Boosters?"

Vandeaga just shook his head.

"Now listen carefully and don't repeat what I am about to tell you because this information is only privy once your training is complete. Do you understand?" Josef smiled again when Vandeaga nodded.

"Good, if you prove yourself in battle or live long enough, and that is always a challenge in this world. You are 'awarded' with a Booster injection. This will change who you are at the core. You will become stronger, quicker and just more than what you are now. The added bonus is that you age at a much slower rate. The only problem with them is that sometimes they need to be replaced but that is very rare. Do you have any last questions? As I'm afraid that will be the end of this conversation, because I am still an Officer and in charge of your dorm. I am not meant to be talking in such a friendly way to a recruit." Vandeaga swallowed and thought for a moment but only one thing came to his mind.

"How old are you sir?" He asked and Josef sucked air through his teeth.

"Now that is something I'm not allowed to talk about. You see, even Officers don't like to know the age of their peers, it's a simple but old tradition. It's just something we just don't need to talk about, you understand of course?"

Vandeaga nodded once again but felt a little deflated by the rejection of the question. Josef grinned as he slowly shook his head. He knew he shouldn't but couldn't help himself. He turned his head a little and leant forward, and said something that wouldn't even be called a whisper. "I'm sixty-six, don't tell anyone."

Vandeaga's eyes went wide as he turned to Josef. If anyone he knew had asked him how old he thought Josef was he wouldn't have said past thirty-five. Josef stepped forward and shouted as the last sets of lights started to come towards them.

"Right the last transports are coming so line up, I've been too good to you lot, breaks over." Larooa and Mike stood behind Vandeaga.

"Guys you ok?" Vandeaga looked past them and scanned everyone present. "Where's Muncher? Please tell me he's alright."

"Yeah the twats fine." Mike said with a laugh, but abruptly stopped when Josef glanced at him. When Josef turned back, he continued.

"He went on an earlier transport. On the way out he tripped and broke his wrist."

"Damn, that guy has some bad luck." Vandeaga said with a grin. If something bad was going to happen, it was going to happen to Muncher. The A.I. controlled vehicles pulled up to the pavement and opened their doors towards the sky. The two Minders that were left, separated and stood by each car.

Vandeaga nodded at the one next to his transport, it still hadn't been fixed. The two groups started to board. As Vandeaga was at the front he stepped to one side. "After you guys."

"Why thank you kind sir." Mike added a fake bow as he stepped inside.

"Thank you," Larooa smiled at him, but deep down it was more than that. She touched his arm as she passed but Vandeaga winced as something heavy struck his shoulder and bounced into the vehicle. They all looked at it for a millisecond as it came to rest next to Mike's foot.

"GRENADE!" Vandeaga screamed, but before he could finish that word the damaged Minder pushed its way past him. Larooa was forced into the vehicle and blocked by the Minders ample frame. Vandeaga tried to pull her arm but the Minder didn't move as it tried to get to the grenade, or to shield him, but he'd never know.

Larooa cried out something as Mike looked at Van and closed his eyes. Broo had seen the grenade strike Vandeaga, but instead of getting out the way he jumped in front of Vandeaga and tried to grab Larooa too.

The explosion threw Vandeaga backwards as his vision went white and his hearing blew with a scream. He landed hard but he didn't touch the tarmac. He rolled off another body and tried to stand but his knees gave way and he fell onto all fours.

Vandeaga tried to speak to Broo but his unblinking eyes didn't move, a large lump of something metallic stuck out of his forehead. Most of the recruits had hit the floor when Vandeaga shouted the warning but some took the full force of the blast. His friend's bodies combined with the Minders partially shielded him, but it wasn't enough.

He tried to focus past the double vision and looked down at the piece of shrapnel that was sticking out of his chest. He forced his eyes shut when he realised the object wasn't a lump of metal, it was a shard of thigh bone. He tensed his throat and forced himself not to throw up and without thinking pulled the large shard from between his ribs.

Josef was laid face down on the floor and wasn't moving. Blood started to flow from Vandeaga's nose and he started to shake uncontrollably. He couldn't hold it back any longer and puked over his hands. Blood run down the side of his head, this added to the fluid from his nose and splashed into the contents of his stomach. There was a loud bang as something detonated within the burning transport vehicle. The smell of burnt plastic, clothing and flesh filled the air.

That's when Vandeaga saw him. Taradin stood there with his face twisted in pure hatred, he shouted something but Vandeaga's hearing was still blown.

How could Taradin have that much hate and anger contained within him?

Vandeaga was about to join him as he pushed past the pain and clenched his jaw so hard something cracked. Taradin looked down into the bag that was over his shoulder and rummaged through its contents. Vandeaga wrenched himself onto his feet and with a huge breath, charged.

Vandeaga covered the distance between them before Taradin had even started to look up. He grabbed Taradin by the waist and body slammed him into the floor. The bag broke and multiple grenades rolled across the tarmac, all of them still had their pins in.

Vandeaga didn't see it at the time, but Taradin had already taken more than a few beatings himself. His skin was a mixture of new and old bruises. Whether Taradin didn't expect it or didn't care, he didn't try to fight back. Vandeaga had pinned his arms down with his legs and started to repeatedly punch him in the side of the head.

Die you fuck! This was it, Vandeaga was going to kill him, his first point was going to be a fellow recruit. It wasn't to be as something struck him hard in the back of the neck. He went ridged with the strike and toppled off his prey. Before he blacked out Josef said something to him but he didn't hear it.

Chapter 19

It had been four days since the incident at the arena and Josef was once more called into a meeting. He walked into the room and saluted those present. Tyler, Chrisa, and Chancellor Torn, she nodded but the other two didn't even look up. He pulled out the chair and sat down at the large table.

"You have been awarded a recommendation, Officer Josef." Chancellor Torn passed the paperwork to her man, and he passed it to Josef.

"Thank you, Chancellor, but this is not required. I was hoping this was to do with the arena and why The Dean killed so many people."

"I wouldn't call them people." Chrisa said with a smirk, he didn't even bother to look up from his papers. Josef slapped his hands on the table.

"We are supposed to train them, not kill them. Are you stupid enough to forget that Officer Jenna was also killed in that mess, you insignificant Kank!" Josef didn't shout, but he didn't have to. Chrisa shook his head and looked towards the Chancellor.

"That had slipped my mind but he can't talk to me like that, can he?" Before Chancellor Torn could speak. As Josef stood his chair slid back with such force it travelled a good ten feet before it tipped over, and pointed at Chrisa.

"With honour and blood, I challenge you to death. My challenge means your choice of weapon." Josef hadn't challenged anyone in over ten years but this had to be done, this was for Jenna's honour. The Chancellor turned to Chrisa with a disappointed shake of her head. Josef could feel that every fibre of his body wanted Christa's blood.

"You need to leave now, and Josef you need to calm down." Josef didn't speak until the walking trash had stood up and left the room. Her man had walked over and picked up Josef's chair, and placed it behind him. Even though the incident was over, the chancellor's man was ready and was very close to having his hand on his sidearm.

"I'm sorry, I should not have done that in your presence. I apologise for the upset but the challenge will stand unless you interject on his behalf." Josef bowed with his apology.

"We shall see, but back to your original question. We have no idea why The Dean acted the way he did, but his program has been removed from the commands database. The central computer tried to get it under control, but every attempt failed.

"One of the three was on site at the time but even he could not take back control. Your decision to act and have the power cut is the only thing that stopped it. Now the problem we face is that the arena needs to be cut from the region before any power can be brought back online. The only other major building in that area was the Shell," Josef nodded.

"Speaking of the Shell, when will Taradin face execution?" Torn shook her head as she was not pleased with the ruling.

"He won't," she said with a vile taste in her mouth.

"He killed four recruits! And how did he manage to get out of the Shell in the first place?"

"I have been told that someone with that skill set will be useful. I was overruled on my proposal for liquidation. We are however looking into his escape as it does seem he was given door access. He was also given information on the training session's dates and the logins for the grenade storage. He has developed a rather intense hatred for Vandeaga."

"And we have no idea who helped him do we?" Josef asked.

"Not yet," the larger man at the end of the table answered before anyone else could, "Sorry, I'm Drake and I'm in charge of this shell. This situation is something that should never have happened." His longer than average salt and pepper hair swished as he bowed his head.

"I agree but if they cover their tracks this well, I doubt we will find who did this." Josef knew he wouldn't be told even if they found out who it was, his rank was far too low for this information.

"We will catch the bastards if it's the last thing I do." It was Drakes turn to slap his hand on the table.

"Do we have any information about 454376AHF? He has not returned to normal training yet, and as I oversee his dorm I would like to ask why?" Chancellor Torn looked down at her notes.

"He is still in the medical wing, sedated." She turned the paper over and put it to the back of the pile.

"He had no lasting injuries to justify this amount of time, and why is he sedated?"

"If he stops screaming and attacking staff, every time he wakes, he wouldn't need to be sedated." The second man spoke up. Josef didn't recognise him at first but he was Turner the second in control of the medical block.

"We need to make a decision about him soon as it's a waste of resources keeping him this way." When he finished Chancellor Torn sat back in her chair and breathed a heavy sigh with an added shake of her head.

"This whole season has been one disaster after another. We are down to twenty-two percent of the starting recruits and I doubt many will actually make it to the field. The AI is a mess across the whole city."

"We ran too many tests," the whole group looked at Tyler. "I know I was the one to push for the extras for this new facility, but it has been too much for them to bear. Even the clones have been the worst batch since I can remember. Some snap if you ask them their name too many times, and that is something I cannot explain." The group nodded, whether they wanted to admit it or not, it was still the truth.

"We need to ask you Josef, if you think it is worth trying to get 454376AHF back into training, or have him removed?" Josef was almost shocked at the question.

"Have you even looked at his record?" Josef pointed at the mass of paper. He knew that information was in there somewhere.

"Yes, we all have, and it's very good apart from the last two months."

"Then you can see he is more than capable of completing the course. He will give you all the data you need for future clones."

"He is not a clone," Turner interrupted Josef.

"You've lost me, he's not a clone?" Josef asked with a puzzled look because as far as he was aware, they were all clones.

"That's correct. He is part of the unwanted, unplanned pregnancies between the lower ranks and civilians," Turner shrugged. It didn't make any difference to him but it was still a fact.

"If you're gonna use it, get a permit." Drake said, this gave them all a smile. It was a stupid commercial but it seemed to work.

"I guess we have no data on the parents?" Josef knew the answer but he had to ask.

"As you know, that information is scrubbed from the system straight after the birth. It is a pity as he is very good at what he does, but that doesn't help us," Tyler said and glanced over to Turner. He nodded with agreement.

"Which ever squad he ends up in will have a valuable asset, he can do anything. He would progress with the right push." Josef wanted them to see him for what he really was and not just the problem he had become.

"It is very unlikely he will get that far. You know how short the life span on the front lines can be."

"Yes, I was told the same."

"You are different," Chancellor corrected him.

"So is he," Josef wasn't going to give in easily and Chancellor Torn gave him a smile.

"So, what do you propose?" The whole conversation was being recorded but still each person present took notes.

"Send him back into training but give him the choice to take the test early."

"Really?" Tyler's interest had picked up by the suggestion.

"If he can't finish the training because of everything that has happened then he can take the test. If he fails, use him for more tests but if he passes, he gets transferred as a normal recruit and not a research puppet. You also tell him he would be put forward as a leader but don't say when. He can be so much more than this."

"Who is going to try and get through to him, as I said, he attacks the first person he sees when he wakes up?" Turner wasn't going to send another member of his team into that room unguarded.

"I have a spare ten minutes, so I can do it," Josef requested. Chancellor Torn smiled at him once more, how far Josef had come from his lowly beginnings.

"I wish we had more like you, this war would already be over if we did."

"Thank you, Chancellor," Josef stood, bowed and left the room. Torn's man picked up the recommendation that was left on the table and handed it back to her.

"How many times has he left that behind now?" She stared at it for a moment.

"This is the sixth time, but one day he will take it with him."

*

It was a short walk to the medical block but Josef took a moment to speak to Max. They saluted each other first then shook hands.

"How are you doing?" Josef asked. Max looked somehow different today.

"I'm as good as I can be. I had the power unit fitted so that's one thing off my mind." Max patted where his stomach should be.

"Why are you taller?" Josef gave Max a once over.

"Because of the added weight, I have had enhancements done to my legs, so just a slight height increase."

"Knocked your head much?" Josef said and they both laughed.

"Not yet but I feel like I need to duck under doorways. Where are you off to?"

"I'm going to see if I can talk some sense into Van. He's confined to the Medical block."

"Need support?" There was a low hum as Max clenched his fist.

"No, it'll be fine. They're having drinks tonight so I have to know if you are coming?"

"I'll think about it."

"That will be a no then," Josef said with a grin.

"Most likely," Max said as he smiled and they shook hands once more. They parted ways and Josef walked into the medical block. He swiped his hand over a number of secure doors and approached a desk. The woman behind it gave him a sideways look then realised who he was and stood up with a start.

"Hello Officer Josef, how can I help you today?" She wasn't sure if she should salute or not but she half attempted one anyway.

"I need a word with 454376AHF as soon as possible." Her fingers flashed across her keyboard a dozen times before she answered him.

"That might be a problem as he is not very talkative."

"I know he is sedated so I need him brought round so I can talk to him."

"I don't know if…"

"I have come from a meeting with the Chancellor and it is part of a request I talk to him so can you please get that started."

"Yes, Officer Josef. Take a seat and we will see to that immediately." The woman gestured to the only chair in the room, Josef didn't look at it.

"I will stand, thank you." Josef could feel that niggling feeling of his temper starting to rise. He was too used to people doing what he said without asking dumb questions.

The woman tapped her temple and began to talk to several people at once. Josef paced the room before he stopped and started to pick bits of fluff off his jacket. He only looked up when the woman spoke directly to him.

"He is in the secure section. Straight down that corridor and take the tenth right. Security will let you in."

"I know where it is, thank you." Josef walked down the white painted corridor and followed the signs. He arrived at a set of hardened glass doors that a member of staff sat behind. He stood up and saluted when he saw Josef turn the corner.

"Good morning, Sir!"

"Good morning, I'm here to speak to 454376AHF. Is he awake yet?"

"Not yet, they are bringing him around now." Josef nodded to himself but soon realised the doors still hadn't opened yet.

"Is there a problem with these doors?" Josef said through the intercom and started to randomly press the buttons on his side. "I'm going to assume this is working."

"I'm sorry Sir," the guards salute still hadn't wavered.

"Then why are they not open, and why am I still stood here talking to you about this?" Josef gave the guard one of his looks.

"Sir, I was asked to delay you as they are having difficulties finding the right mixture to wake him up."

"I have been delayed enough. I suggest you open these doors before I open them from my side and I will not be cleaning up the mess."

"Yes Sir," The guard pressed a button and the doors slid to one side.

"Which room is he in?" asked Josef, the guard didn't speak, he just pointed at a room number on the wall behind him.

"Thank you, you have been most helpful." Josef couldn't hide the sarcasm in his voice as he walked past the doors.

He arrived at a secure room with 117 printed on the front of the door. He checked the corridor but there was no one around. He then checked the ceiling and nodded at the multiple cameras which had tracked his movement. Josef grasped the door handle and with a click the door swung inwards. He strolled in and gently closed it behind him.

Vandeaga was laid on a white medical bed, his eyes were open but he stared blankly at the ceiling. When he heard movement, he tried to sit up but the restraints on his arms and legs kept him in place. The restraints themselves didn't look that secure as they had the appearance of strips of woven fabric. However, no amount of brute force could ever break them. Josef circled the room so he could see Vandeaga's face, he looked less than calm.

"Morning Van, I hear you have caused some trouble?" Vandeaga didn't turn his head, he blinked a number of times before he answered.

"I'm not sure."

"Do you know who I am?" Josef leaned over the bed so Vandeaga was forced to look at him.

"I'm not sure," Vandeaga said with a squint.

"For fuck sake, stupid fucking people." Josef swore to himself and resisted the urge to punch something before he tapped his temple.

"Someone from the Medical block talk to me." Josef tried to keep his voice low but there was a certain edge to it.

"Hello Josef, this is Turner. I have just walked into the block. Are you ok?"

"I'm here to speak to 454376AHF, but he is STILL under."

"I will send someone down immediately."

Josef had only taken two steps across the room when a man and a woman entered, they both stopped when they saw him. Both of them were dressed in white like everyone else, but the woman held a silver case close to her chest.

"I'm going to assume you are here to wake him up? Or you can leave."

"Yes sir, sorry about the wait," they approached as one. The woman popped open the case and took out two vials from the selection. The man pushed the vials into an injector and jammed it into Vandeaga's arm. "He will come around shortly," said the man.

"How long is shortly?" Josef questioned him.

"About five minutes," the woman answered.

"Good, you may leave now." Josef waved his hand at the pair.

"We have been asked to keep watch just in case—" Josef didn't let the man finish.

"In case of what, what do you think will happen? He is tied to a bed. I will say this one last time as I am starting to feel irritated. You will leave now." Without a word both of them bowed and left the room. Josef rubbed at his eyes.

It's one of those days. Josef noticed that Vandeaga had started to blink rapidly and tried to move against the restraints.

"Morning Van, I hear you have caused some trouble?" Josef repeated. Vandeaga looked down at the restraints and then across the room.

"Why am I tied to a bed?"

"Well, I have been told you have given the staff here a hard time, hence the restraints."

"I don't really remember, most of it is a blur." With a flash Vandeaga recalled all of the memories he didn't want, why he was here, why he didn't want to carry on.

He clamped his eyes shut but still saw their faces and tears rolled down his face. He wasn't upset, he wasn't just angry, he was filled with hate. Hate for the facility, hate for the people that made it work and most of all, that bastard Taradin.

"It wasn't your fault," Josef said.

"I let them go first," Vandeaga spoke in more of a splutter.

219

"You wouldn't have known what was going to happen, it wasn't your fault." Josef made each word stand out to emphasise his point.

"If you had of gone in first you would have died with them both."

"I don't want to do this anymore." Vandeaga shook his head because he was done with all of this.

"You can't say that Van, especially not to me."

"You didn't see his eyes Josef. Mike looked straight at me and I saw disappointment." Vandeaga had that image burned into his brain, he would never forget their faces. All the good times and the laughter had gone; all he would think about was that singular moment.

"Mike thought very highly of you."

"I didn't hear what she said." Those words could have been anything but he would never know.

"Who?"

"Larooa said something to me just before she died and I didn't hear it." Vandeaga tried to cover his face but his arms couldn't move.

"Why am I here?" he shouted and started to pull with more force.

"Calm down, this is doing you no good. You need to get back out there."

"Why would I want to go out there again? I don't want to do this shit anymore."

"Then you will be melted down into a paste and fed to the cattle." Josef didn't need to make a threat because that was the truth.

"Then tell me how do I do that? How can I just move forward again?"

"Do you think I have never lost someone? Do you think I haven't made bad decisions and got people killed? You learn from your mistakes. You suck it in, get the fuck up and walk it off." Josef's voice became more aggressive the longer he spoke.

"I'm not an Officer, Sir."

"Neither was I. I wasn't even trained as an Officer. I was a fucking combat medic. I had to fight all the way to where I am now."

"I thought you couldn't change your role in life." Vandeaga tried to recall all of the information he could remember to make sure he was right.

"You can always change your fate. I watched my squad leader screw up and get himself killed, there was nothing I could do to save him. As the rest of the squad unravelled. I had to do something and that is what made me different. That is what made me shine above the rest, I kept fighting until I got where I am now, and believe it or not I'm still fighting. There is always a challenge to overcome."

Vandeaga didn't say anything but Josef could tell he was listening. Josef took a deep breath as his own voice was getting a little too loud.

"Jenna was lost in the arena and she was my support. If I let it consume me, me and you would be in adjoining rooms, but I won't, because I have to keep going. If I gave up, I would be disrespecting her memory and I would never do that. I'm sure you don't want to disrespect their memories either?"

"No sir, I wouldn't," maybe Vandeaga was wrong, maybe everything was about him.

"Good, now you can get back out there and finish your training or you can take the final test. If you pass you will be put forward for leader training, if you fail, you will be liquidated for trying to pass the test before your time."

"Why would I take the test early?" Vandeaga tried to shrug but couldn't.

"I'm just giving you the choice. It also depends if you can stomach this environment any longer or if you want to move on."

"Can anyone take the test early?" Vandeaga did want to leave but he couldn't help but think about the rest of the people in his dorm.

"Yes, but few know that they can. It has been passed in this way a number of times, but it is rare." Vandeaga nodded as he would need to put a lot of thought into a decision this big. It could change everything or just get him killed.

"Sir, why do you call me Van instead of Vandeaga?" Josef smiled as he did this a lot without ever noticing.

"I shorten people's names, I'm not sure why it's just something that I do. So, are you going to calm down?" Josef realised Vandeaga's face had turned red and he clenched his jaw, he slowly stretched against the restraints.

"What about that piece of shit Taradin. I will only be calm knowing he is going to get what is coming to him. If I get the chance, I will finish the job myself."

I can't tell him the truth. Josef took a couple steps away from the bed before he turned.

"It has already been done, for the murder of four recruits and the attempted murder of an Officer. He was liquidated, his information has been wiped and he will be forgotten."

Vandeaga said nothing, he didn't feel any different. The pain and the hate were still there, it poked at him until he forced the memories and their faces away. This was just the beginning of that downward spiral that he would learn to live with.

"Good, when can I get back to work?"

"You will need to be evaluated, but if you remain calm while doing the tests you will be out in a few days."

"How's the new arm, Sir?"

Josef looked down at his right arm and flexed his fingers.

"This is just a temporary solution. My custom build is on its way. It should arrive and be fitted in the next two days. So, you are good?"

"Thank you, sir," Vandeaga didn't turn his head, his eyes remained on the ceiling. Josef gave him a nod and left the small room, when he was some way down the corridor, he tapped his temple.

"Turner, are you receiving me?"

"Yes Josef. How was your talk?"

"Not as well as I hoped but he is willing to get back to training, but we will need to keep an eye on him. That's if he doesn't go for the test straight away."

Chapter 20

The evaluation tests were quite simple. Vandeaga had to answer questions as honestly as he could and reframe from aggressive thoughts or actions. It took more than a couple days but he was released from confinement.

What a waste of time. He thought on the way out of the medical block. The entire training facility was still talking about what had happened at the arena. Everyone lost someone they knew. When Taradin's actions had become public knowledge, his name was blackened and it wasn't mentioned often.

As Vandeaga walked past other recruits, many of them saluted him. He nodded his response and headed for the dorms. He pushed open the swing doors and the room went quiet. You could have cut the atmosphere with a sharpened blade.

"Good evening," Vandeaga saluted them all and walked to his bed. Everyone carried on in silence as this was now their way. Vandeaga glanced round and noticed Muncher's bed was empty. He walked over to Terry and shook his hand.

"How are you doing?" Vandeaga asked him in a whisper.

"Getting there, big shock about Mike and Larooa." Vandeaga had to force the urge to punch something deep down inside of him.

"Where's Muncher gone?" Vandeaga gestured towards the empty bed.

"He requested a transfer," Terry said with a slow shake of his head.

"Really?" Vandeaga wasn't sure why but this almost set off his temper more than anything else so far.

"Oh yeah, he didn't talk to any of us about it, he just said he wanted to get away from this room and left."

"I need to talk to him."

"I don't even know what dorm he's in."

"I'm going for a walk. We have a couple hours before lights out so I will see you all later."

"Good luck," Terry said as Vandeaga left the room. Karl caught his attention with a stern look. "What?"

"You didn't tell him?" Karl asked.

"No, I didn't. If you want to call Vandeaga back and tell him that Muncher thinks he's the bringer of death, then be my fucking guest." Terry went back to organising his footlocker at the end of his bed. This was now the tenth time he had put his socks in order.

Vandeaga walked the dorm corridors and made his way to the Food Hall. As he approached the doors they opened by themselves with an electronic hum.

That's new, he thought, *and what a waste of resources.*

He scanned the food hall and spotted Muncher sat down at a crowded table. As he got closer to the group, they all turned towards him. He gave them a quick salute but only a few returned the gesture.

"Muncher, can I talk to you please?" Muncher didn't even look round; it was as if Vandeaga wasn't there.

"He doesn't want to talk to you." The guy who sat next to Muncher spoke in his place. Vandeaga heard him and spoke to Muncher again.

"If you do not want to speak to me then all you have to do is say so and I will leave, and I will apologise for disturbing you." Muncher shook his head and stood up.

"I will be back in a second," Muncher said to his group and most gave him a nod, "I guess it's private then?" Muncher walked past and sat at an empty table. Vandeaga sat in the chair opposite him.

"Can I ask why you wanted a transfer?"

"That's not a straight forward as you would think. Have you ever noticed just how fucked up things go when you are nearby?" Even now Muncher would not look Vandeaga in the eyes.

"I don't understand what you mean?"

"Things go wrong, that is just the way it is, but quite often you are there when it really does. Don't misunderstand me because I'm not saying you have directly caused anything, but you sure as shit were there every time. Jake, Mike, Larooa all dead, all our other friends have vanished. I can't shake this feeling that it's to do with you. I'm missing a lung from where Taradin stabbed me and that was down to you." Muncher banged his fist into his chest.

Vandeaga could feel his face start to heat up and redden. He wanted to jump the table and give Muncher a slap.

"You believe what Taradin said about me?" Vandeaga said those words through gritted teeth.

"No, but he had a point, and I can see the change in you."

"A lot has happened in the last few months so of course I've changed." Vandeaga pointed to Muncher, "You have too." He shook his head as Muncher pushed his chair back and stood up with a stretch.

"We all have and not for the better, good luck Vandeaga, it's only going to get worse from here." Muncher left Vandeaga and re-joined his new dorm mates and as a group they vacated the Food Hall.

Vandeaga remained where he was for a few minutes. He had clamped his fingers around the table leg and squeezed with all of his force. It must have worked because he hadn't tried to strike Muncher once.

Why do I care for these people? Vandeaga hadn't questioned his feelings before, he just acted on them. He released the leg and pushed himself away from the table. He already felt drained. He scanned the hall and only a few returned his gaze. *I think it's time for me to go.* He walked across the hall and back out of the double doors. He approached the closest Minder and greeted him with a salute, the Minder remained motionless.

"I need to speak to Officer Josef urgently. Could you take me to him please?" The Minder's head twitched for a couple of seconds as it sent and received information. It signalled with its hand and walked up the corridor. Vandeaga followed but not too closely as he didn't want to provoke it.

Why are we going outside? Vandeaga thought as they passed through a set of doors and into the fresh air. He'd never had a reason to walk this way before.

It was only a short walk round the back of the Officer's Block. As they turned the last corner, Officer Josef was leant against a doorframe and inhaled from something in his hand. The Minder stopped as Vandeaga walked past.

Vandeaga greeted Josef, but the Minder remained motionless until it was signalled to leave and returned to its original station.

"Good evening, Van," Josef said with an exhale of light blue smoke.

"Evening Sir. I've made my decision."

"That was quick. I expected you to give it at least to the end of your first full day." Josef put the oblong shaped object to his lips and squeezed it with his thumb. It hummed as he sucked air through the small hole at the top.

"With what has happened, I feel like I need to leave this place one way or another."

"Is this about Munch?"

"He definitely helped me come here sooner. Sir, may I ask what that is?" Vandeaga gave the object a loose point with his hand. Josef held up the item with another cloud of blue.

"This is one of the least addictive substances that we are allowed to take on site. I would highly suggest that you take my advice and don't start. The only reason I am telling you this is because the withdrawals are a pain to deal with if you cannot get hold of a good supply."

"Why are you outside?"

"It's also best not to let everyone know what you are keen to try, anyway let's get you prepped. You will not be thrown straight into the test so you will be given seven days, but you will not be allowed to walk around the academy. This is so you can't unload any information onto your peers. Is what I have said so far, clear?"

"Yes sir," Vandeaga nodded more to himself because if he was honest, none of it made any sense.

"So, as a reminder, if you pass you could become an Officer and if you fail you are liquidated. Is that also clear?"

"Yes Sir, but what if I don't want to become an Officer?"

"You know that decision is out of your control. You have been picked for that role based on your scores and that is what you are trained for. There is nothing I or you can do about that right now."

"I don't know anything about the test, Sir."

"That will be explained later. Let's get you to your private quarters. Is there anyone you would like to speak to before you go, you will not get another chance?"

"I think it's better this way sir." Vandeaga let out a heavy sigh before he saw Terry come marching round the corner. Josef slipped his inhaler into his back pocket. Terry approached the pair and saluted before he held out his hand. Vandeaga looked at it for a second before he shook it.

"I hear you are going for the final test early?" Terry asked, Vandeaga gave Josef a sideways glance.

"Don't look at me I've not mentioned it to anyone," Josef laughed as he wouldn't have told Vandeaga anyway.

"How did you find out?" Vandeaga said with a confused look.

"It spread across the dorms about a minute ago. No one knows where it started, but we all wish you luck. If anyone could pass the final early, it would be you."

"Thank you, Terry."

"Is there anything you want me to pass on?" Terry still hadn't released Vandeaga's hand.

"Tell everyone they can do anything they put their will to."

"Will do, I will never forget you Vandeaga," he turned to Josef, "Sir." Terry saluted once more and walked back to the main block. Officer Josef clapped his hands with a loud slap.

"Right, let's get you to your quarters, follow me." Both of them walked around the leaders block and towards a smaller building. This was only one storey and had no windows that Vandeaga could see. Josef tapped at the door panel and it slid open. He turned towards Vandeaga and placed his hand on his shoulder.

"This is where we part ways. This building is set up to take ten people to the final test but there has never been more than one person in there at a time. As you have chosen to take the test early you are in lockdown. The next people you see will be on your test day. Who they are will depend on whether you pass or fail? Head inside and make yourself comfortable. It's up to you now, you can sit on your arse for a week and hope for the best or use the whole facility and train like there is no tomorrow." The door opened onto a white tiled corridor with pale blue back lighting.

Vandeaga nodded and walked through the door, he stopped and turned.

"Was this a bad idea?"

"No, it has been done before. I won't say good luck because luck has nothing to do with the final. You will make a fine Officer one day, Vandeaga."

Vandeaga nodded his thanks as the door slid shut.

"Welcome to the final exam facility." The electronic voice boomed down the corridor in front of him. Vandeaga was forced to place his hands over his ears.

"Fuck me, can you turn the volume down please? You're a bit loud." Vandeaga said as he lowered his hands from his ears. He threw them back up as there was an even louder blast of static before the voice repeated itself but at a more agreeable level. Vandeaga was never sure, but he swore that he heard Josef laugh behind door.

"We will take you on a tour of the facility, please follow the blue line and stop when instructed. If you do not comply you will be immobilised." Vandeaga felt like he needed to put his hand up and wait to be ask something, but he didn't. As he spoke Vandeaga checked all the surfaces he could see. He wasn't sure what he was looking for, but it was all very clean.

"Question, what do you mean by immobilised?"

"You will be electrocuted. It's not a fatal charge, but I am required to not recommend it." Vandeaga grinned to himself and started to follow the blue line. It went straight up the short corridor and turned left at the cross section. A small flat robot appeared through a flap in the wall. It hoovered up the small particles of dirt that had dropped off Vandeaga's boots. When it had finished it seemed to point towards his legs and growl before it shot back into the wall.

"Now Stop! To your right is the wash area. Everything you require to keep yourself and your clothes clean. Ahead of you is the gym, which is fully furnished with everything you need to keep you at your peak. You may now continue to follow the blue line."

Vandeaga strolled around the bend and was instructed once more.

"Now Stop! To your immediate left is the shooting range." That's where Vandeaga wanted to be, he knew he was going to spend many hours in there.

Would they really let me use live rounds on my own?

"To your right is the information room, and this is where you will study and expand your knowledge. You may now continue to follow the blue line."

Vandeaga walked towards a dead end and only stopped because the doors didn't open.

"These are the personal quarters where you can discuss the final test with your fellow recruits." Vandeaga looked behind him to make sure there was no one else there. The doors took an age to open and for a moment he felt nervous; what if there was someone else in there? What would he even say to them, or would he even want to? When the doors finally parted he walked inside and looked down another corridor.

"Pick a room that is green and place you hand on the scanner. After you have been verified, you will be given access. The computer inside will be preloaded with all the information for your class. Do you have any questions?" The voice, through its own accord or not, seemed to be getting louder each time it spoke.

"Will I be monitored while I am here?"

"No, but if you do not respect the facility you will be immobilised."

Vandeaga nodded to himself once more and walked towards the first room and of course the door was lit around the edges of the frame with green light. With his hand on the scanner his name appeared above the door as it slid to one side. The room was all white with a tiled floor. He had a double bed to himself, a desk and a very high spec computer, or at least it looked better than the ones he had used before. There was a door with a sign for a toilet and a work surface with a selection of coloured cupboards.

"Now that's nice, wait, hold on?" Vandeaga stepped back out of the room. "Question, where do I eat?" He had already pushed his fingers into his ears for the upcoming blast of static.

"There is a food dispenser in your room. It is next to the fridge behind the blue door."

"I have a fridge? Thank you!" Vandeaga shouted as he rushed into the room and pulled open the blue door with so much force the hinges cracked. He was presented with a box with an opaque glass front. To the left of the glass was a panel with multiple buttons and a crystal display that flashed hello at him. He pressed a random button and a menu popped up. It wasn't great but at least he could eat when he wanted to. He pulled off his boots and threw himself onto the double bed. Whether Vandeaga planned to or not, he was asleep within minutes.

*

Vandeaga's body needed to sleep, it needed to rest far beyond he knew, but his mind didn't stop the tormented cycle. He was back at the arena once more, but each time he dreamt about this place it was different. This time nearly every surface was on fire and the black plastic and metal hands were so tall they blocked out the sun, everything had a burning shadow cast across it. It was strange to be on his back but not know how he got there, he rolled onto his knees.

Two recruits ran past him and smiled, both of them seemed oblivious that they were ablaze. Their clothes and hair crackled as their skin melted with the heat. Vandeaga spun in place to look for Larooa, like he always did and unfortunately every time, he found her. He tried to stand but stumbled back onto his knees, he looked down to the bloodied stumps that were his feet. He couldn't have known this pain, but his mind tried its best.

He looked away from the splayed bones and crawled forwards to grasp her hand. Her unblinking eyes stared skyward. He tried to ignore the fact that the bottom half of her torso had been opened to the air and her intestines trailed for miles into the distance.

"You are going to be ok! You are going to get through this!" He had said this each time and never did he believe it. Her head slowly turned towards his but her eyes remained fixed on the sky.

"You failed me," as she spoke, blood and shit poured from her mouth.

"I did my best…I," Vandeaga tried to stay calm but his voice broke away before he could finish.

"Your best got us killed." Her eye flicked towards the remains of Mike. His body was smeared over a large area, none of his extremities were attached to his torso. Mikes left arm rotated on an invisible shoulder joint and gave Vandeaga the finger. The ground began to shake as a blast of sound raced towards them. He turned back to Larooa as her eyes filled with silver.

"If you lead, people will die and you will become a shadow of your rightful self." The floor shook as a thousand floor building that stretched past the clouds toppled in the distance. The monstrous skyscraper screamed as it folded under its own weight and smashed to the floor.

"I can't get away from my fate."

"You're right," Larooa tilted her head towards the sky. Vandeaga followed her gaze as the huge metal hands turned and plummeted towards the ground. He had enough time to cover his face before they hit.

*

Vandeaga woke up with a start and threw himself off the bed and raised his fists to defend himself. His T-shirt was soaked with sweat and he had a headache like he had never felt before. His fists were clenched so tight they started to hurt.

"Heightened levels of aggression detected, please remain calm." The voice crackled over the speaker system. Vandeaga screamed as loud as he could and sprinted out of his quarters and towards the firing range. The buildings artificial intelligence must have known where he was headed as it proceeded to instruct him on how to use the range.

"The range uses simulated weapons, which are for all intents and purposes, are 100% accurate to their real-life counterparts. They fire life-like projectiles so do not aim the weapons at yourself. If you do you will be immobilised. When you are ready to begin, request the number of targets, movement parameters and the required distance for the firing line."

Vandeaga stopped just inside the door to familiarise himself with the layout of the range. In front of him were ten booths, each had a large shelf with ear and eye protection. To his left was a very long cabinet which contained a large number of rifles and pistols. Below each weapon was a deep box with one magazine and the ammunition that needed to be fed into them.

Most of these weapons he had never seen before, he hadn't spent much time with pistols so he grabbed himself a battle rifle. It was a standard issue, fully automatic, fifty round machine gun. He pulled the magazine from the slot and another one slid into place so he took that one too.

"Ten targets, random position and movement, and go!" Vandeaga shouted as he walked towards the middle booth. Red discs the size of a person's head appeared down the range, some of them moved across the space and some were stationary.

Vandeaga didn't bother with the eye protection as he looked down the iron sights and fired. Eleven shots and ten targets down as Vandeaga placed the weapon on the work surface. He walked back to the rack and stared at a huge pistol. It looked more like a Hand Cannon than a pistol. He picked it up and held it in one hand, the weight felt good.

There was no place for a magazine or a slot for cartridges to be pushed into. It was dull silver with thin pipes that ran across the surface. He went back to the booth as the AI introduced him to the weapon.

"The Thor is a prototype energy weapon that is not in circulation as of this date. It fires superheated slugs of pure energy. The mechanics of the weapon are still classified, the weapon you hold does not fire the slugs but does have the same recoil and fire rate. It is not recommended to use this weapon with one ha…"

Vandeaga aimed down the range and fired, as he only used his right hand the gun recoiled like a maul. He had to pull his head to one side or it would have slapped him clean in the face.

"Wow, that is awesome," He switched hands and looked down at his wrist, "that is going to be sore tomorrow." He looked over to the wall of guns. "What do I call you?" Vandeaga asked.

"It does not matter what you desire to call me. It will not change my job role or responsibility."

"I'm going to be here for seven days so I need to call you something other than the A.I." Vandeaga stared at the ceiling. It would have made more sense for him to ask the camera directly but that made him feel a little uncomfortable.

"In the past, I have been called Jolly Joe." Jolly Joe's voice seemed to lighten when he said his own name.

"Ok Jolly Joe, tell me about every weapon on the rack." If a computer that had no face could smile, then Jolly Joe just did.

Chapter 21

Vandeaga spent an entire day playing with his new toys. At one point Jolly Joe had to remind him to put the empty magazines into the recycling bin, as the dozens left on the floor could become a trip hazard. He had begun to feel tired but he couldn't bear to have those dreams again so he made himself some food then hit the gym.

He had no surprises here as Vandeaga had seen all of this equipment in their old dorm. No matter what Vandeaga said, Jolly Joe gave him a running commentary of instructions on how to use each piece of equipment. He only spent a couple hours training before he went to see what was in the knowledge room. On the way, Vandeaga stopped as he had a strange urge.

"Jolly Joe, can I ask you a question?" Vandeaga tilted his head to one side. He still wasn't sure if this was a good idea and tried to think of the best way to ask.

"Of course, I am here to help you." Jolly Joe seemed to have sorted out his volume problem, because his voice, for the moment, was at a constant level.

"Have you ever had to immobilise people before?" Vandeaga didn't need to know but he was kind of curious.

"Yes, I have," Vandeaga looked behind him and back again as he tried to find where the shock could come from.

"How painful is it?"

"The data shows that it is excruciating, but I can confirm that there is no permanent damage caused to the body of the subject."

"I have an odd request. I would like to know how it feels, so, could you immobilise me?"

Vandeaga thought that there would be some sort of exchange between Jolly Joe and himself. Maybe Jolly Joe would ask him if he was sure or even try to talk him out of the suggestion, none of that happened.

"Coming right up sweet heart!" If the walls could grin, they would have.

Vandeaga gave the closest camera a weird look as a mini turret shaped like a football dropped from the ceiling and fired two darts into his chest. The noise that passed through Vandeaga's mouth as his muscles turned solid was not voluntary. His body stayed straight as he landed onto his back, his arms remained pinned at his sides for a full minute. As the pain started to subside Vandeaga sat up.

"What the hell Jolly Joe! You could have warned me you were going to do that straight away. If I ask you to do that again, say no!"

"Ok, this information has been noted and a reminder has been set. On a positive note, your heart did not stop". Jolly Joe was an Artificial Intelligence but for some unknown reason he almost enjoyed doing that to people. Vandeaga looked down and pulled the two darts out of his skin. The turret had already retreated back into the ceiling.

"Please keep the corridor tidy and place the probes and loose cables into the closest refuse bin." Vandeaga looked up at the closest camera with a puzzled look.

"What about my heart?"

"There is a 0.5 percent chance that your heart would stop while being immobilised."

"Why the fuck didn't you tell me?"

"You did not ask, and please use respectful language."

"Ok Jolly Joe, I'm going to the knowledge room now." Vandeaga began to wrap the thin cable round his hand. Just before the turret disappeared it must have ejected both lines.

"There is a bin on the way to the knowledge room."

"I know, thank you," Vandeaga rubbed at his chest where the prongs had struck him. His entire body ached and he knew it was going to hurt for a while.

Vandeaga had to smile to himself as he walked through the door. There were ten desks that faced the back wall, he thought they were the same as the other ones he had used. On closer inspection, these had a lot more tech inside them. As he sat down the screen lit up and asked him for his hand print, it then asked him to place a piece of paper on the laser imprinter.

He watched the device flash as all of his details were etched onto the paper in under a second. He grabbed the paper as the screen flashed up the modules that it recommended for him to work through. Before he had touched his pen to paper Vandeaga sat back in his chair.

Why am I doing this?

He thought about the dream that he kept having, yes, it was just a dream, but there was something in there that he knew to be true. His fate was to become an Officer, but that was not what he wanted. The last year had proved he couldn't handle loss purely based on his decisions. The main problem was, he couldn't fail the test. If he did, he would be executed but if he passed, he would become an Officer.

I'm not giving up, but I don't want to pass.

He tapped his chin with his pen and thought about his problem. He started to list all the ways he could get around it. He knew the pass mark was 92 percent. Apart from the last modules, he knew the rest like the back of his hand, so that target was easy to achieve. If he scored 100 percent, it wouldn't change anything as he would just get honours before he was promoted. If he scored zero, then they would believe he was being difficult and just execute him.

What to do? Vandeaga ran his hands through his hair and looked to the ceiling. It was at that point a realisation kicked in and he knew exactly what to do. It would be complicated but if he pulled it off, he would confuse the hell out of the system.

He flipped over his piece of paper and started to make a plan for the rest of the week. He would have to spend almost all of the time he had left in the knowledge room, but he knew it would be worth it. Of course, he would go to the firing range again at least once more, maybe twice.

Chapter 22

It had been a week since Officer Josef had last spoken to Vandeaga. To be honest, Josef had almost forgotten about him. Josef was in the middle of a late lunch when he received the call to attend a meeting. He brushed past a Minder and handed it his plate that contained what he couldn't eat.

He didn't usually eat with the recruits but an Officer was always needed on hand and today was his turn. The Minder glanced between the plate and Josef a number of times. It growled to itself and walked back towards the Food Hall. Josef tapped the side of his head.

"Come in," a voice echoed through his inner ear. He pushed through the door and saluted the people present. Apart from Chrisa, the same faces were sat at the table, maybe they had nothing better to do than to hold meetings in the first place.

He once again pulled up his chair and sat at the table that faced them. The table was covered in paperwork and figures, but then he spotted the picture of Vandeaga in front of him. He was stood in the firing range with a mass of equipment and discarded magazines at his feet. Vandeaga's face was twisted into a scream as he unloaded the weapon in his grasp.

"What has he done now?" Josef asked as he flicked through the papers.

"He has made a fool of the system," Tyler said while he glanced over similar paperwork.

"How so?" Josef said while he tried to speed read through the mass of printouts.

"He didn't pass the final test Officer Josef." There was no emotion in Chancellor Torn's voice.

"What! How could he not pass, the final test is a joke for someone of his skills." Josef couldn't hide the shock on his face. He finally found Vandeaga's scores and when he read them, he couldn't stop the laugh that forced its way out of his mouth. "How did he manage that?"

"This isn't a laughing matter Josef," Chancellor Torn couldn't hide the frustration in her voice any longer.

"I'm sorry, that was an impulse reaction. I'm just confused on the situation."

"He didn't pass but he didn't fail either. 92 percent is a pass; 91 percent is a fail. He scored 0.5 percent under the pass mark, but the system isn't designed to register 0.5 percent in any situation. So, the computer recorded his mark as a draw." Tyler said but didn't look up from his paperwork. It was at this point that Josef became certain that the paperwork Tyler held had nothing to do with this situation.

"Over the last four months his scores have been all over the place. He could easily get top marks, but we believe he was purposely doing this so he could work out the scoring system. Which is how he managed to get his score to that exact figure. Now let's speak of how he managed to confuse the system to give him a 0.5 mark. He managed to get the laser to print his name wrong." Chancellor Torn gave Josef one of her looks.

"But isn't that a 1 percent markdown?" Josef asked. It was at that point he realised he'd interrupted the Chancellor Torn mid-flow. "I'm sorry, I will remain quiet until you ask me a question". He held up both of his hands as an apology.

"Thank you, then I will continue." She glared at him for almost a full minute before she started to speak again.

"He dropped a spot of blood on an exact point on the final test paper. The laser failed to print one line of one letter of his name. So that is how he confused the system. Tell me Josef, what are your thoughts on the situation?"

"If I'm honest I think he is a clever little bastard."

"This is no time for jokes, Josef."

"That wasn't a joke Sir. He is proving how good he is. His intelligence is through the roof and just looking at his range scores." Josef held up a piece of paper. "He is almost perfect on his accuracy. The only thing that confuses me is why he has now started to favour pistols over rifles." Other than the Chancellor everyone at the table started to speak at once.

"We cannot let someone as difficult as him become an Officer."

"That may be so, but I am sure he could work up to it."

"I vote for liquidation. He will cause too much damage to the way things are, he's too different." Tyler was still focused on his own findings.

Josef looked towards the Chancellor and waited for her to intervene but she didn't. He had to make a stand if no one else would.

"That would be a complete waste of talent. Yes, he wouldn't make a good Officer right now but he would make a fine soldier, given he also shows none of the normal sadistic tendencies that we are used to. He could easily rise through the ranks if given a purpose, he lacks drive here. Dump him on the field and see where he goes if you must."

"Why do you have so much faith in this one recruit?" Chancellor Torn shook her head.

"Officer Faleama had faith in him, and if she sees something then whatever it is gets my support."

"Thank you for your input, Officer Josef, you may leave now. We will make our own decision on the matter." Josef almost forgets to stand up, but as he slid his chair back, he had to ask.

"May I ask one last question?"

"Yes, Officer Josef."

"Is there a reason Chrisa is not here?"

"That is confidential, Josef, and will not be discussed." Josef smiled to himself, he knew what that meant, and it was never good for the person involved.

"Thank you," Josef saluted and left the room. When he had gone the Chancellor rubbed her temples, and tried to ignore the headache that thumped in the centre of her brain. It seemed it was going to be one of those days.

"You know this information will get out sooner rather than later, it always does." Turner said. "I suggest we give them all what they want to hear and then deal with this in our own way," Turner started to pack away his papers, "but that is just my suggestion."

"How would we do that?" Tyler asked with one of his grins.

"We will grant him a pass and say he was sent to a far reach sector of the planet," Chancellor Torn said.

"What will we really do?" Tyler pushed the papers that didn't matter to him, which was most of them, into the bin.

"Delete his file and dump him on the front line as a Low. Then time and battle will sort itself out." They nodded in unison at her wise decision.

*

Vandeaga's dorm celebrated when they heard the news and promised to make him proud. Each one of them hoped to follow in his footsteps and to meet him again. Over the next month they trained and fought like their lives depended on it, and it did.

Chapter 23

An armoured transport roared down a narrow pass as a group of vehicles chased after it. Each fired every weapon they had after their intended victim. The dull black armour was charred in a number of places and both of the roof-mounted guns swung on damaged joints and cables.

With great skill, the driver didn't slow as this large transport skimmed jagged rocks. He tapped at the control panel in front of him, and a speaker symbol lit up on the front wind shield.

"Emergency pick up has been made, but I have taken damage and lost both of my escort drones. I'm cutting through sector 15665 by rocky strip, but we do have some clingers which are refusing to turn back. I require support or information, over."

He waited for a response as he listened to the rattle as hot lead and uranium ricocheted off his baby. His gloved hands gripped the controls a little tighter than he intended to.

They're going to regret that.

The door that connected to the rear compartments slid open. A soldier pulled himself through and sat in the only vacant seat. His armour was covered in blood but none of it was his own. He tried to wipe his hands on his legs but it was a pointless exercise. As he slumped down, he breathed a heavy sigh. The driver didn't take his eyes off the terrain as he spoke.

"Are your guys doing alright back there?" The soldier shook his head.

"One took a clean hit to his face and most of his jaw is gone, he's lost a lot of blood. Barren took a hit to the chest, but Marcus said he will be fine. That guy hasn't stopped since the shooting started. We had to leave some of our people behind."

"Marcus? What's his second name?" The driver knew he had heard that name before but couldn't remember where.

"What?" The soldier gave him a sideways glance.

"It's rare to have a second name, did he tell you it?"

"Erm…yeah, he's Marcus Dean." He shrugged and began to check his mostly empty pockets.

"Marcus fucking Dean is riding in my baby, damn I'm going to have to get him to sign something." The driver gave his dashboard a quick glance for anything of his that could take a signature.

"I'm new to this squad and you are the second person to mention him. Is he good or something?" The soldier shrugged again and glanced over the numerous lights and buttons in front of him. The driver laughed at the poorly chosen words.

"Good ain't the fucking word, mate, this guy is a living legend. He could stop you dying if your head was removed from your body, he is THAT good." The transport swerved around a column of rock as a chasing blast of auto-fire shredded it into pieces. The speaker symbol flashed on the console again. "Waiting for instructions, over."

"Follow the line for three miles, two hornets on route." The robotic voice broke up slightly as it spoke.

"Straight three miles, hornets stationed, over." The driver tapped his heads-up display and a marker appeared on his map. He took no notice of the distance tracker that popped up alongside it, as he knew where he was.

"Blood and honour, you are what makes us."

"Blood and honour, Command, out." The driver turned to his passenger and gave him a slight smile.

"If they are still on our tail when the Hornets get here, they're screwed."

"If Marcus is that good, how comes he is not an Officer yet. Doesn't outstanding achievement get you promoted?"

"I'm not in a position to ask and as you are in his squad that's down to you." The driver turned and Marcus had his head through the door, his unblinking eyes shone like emeralds. His silver hair stood almost upright with no assistance required. Marcus would say he never did anything with his hair. Even though, it did look like he used spray paint instead of hair spray. This was one of the rarer side-effects of a Booster implant.

"Apparently, I'm too unstable," Marcus turned to the passenger, "Danny, what blood type are you again?"

"As far as I can remember I'm AB+," Danny said.

"That's no good to me." Marcus shook his head but Danny gave him a shrug as he couldn't have said anything else.

"I'm O+ and you can take four pints before I start to feel it."

"Are you boosted?"

"Oh yeah," the driver said with a larger-than-life smile.

"You have become my new best friend, let me get my bag." Marcus disappeared back through the door.

"Oh damn," the driver bounced up and down in his seat. "Marcus Dean is going to take my blood," the large smile tried to get bigger but couldn't, "this is a good day."

"How many are following us?" Danny asked. The driver's fingers flashed across a number of buttons. A small portion of the windscreen lit up with a rear facing camera, they could see at least six heavily armoured vehicles that were in pursuit. Each one had an array of weaponry attached to it. There was a small red blip on a different monitor and the driver flicked his eyes to it. He swerved and started to grind the transport against the side of a rock wall.

"What are you doing?" Danny shouted as he grabbed hold of his seat for support.

"I'm picking up movement in there and I'm hoping to piss something big off, and here it comes." The driver steered clear of the rocky wall as a monstrous worm that was twelve feet across burst through it with a shower of rubble. It's mass of teeth barely missed the transport but quickly turned its attention to the following vehicles. They had to turn their guns on it first but the worm half swallowed one of the vehicles before they could kill it and keep up the pursuit.

"That's a lot of company, what was your mission?" The driver wasn't really interested but as it was rare for someone to bother to come and sit with him, he might as well try having a conversation for once.

"We were tasked to take a fuel depot but we had to blow it up instead."

"That would explain why they are so pissed." The driver laughed to himself, but soon grimaced as something large struck the side of his transport with a massive explosion.

"What the hell was that?" Danny shouted and looked round for the damage.

"Front facing mortar, son of a bitch damaged my girl, hold on!" He hung a left at full speed, Danny almost slid right out of his seat. All twelve wheels of the transport screeched on the rocky ground for purchase. In the brief moment, they were out of view the driver pressed a button and released a scatter of black discs from the back end of the transport. The lead car couldn't avoid them and erupted into a ball of fire as several mines tore through it.

The vehicle broke apart as metal and organic material rained from the sky. The chasing vehicles smashed the burning shell out of the way and continued after their target. Danny had to ask the obvious.

"What are the chances of getting out of here?"

"With the power they are packing and the damage I have taken, I would say quite slim, but fuck it I'm not going to just stop!" Ten Gatling guns sprayed the back and side of the transport as he turned right into an open stretch of ground. A top-down view of his vehicle appeared on the display as a number of sections turned red.

"Is that bad?" Danny leant forward to get a better look at the images.

"My girl has some meat on her but her armour is failing." A second explosion forced the right set of wheels off the ground. They landed back down with a crash as the driver regained control.

"Shit, I'm losing wheel seven." Within a second, his hand flashed across a series of buttons which ejected the entire thirty-two-inch wheel. It shot away and rebounded off a rock wall then back into the path of the chase vehicles. The front four parted to avoid the wheel but the last car took it full force to the windshield. The hardened glass couldn't take the impact and was crushed into the occupants inside. The damaged car slowly rolled to a halt.

"That was lucky," Marcus dropped his bag next to the driver, "which one is it then, and I never asked your name?"

"It's Ennis and it has to be the left, I have too many modules in the right." Ennis said and held out his arm. Marcus began to roll up his sleeve.

"How far till support arrives?" Marcus pushed the needle into Ennis's vein.

"About a mile to the hornets," Marcus nodded with acknowledgment.

"Keep an eye on that and don't let it drain more than three and a half pints. I will be back in a minute."

"Isn't three and half pints of blood a lot to take in one go?" Danny asked but Marcus had already gone.

"Not for me, I was Boosted a long time ago," Ennis said.

"What's Boosted?" Danny asked with an intense stare.

"You are part of a hit and run squad and you don't know what Boosters are? Damn you are green." Danny stared at the side of Ennis's head as he spoke but his eyes remained on the road.

"I'm not explaining it to you, unless you have forgotten, I'm the one driving," Danny smiled to himself.

"I'm only screwing with you I've not got mine yet," Danny shrugged. It wasn't like Boosters were a cure-all that kept you alive no matter what. He had seen too many people fall to know better than that.

"Stay alive long enough and you will, it's just a matter of time." Danny nodded and looked down at the blood pump.

"I think that's done. Marcus! Your bloods ready."

"Fantastic!" Marcus appeared from the back and removed the blood collection kit. The display lit up as some of the red panels turned black. Danny was about to ask about the display when a huge impact exploded the side window and rocked the whole transport. Deadly shards of glass and metal blew across the cab.

Before the window had begun to crack Ennis had raised his arm to protect his face and neck. His armour and exposed flesh caught most of the glass and shrapnel. However, some of it passed through the plating. Marcus grabbed Danny's body by his jacket and started to drag him into the back compartment.

Ennis leant forward and pulled what was left of Danny's arm off the dash board and tossed it behind him. Ennis could feel the side of his chest was starting to dampen his clothes with blood.

"Is he dead?" Ennis shouted over the noise of more gun fire; he sprayed a small fire with an extinguisher. Danny's face was a mess and his arm had been removed near to his shoulder. Marcus just laughed.

"Nope, but he sure as shit won't be the same when he wakes up. Are you alright?"

Ennis looked down at the screen that showed his vitals.

"It's not fatal, I can wait until we get back."

"How long until the hornets come and save our arses?" Ennis didn't get a chance to speak as he was cut off by the sound of a jet engine.

The hornet was shaped like a wasp but was the size of a minivan. Ennis swerved, as the hornet passed, it took some paint work with it. It unloaded ten rockets before the chase vehicles had a chance to react. Each one flipped with a thunderous blast of flame and smoke.

"I guess that answered my question. Good, Ennis, I will be back in a moment as it looks like you are leaking." Ennis was more concerned about their ride home as Marcus dragged Danny's almost lifeless body through the door. Ennis shook his head at all the flashing symbols and lights across his dash board.

"This is going to take fucking ages to fix."

Chapter 24

The transport limped over the perimeter of their forward operating base and pulled onto the drop-off point. This base was a lot smaller than most as it was designed to be undetected. There was a maximum of three-hundred personnel that called this place home.

The perimeter was a make shift wall that surrounded the base, a multitude of weaponry pointed over the top of it into the rocky landscape. What vegetation that had once been here was blasted away decades ago by conflict. They were greeted with a dozen stretchers and medical staff.

The members of the squad that were able to walk were called into a debriefing. Several members of the medical team joined them to treat what wounds they could. Squad leader Carlos pushed one of the medical team away with a polite shove. She had tried to treat the deep wound on his face.

"I'm fine it's only a flesh wound. I will get treated later. On me people, we debrief then we get fed." He pushed through two sets of doors and into a large room filled with computer screens and staff. As his squad pulled up chairs, he remained standing and saluted his Officer.

"Squad Leader Carlos reporting in Sir," Officer Braker smiled.

"I see you have promoted yourself to squad leader."

"I was forced to, under the circumstances. Deaktree took a bullet to the back of his neck and Marcus couldn't save him."

"I thought Marcus was the best?" Braker glanced across the room for their first medic but he wasn't there.

"There wasn't much left of Deaktree's head to put back together sir."

"That will explain it then," Officer Braker turned to everyone that wasn't part of the squad, "I need the room please." Without question, without hesitation, the room emptied until the squad and their Officer were alone.

"Explain to me what the fuck happened?" Officer Braker couldn't hide his anger any longer. It had been boiling over since he received the transmission to say the operation had ended under dubious circumstances.

"I don't understand, sir."

"The objective was to TAKE the fuel depot, not blow the fucking thing up. How did that set of instructions get mixed up? The ongoing campaign needed those resources. Our commander has even expressed his concerns on the matter."

"The intel was wrong Sir. We did send a number of messages to Command."

"The only message that we received was for emergency pick up and the information was sourced and selected by the Drill, it couldn't be wrong."

"The information we were given, was to take control of a civilian fuel depot. It was a five square mile facility with no outer defences."

"That is the same report that I was given." Officer Braker picked up a file of papers and threw it across a desk.

"The facility was easy to take, only because there was no one on the outskirts, or on visible guard. When we were inside and began to set up, we were attacked from every angle. These guys had every weapon that I could imagine. Our transports, antimissile barriers ran out of charge in minutes. It was Squad leader Deaktree's order to plant charges as we fought our way out. We lost the transports and Deaktree took a hit to the head, we lost over half of our people. We requested a pick up and fought to the extraction point and I set off the explosives. That is everything that happened and many of us that survived were recording so you can check the footage." Squad leader Carlos hadn't moved from where he was stood, and saluted when he was finished.

"We have to check all available feeds. Would you say that they knew you were coming?"

"I believe so Sir, yes."

"Go get some food, get cleaned up, but make sure your footage is downloaded by the Techs first."

"Yes sir, on me people." The entire squad of eight stood and saluted their Officer before heading for the Food Hall. It wasn't long before Braker was the only person left in the room. He tapped the side of his head twice.

"Back to your stations." He rested his hands on the main console as a Tech walked up to him.

"It was bad intel, wasn't it?" Braker looked across to his lead Technician.

"What a fucking mess this is, Vicks." Braker said in a low voice, he bit his bottom lip with a long exhale of breath. Vicks moved a stray red hair from in front of her face.

"I have been over this base's A.I. a dozen times and I cannot find a problem. Every single check comes back clear.

I've even had other people take a look but the result always comes back the same. Unless it's a problem between our local A.I. and Command."

"Could it be in the code, a corrupt line maybe?"

"If that is the problem and the checks can't find it then a manual visual check would need to be done."

"Is that even possible?" Braker turned and leant back against the desk.

"Yes, anything is possible, but even with these." Vicks tapped one of her plastic eyes. Her pupil reacted to the impact with an expansion and a rotation.

"It would take a team of over a hundred and a decade, but even then, we might not find the fault."

"Please don't do that, it creeps me out," Braker had to avert his eyes from Vicks.

"What?" She asked.

"When you tap your eyes," Vicks couldn't help but laugh.

"Oh sorry, I don't notice I do it half the time. When does your relief start?"

"Sasha should take over from me in three hours."

"Well, I'm done here so we will meet up later?" Braker had to think for a moment to make sure he hadn't already said he would be with someone else.

"That's good for me, I will let you know when I'm cleaned up." Vicks saluted and walked out the operations room. A number of screens flashed up with errors. One of them made Braker look round the room. It stated there was a large fire in the operations room. As this was the room he was stood in, he was sure as shit there was no fire.

"I hate this crappy system." Braker muttered to himself before he raised the incident with the Tech team.

Chapter 25

Marcus walked into the Food Hall and sat down with his squad.

"Where have you been? And why did you not attend the debrief?" Carlos pushed aside his plate of food. Marcus completely ignored him, with a sigh he left his chair and walked back towards the food processor. He threw a tray into the machine and hit a few buttons. The machine filled the separate compartments with hot gloop.

Why does this smell so good but look so rank?

Marcus picked up the tray and went back to the table. Carlos hadn't moved and still waited for a response, but he didn't get it as Marcus stuck a fork into what shouldn't be called meat.

"Didn't you hear me?" Carlos asked, he never took his eyes off Marcus. Marcus looked up and smiled.

"Sorry, I didn't catch what you said."

"Then I will repeat it for you. Where have you been? And why did you not attend the debrief?" Marcus shrugged and went back to his food. Carlos looked round at the other members of his squad and a number of them gave their medic a series of disapproving looks.

Marcus shovelled as much as he could into his mouth and pushed the empty tray away. He held up a hand as he chewed, he only lowered it when he swallowed.

"Right, we had members of our squad that needed treatment. I have more expertise than anyone here and I did a fucking good job." His tone changed as his eye twitched. "They won't be the same but they're all still breathing. What's the point of being at the debrief anyway, they tell us what we did or didn't do then we get sent out again?" Marcus leant across the table so he was closer to Carlos, but his face twisted into a smile.

"It doesn't fucking matter," he stared into Carlos's eyes, "you seem tense, let me make you feel better." Marcus raised his hand. As Carlos stood up; his chair fell backwards. The clatter made a couple of the Officers look over to their table.

"Don't touch me Marcus," Carlos said.

"Not scared of me, are you?" Marcus gave him another smile. After all, he was just trying to be friendly.

"I don't want your help or you trying to screw with my head." Marcus slowly lowered his hand.

"No need to be like that. Also, it's quite silly telling a medic you don't need his help. Anyway, you really should check how many points we have to get our squad up and fighting," Marcus stood up and stretched, "I'm tired, wake me if anything happens, and no I don't want any implants."

He turned and walked out of the Food Hall. It was quite strange to see the number of soldiers that had stepped out of his way as he passed. Braker walked over and stood next to Carlos.

"Is there a problem?" Braker asked.

"Nothing I can't handle Sir, but I do think he is getting worse."

"He has been doing his job for a long time so it is possible he could be close to a slip," they nodded together, "however, he does have a point."

"Sir?" Carlos's eye brows scrunched up in the middle as he turned to his Officer. He'd never heard of points before.

"You need to check in with medical and get your points allocated."

"I'm new to this role sir, I'm not sure what that means."

"That's very true as you have not been briefed, you can't be expected to know everything." Braker was about to suggest they head to the training area before he remembered that he had an appointment to keep.

"Speak to me tomorrow as I need to take a meeting in the next twenty minutes."

"It must be important?" Carlos asked as Vicks walked past the twin doors and glanced through the glass. It was just enough time to catch Braker's eye.

"Yes, it is," Braker said as he left the hall with such a pace it would almost be called a jog. Carlos sat back down and pulled his tray towards him, but his appetite had long gone. The soldier sat next to him cleared his throat, a bandage was firmly attached across his face.

"He does do a good job," Carlos smiled but stared at the tray.

"I'm not saying he doesn't but he refuses to follow orders and does not listen."

"Deaktree just let him get on with it."

"Only because he used Marcus to take away his nightmares so he could sleep." Officer Sasha walked into the food hall. Carlos looked at the clock on the wall.

I thought she was on duty?

She walked over to their table and placed her hands on the top.

"Have you seen Officer Braker anywhere?"

"He left about a minute ago."

"Did he say where he was going?"

"No sir."

She clenched her hands into fists, she almost growled her words and left shaking her head. The squad watched her march through the doors, they slammed open with some force.

"Not sure what she was so pissed about?" Carlos said this more to himself than anyone present.

"Really, you couldn't tell?" He turned to his squad mate, she looked him straight in the eyes, her dark hair was cut near to her ears.

"Not a clue, Bella." He said with a shrug and she smiled.

"The soldiers are mostly an even split but the Officers working out of this base are nearly all female."

"So?" Carlos was far from stupid but this went straight over his head. Bella clenched one hand into a fist and tapped it into the palm of her other hand. Carlos smiled to himself when realisation dawned on him. "Ok, I get it."

"Why doesn't she just grab one of the other males then?" The soldier with the bandage grunted his statement.

"You can't step down or step up. Those are the rules and they can't be broken."

"I never really thought about it before." Bella waited for the other soldier to look away before she leaned towards Carlos.

"So, are you free or have you lost your appetite completely?" Bella asked, the words 'I'm tired' almost left his lips.

Don't refuse you stupid prick, it's rude.

"Not being hungry doesn't mean I'm dead, yet." They both stood up and headed for the soldiers' meeting quarters, the bandaged soldier watched them leave.

"No one ever asks me, you know." One of the female soldiers that remained didn't look up from her tray.

"You don't ask anyone though, do you?" She answered him around a mouthful of food.

"No," He would never ask someone for the possible chance that they might say no, even if that was a very low probability.

"If you never ask then people think you are not interested and won't ask you." She took the time to place her tray to one side and look straight at him.

"Yeah, that's possible," he gave himself a nod almost like he knew all the mysteries of the world.

"I'm going to get some sleep." She stood up with an outlandish stretch of her arms.

"Ok catch you later, Clara," he said. Clara wanted to pick up her tray and slap him round the head with it, but instead left him to it.

Chapter 26

The next morning, Carlos pushed through the doors to the learning centre and walked into a rather heated conversation.

"I'm not a machine, I do need some sleep." Braker gripped the back of a plastic chair and rocked it with each word.

"You said we were meeting and you fuck off with someone else."

"Fuck me, I'm going to need a rota for all this, I can't keep up. I said we were meeting today after your shift, not yesterday."

"Your grunt's here," Sasha and Braker turned to Carlos, he had no idea what they had just said so he just saluted. "I will see you later then?" Sasha asked as Braker ran his hands through his hair.

"Yes, I will, but you really need to ease off and relax."

"Maybe," she marched out of the room with that same heavy thud of her boots.

"Officer Sasha didn't sound too happy Sir," Carlos said. Braker shook his head with a smile.

"Officer Sasha is a very complex person and she can sometimes let small things irritate her. Given time, she will be fine. Did you get the service pack last night?"

"Yes Sir, I had a brief read through it."

"Good, because you need to be up to speed before you take lead on the next assignment. It's not all about screaming orders at people."

"Yes Sir."

"Do you have any questions?"

"The points system still doesn't make sense to me."

"It can seem very complex if you start looking at the ratios and break downs but I will simplify it for you." Braker tapped at the computer he was sat next to and a number of pie charts and figures flashed up on the screen.

"Just look at the end section for each soldier. Depending on kills, time served and supporting the squad, they are awarded points. You know, as well as I do, that everything is recorded. If a soldier takes any injury, for example if he or she loses a hand, you can allocate them points to have an upgrade so they don't get a basic replacement. Soldiers don't need to be injured to receive upgrades. Teal, your sniper had the superior eye implants, his range and accuracy went through the roof. That cost Deaktree a lot of points but it was worth it. On the other hand, you don't give upgrades to someone that you believe won't last long. That's hard to work out because anything can happen on the battlefield".

"That makes more sense now." Carlos said with an inhale of breath, he knew he should have written this all down.

"Good, have you heard of Officer Max? He is currently stationed at one of the research facilities," Braker asked.

"Isn't he the android?" Carlos said, he was shown a picture once, the guy was huge. Carlos didn't take Braker's chuckle as an insult.

"He's not an android, but he does have many more than the average amount of improvements. He held an outpost primarily on his own for two days before support arrived. He was awarded more points than you can imagine. What he's had done cost him a lot of points, but with a good record you get looked after, understand?"

"Yes sir."

"Good, you will get a rotation tomorrow to fill the empty places in your squad. Spend some time looking through the enhancements for your squad and their points before you get rested and wait for the next assignment."

"Yes Sir."

"Before I forget, have you seen Marcus since yesterday?"

"No sir, he seems to have confined himself to private quarters again."

"At least he cannot cause any trouble while he's in there." Braker thought about what he had said and quite quickly, realised he was wrong.

*

Marcus had spent the last twelve hours staring at the mirror above his sink. His knuckles had drained of colour with the amount of force that he held onto the metal basin. He couldn't sleep for the sounds of gunfire and screams, but his room was silent.

The voices were getting worse too, they told him things he didn't want to hear. His face had gone pale as the pain in his head had increased. His emerald eyes flicked down to the collar that was fastened around his neck. The charred mess that used to be a person vanished from behind him as he looked away.

His tensed muscles cracked as he struggled to get the armour and medical harness off. He wrenched everything off in one go and threw it against the closest wall. He'd begun to sweat and before he turned back to the mirror, he could feel the moisture dripping off his chin.

He grasped the sink once more, maybe he wanted to keep himself grounded or maybe it was simpler than that. He just wanted to prove to himself that this was real amongst a room of ghosts. He didn't remember having removed his undershirt but he was bare chested.

Other than the sunken points over his body where he had been injected with Boosters, there wasn't a mark on him. Over countless battles and firefights, he had never been badly injured. Marcus had, however, had a number of near misses over the years but his body was unchanged.

Due to his long service, he had been witness to too many of his people losing their lives. He'd lost count of the people he had saved with his expert skills, but that is not what he remembered. The faces of the dead and dying were always there, always talking to him. His harness bleeped once as a warning to show the explosive in his head had been armed. His eyes darted to the LED as it turned from green to red.

"Fuck you, you piece of shit!" He muttered to himself and released the basin. The blood rushed back to his hands with a tingle. He waved a hand in front of his eyes as one of the twisted faces hovered too close.

"Go away!" The broken face gave him a wink and disappeared into the closest wall. He turned and sat on the only bed in the room, he placed his hands on his knees.

Marcus tried to calm his heart rate as with each thump it began to ache.

He didn't want to take any of his own supply but he needed to sleep. This feeling only seemed to catch up with him when he was on his own. Marcus left the bed and wandered over to his harness. He picked it up with a shake of his head and sat back on the bed. He pulled it onto his legs and started to rummage through the assortment of pockets.

He picked a selection of coloured vials and dropped them onto the bed, then tossed the harness back onto the floor. He took a small amount of each fluid to make a very powerful blend. He pulled the syringe out of the last vial and squeezed out the small amount of air before he injected the contents into his arm.

He didn't even look down as he pulled the needle from his vein. A large smile spread across his face as he fell backwards onto the bed. The people that used to be alive disappeared from his presence and were replaced by a cascade of colours and patterns.

At first, he tried to keep his eyes open but as his mind went blank, he closed them. If someone had asked him his name, he wouldn't have been able to give them a coherent answer.

You are destined for greatness.

Marcus ignored the voice. What or who this was always seemed to try and speak to Marcus at the worst times, normally when he was off his face.

You will be remembered for what you will do and the lives you will save. Marcus giggled to himself. It felt like someone was tickling his brain. As he giggled long strands of saliva dribbled down his chin.

"Good night!" Marcus said to the voice in his head.

You will remember my words. The voice tried to sound stern but nothing would have an effect on him right now.

"No, I won't," Marcus said moments before he blacked out.

*

WAKE UP!

Marcus sat bolt upright and reached for his gun, but couldn't find it. He was sprawled across the floor rather than the bed. He wasn't sure if the voice was real or not, but he checked the room regardless. He blinked his eyes a number of times to try and make them focus, his quarters were empty.

His armour was still in the same place and none of his friends had said hello yet. He painfully raised a hand to his head but that just made everything else hurt. It took him a minute to stand as his legs wouldn't cooperate. He staggered over to the basin and turned on the tap.

He grabbed a white capsule off the shelf and popped it into his mouth. He bent down and took a mouth full of water from the tap. The capsule started to foam and buzz around his teeth. Marcus looked into the mirror and waited for the capsule to finish its job. The capsule buzzed twice and Marcus spat the contents into the basin. He looked down at the large splash of blood mixed with saliva and white foam.

"I really need to stop taking that shit." He muttered to himself and washed the red fluid down the drain with his hand. He stared at the pale coloured skin on his fingertips as the feeling started to come back to them.

His intercom gave out a loud bleep. He looked round the floor and found his earpiece under the bed. He placed it into his ear and tapped it twice.

"Yes!" Marcus said but even he didn't recognise his own voice.

"Marcus?"

"Yes, who else could it be?" Marcus swallowed a mouthful of bile as he tried not to empty his stomach.

"Our presence is required," said the voice.

"I was asleep."

"You have been in that room nearly thirty hours. Have you been mixing your chemicals again?"

"Yes, I have. Tell dickhead I'm on the way."

"Who?"

"Tell Carlos I'm on my way."

"You are speaking to Carlos."

"Tell yourself I'm on my way and yes I called you a dickhead." Marcus pulled the earpiece out and tossed it onto the bed before he had a chance to hear a response. He thought about putting on his armour and harness, but decided to have a wash first.

Chapter 27

Marcus walked into the operations centre and stood with the rest of his squad. More than a few of them were replacements for the people they had lost. He wasn't going to try and remember any of their names as they would only get replaced by someone else. Braker looked towards him, Marcus gave him a simple nod.

They sat down and proceeded to be flooded with information about their next target. Marcus wasn't really listening as his job role never changed. They could be tasked to hijack a ship or raid a local town for captives, but all he had to do was keep everyone alive. Marcus still didn't understand how their base hadn't been assaulted yet, being this far behind enemy lines was always a risk.

"Are we clear?" Braker shouted across the room.

"YES SIR!" echoed round the room, Marcus looked up and nodded again. Every one stood and began to filter out of the double doors and head towards the ready area.

"Marcus, I need to speak to you," Marcus stopped and gave Braker a sideways glance, "right now."

Fuck sake, I bet dickhead had something to do with this.

Marcus turned and walked down the room. Each step was an effort as his legs still ached and burned. He stood in front of his Officer and gave a formal salute.

"You require my presence, sir?" Marcus asked, he tried to make his speech as clear as possible but it was difficult.

"At ease, I guess it's time we had another little chat, don't you?" Marcus said nothing, his eyes scanned the screens behind Braker. "Are you taking your own medicine again?"

"Yes sir, I am," There was no point in even trying to lie. Braker could find out in any number of ways what Marcus was up to.

"You know there are other ways to get rest."

"Yes sir."

"Then why take it in the first place."

"Because it is easier than going to get other drugs that do the same job. I also don't need to take a full assessment and then have to wait in a que."

"Those chemicals are killing you; your read outs are off the charts."

"I can control it. I just need to change the dose." Braker shook his head at the response.

"It's not always about what drug you take and you know that. How many times have we had this conversation?"

"At least five times sir." Something hovered in Marcus' peripheral vision, he ignored it.

"Ok, if the read outs look like this again within the next month you will have your harness locked inside the room you are in."

"That's a bit drastic, don't you think." Marcus shook his head as he could feel the urge to hurt something start to build up in him.

"No, because you are needed here and you are killing yourself and that will affect a lot more than you think."

"Is that it, Sir?"

"No, did you call Carlos a dickhead?"

"How many times?" Marcus asked with a grin.

"What?" Braker didn't want to lose his temper but Marcus was pushing his buttons today.

"Do you want to know if I called him a dickhead or how many times I called him a dickhead?" Marcus shrugged as neither answer meant anything to him.

"Just tell me yes or no."

"Yes, and twenty-two."

"Why?"

"Because he is a dick head."

"Just give me a straight answer Marcus!" Braker slammed his hand onto the closest desk. The already damaged top splintered with a loud crack.

"I will assume that you have read the reports and the footage has been seen. You know that Carlos ordered two soldiers to be 'Put down' due to their injuries." Marcus' demeanour changed as his shoulders tensed and the pain in his head returned. Something in the room screamed, Marcus didn't react as he presumed it was coming from inside his head.

"I'm am aware of the circumstances, and they were not as blunt as that."

"If that dickhead had waited, I could have saved them both and got them back here, but instead he chose to just shoot each in the head and then had them liquidated."

"The entire squad was in danger. That was the smartest solution to get as many of you out as possible. Leave them behind and leave the area for pickup. You know we do not leave our people to be taken by those scum."

"Let me do my job, I could have saved them!" Marcus pointed with his finger as Braker stepped back. Braker didn't look it but he was ready for whatever Marcus did next.

"I will never stop doing my job until the person is dead, they were still breathing, so they could have been saved!" The room echoed with his voice.

"This is what I am talking about. You need to calm down."

"I am fucking calm!" It was a minor contradiction when he kicked the closest chair across the room.

"You are slipping Marcus. You know as well as I you need to clear what is going on in your head. You can have all the support you need but you need to request it. I will intervene if I have to, and I will be forced to take action against you."

"There is nothing wrong with me!" Marcus shouted every word as he rubbed the blood away from his nose. The chemicals still flowed through his system as his Boosters tried to neutralise each one. He looked down at the red on his fingers and forced himself to take a deep breath.

Braker had taken another step back and placed his hand on his sidearm. Marcus turned and pulled a chair towards himself and slumped into it. He raised his palms to the ceiling.

At the same time, he made an effort not to make eye contact with the scorched faces that looked at him from behind the computer screens. He tried to force a smile but failed. He knew in himself that nothing good would come from him continuing on this well-trodden path.

"You may have a point and I do need support. What do you suggest?"

"A full evaluation and to have all supplies removed from you before you rest."

"How long?" Marcus asked, but in truth he did not want to hear the answer.

"One month, and you will be speaking to the behaviourist every fourth day or when you are available, and you will be available." Braker's hand was now firmly on his pistol. Whether Marcus agreed with him or not he nodded at Braker's every word.

"No juicing for fifty-five days and talk about my feelings every fourth day, I got it, anything else?"

"Yes, as it happens, you will respect the chain of command. You should have a few more strikes against your name but certain ranks have chosen to be lenient because of your profession and your skill. This will not last, so you need to behave or you will be spending time in confinement, and no one wants that. We are together here. We will support you in every way."

Braker had relaxed his stance a little but still expected every outcome of this meeting. Marcus took a few deep breaths as he stood up. His chair scraped across the floor behind him as he made no effort to pick it up.

"No juicing, talk about my feelings, and behave. Yes Sir!" Marcus saluted and waited to be dismissed.

"You are needed here Marcus. Go to the ready area and I don't want to speak about this again."

"Yes Sir, I apologise for my actions, and I apologise for making myself your concern." Marcus gave Braker one last salute and left the room.

What a prick! It wasn't that Marcus disliked Braker for any one reason, he just disliked most people. He chewed his lip as he walked down the grey corridors, he always hated that colour. It was like everything was painted that colour just for him.

He finally pushed his way through the doors he wanted. The ready room was like all the others he had been in before. Most of the available space was taken up by dozens of tables and chairs. Counters and shelves lined the perimeter of the room.

A man stood behind a blast proof screen surrounded by weaponry and medical supplies, several soldiers handed him paperwork and he handed them their weapons. The sounds in the room dipped to silence as Marcus walked past the tables.

This didn't bother him anymore as he had a job to do and really didn't give a shit about anything or anyone else. He stopped several feet in front of Carlos and saluted.

"Sir, I am ready for action. You point us in their direction and I will keep our boys and girls safe. I hope you can forgive me for my actions, I have not been myself." Carlos was slightly taken aback by this. He was more used to Marcus being an arsehole all the time. Carlos checked the safety on his weapon again and placed it on a counter.

"Stock up with supplies, we are leaving in twenty minutes."

Marcus gave a nod and queued up at the supplies station. The guy in front of him turned around.

"You alright Marcus?" Danny asked. The right-hand side of his face was red and scarred and his eye was jet black. Marcus looked down at the metal hand that protruded from his sleeve. Danny's fingers clicked as he flexed them.

"I'm good, I see they couldn't save your arm, how are you feeling?"

"A little sore but yeah, I'm good. I wasn't asked whether I wanted to have the arm reattached, I was just given this one. I was also Boosted as it helps to enhance the use of cybernetics and helps them coexist with the body." Danny sounded like he was reading from a brochure.

"How's it treating you?" Marcus only asked because it would be his problem if something went wrong with the connection of artificial fibres and flesh.

"Yeah, it feels good for now." Danny raised his hand as his wrist spun all the way around and his fingers twisted and turned in ways organic fingers could never accomplish.

"It felt a little odd at the start but I'm getting used to it, same with the new eye. Thanks for getting me out of there, I don't remember much, other than the heat and the shock."

"Just doing my job."

"Thanks anyway."

"No problem," Marcus nodded to himself. Danny lifted his gun and supply bag with only his metal arm. He glanced between it and Marcus.

"I like this more and more," Danny laughed and walked over to a table. Marcus smiled and handed the attendant his paper slip. The attendant had a symbol on his uniform that looked like a wrench with one yellow line on the bottom. This meant this person was a low-level Tech of some kind. Marcus had almost forgotten to get his form from the ops room. The attendant looked at it and gave a low moan.

"Is there a problem?" Marcus asked, his eyes flicked down to the paper work.

"No, there are just a lot of supplies here. I will hand you your weapons but you will have to give me some time to get the rest ready." The Tech said as he scanned the list again.

"How long is 'some time'?"

"Four minutes."

"That's fine," The attendant handed Marcus his guns and grabbed the radio off the counter with a practiced movement.

"I have a large list and need support. This is an urgent requirement." No more than a few seconds passed when a second attendant appeared from a side room and was handed the list. Marcus checked his gun and placed the spare magazines into the pouches on his armour. He checked each one as he wasn't going to make that mistake again. He didn't have the carry space the other soldiers had due to his medical harness being worn over the top. He stepped to one side so other soldiers were given their weapons and supplies.

"Marcus your consignment is ready!" Marcus looked up at the second attendant, he must have been day dreaming, to him only moments had passed. He walked over to a small metal shutter next to the blast glass and a large bag was passed through it.

"Thanks," Marcus found the closest empty table and upturned the bag. A barrage of medical suppliers tumbled onto the table top. There were bandages of various sizes, a suture kit, skin and bone welders plus numerous other devices used for the treatment of injuries. He picked up each item and placed it into its designated pocket without a downward glance.

There was one device that he always had but never used. It was a small cylinder tube with a drill one side and a tube on the other. It was designed to feed blood directly into the patient's collar bone, if no veins or arteries were available. With the technology that they had; Marcus was amazed it was still in use.

His eyes remained on the selection of his favourite pastime. He rolled the different coloured vials in his hand. He didn't consider himself a junkie but he almost put the vials in his back pocket rather than in his harness.

The temptation to just head back to his room and mix them together was almost overwhelming. He put the vials where they were supposed to be. He left a metallic blue vial on the table top. When he had tightened his harness, he picked it up and walked back to the attendant.

"Is there a problem?" The attendant scrunched his eyes together which formed ripples on his fore head. It was rare for someone to come back to him more than twice.

"Yes, there is, why have I been given this? I didn't request it so you can take it back."

"All medics must be assigned at least one 'Kick' regardless of the request form."

"I will not use this, so it is a waste."

"It's not my job to tell you why, it is my job to give you supplies. If you are that unhappy about it then take it up with your squad leader or the appropriate Officer."

"If you had seen what a soldier does when you inject them with one of these you wouldn't hand them out," the assistant shrugged, "thanks again." Marcus said and turned away, he caught Carlos's eye with a nod. Carlos walked over to him and expected the worst.

"What is it Marcus?" Carlos said with a sigh.

"I have been given this," he held the vial in such a way that only Carlos could see it.

"Why did you request a Kick?"

"It was not on my request form, but I was told all medics are assigned at least one Kick. I knew Deaktree's feelings about these so that's why I'm letting you know that I have it and why I have it."

"I know we don't get on but this needs to be kept between you and I, so don't tell anyone else because many of them still want to try that shit."

This is maybe the only time I've agreed with you, dickhead. Marcus couldn't bring himself to say these words, dickhead was fine but the rest would make him queasy.

"Yes sir," Marcus put the Kick in a back pocket and tried to forget it was there. It wasn't long before they were ordered onto the landing pad. The dropship was grounded and waited for them to get on board.

Chapter 28

The squad walked out into the hot moist air, and headed towards the take-off deck. This was located on the roof of the base and a number of Dropships were stationed here, but only one was ready to go. The Dropship's body was about the length of a bus but twice as wide. The stubby wings supported four engines and a dozen mini guns and rocket pods. It sat on legs rather than wheels as this was designed for fast unload and take off when required.

The words 'Blood and Honour' were painted over a red shield on one side. The two pilots were stood near the front of the Dropship and they both had their hands on its armour. As the squad walked towards their transport, Danny nudged the soldier closest to him.

"For blood and honour, whether it is death or glory on this day we are privileged to have you take us there." They took their hands off the machine and grasped the forearm of each other.

"You ready?" the first pilot asked.

"Always, let us get our people into battle. Going in the back?"

"Of course, it's the way." They turned in unison and walked down the side of the drop ship. The first pilot ran his hand along one of the mini guns as he passed. Someone had spray painted 'catch me' on one of the rocket pods, no one would ever admit who it was. They approached Carlos's squad on the way in.

"Good morning drivers!" Danny shouted at them.

"You're a funny fucka," the first pilot shouted back, "You can walk if you want." Danny laughed at the exchange. He always seemed to say the right thing to piss someone off.

"Haven't you got doors on the front or have you forgotten how they work?" Danny called after them. The first pilot wasn't going to say anything but the second couldn't stop himself.

"You always enter the same way you left. Whether it's bad luck or tradition it's just the way we do things." The second pilot's eyes glowed as they changed colour from blue to deep red, his metallic arms began to expand and increase in size.

"Don't piss off the pilots, Danny." Carlos called from the back of the group. Danny held up his hands.

"I'm just messing with you guys." The second pilot smiled but remained enhanced.

"Yeah, I'm sure," he said. The squad boarded the drop ship and secured their gear before they grabbed any available seats. The pilots moved past the chairs and headed for the cockpit. The door moved to one side and they took their places. The first pilot dropped down into his chair and run his hand across the console in front of him.

"Korts, can you stop doing that, it's weird." His arms seemed to relax as he released the build-up of pressure.

"I know but it makes me feel better," Korts said as he did it again, "you have your rituals too and I don't complain, do I Terrin?" Korts said with a smirk.

"That's true, forget I said anything." Terrin replied as he patted his head twice, his heart three times, then the seat once.

"Are we clear?" Korts asked as Terrin's screens lit up. He checked that everyone was in and strapped down. The area around the drop ship was clear of personnel and equipment.

"Yes, we are clear, no obstructions and we have a green light."

"Let's get her going." Korts started the ignition procedure and the engines lit up with a roar before each one rotated from horizontal to vertical lift off.

"All electronics are in the green. Fuels cells are stable and weapons are primed." Terrin checked his harness and all of his controls one last time.

"Command, we are taking our luggage to the drop off area. Do we have any updates or are we good to carry out the delivery?" Korts said as he repositioned his headset and tugged on his harness to make sure it was locked.

"This is Command. Delivery is standard, drop off and return, do not take side streets and do not cause arguments with the guests, no drinking on the way. Blood and honour."

"Blood and honour Command." The radio clicked off and Korts changed the output to the internal intercom. Terrin flipped switches, pressed buttons and turned dials.

"Systems green, weapons green and fuel cells green." Terrin said this more to himself as he replayed his mental checklist.

"Hold on to your seats, we are going straight up. If you have any questions, please keep them to yourselves and if you need a piss, it's too late". Korts broadcast his message to their passengers, "ready!"

"Ready!"

Both Pilots pulled down on their controls and hit the thrusters.

The dropship's engines increased their force and the vapour turned white. The machine lifted off the ground and slowly rotated until the cockpit was aimed straight at the sky.

As the vapour turned purple, it rocketed towards the clouds. It started to level out at two thousand feet, the ground was orange and black rock for as far as the eye could see. Korts set the Dropship to auto and sat back in his chair. Terrin tapped more buttons and scanned the local area.

"Sector 15456 is close to the front line, isn't it?" Terrin asked.

"Yes, it is," Korts said without looking up.

"We don't operate that far east, normally."

"I was thinking the same thing." Their heads-up display turned red with numerous flashing symbols.

"Command, you have incoming to your location, several dozen vehicles and what looks like six mechs. We can—" Terrin couldn't finish as Korts shouted at him.

"We are targeted, incoming ordinance, taking evasive action." Korts grabbed his controls, he pulled and twisted as the Dropship increased speed with a rotation. A twelve-foot-long missile bounced off the bottom armour and detonated behind them.

Marcus grabbed hold of his harness as they went vertical again.

"What the hell is going on out there?" Danny shouted to anyone that might know the answer. Carlos squeezed his radio and tried to get through to the pilots.

"What is happening? Are we breaking off the mission?" Carlos asked but he got no reply. There was a huge bang as something connected with the outside. They could smell the air burn through its armour.

"This is not good," Marcus said to himself. He glanced down the line and some of the others were on the brink of panic. Carlos also picked up on this and started to scream orders.

"We are taking fire, everyone brace! Keep eyes on those closest to you, if we go down, we get everyone out, is that clear?"

"Yes Sir!" The lines screamed back at him.

The Dropship twisted and turned to avoid as much fire as possible. The defensive weapons blew most of the rockets and shells out of the air before they could even come close but there was too much. Within a minute the ammo for those guns was running low.

"I can't reach command. Something is blocking our transmission." Terrin pressed some more buttons and tried every frequency but nothing worked.

"We continue as far as we can and try to outdistance their guns. We go low and get something between us and them."

"We have fighters inbound," Terrin grimaced at the blips on the radar.

"Fuck me, this is a full-on assault. Broadcasting over all emergency channels, command there is an army heading towards sector 15600 forward base. Command please respond, over".

"We have to go back and warn them." Terrin knew they couldn't but it slipped out before his brain had thought up.

"We wouldn't make it all the way back before we were torn apart. We have to get these troops on the ground, anywhere away from here."

"Today's the day brother," Korts turned to Terrin and gave a grin.

"It seems that way, how about we take as many of them with us?"

"Good plan, all weapons primed, lets blow some shit up."

More enemy vehicles and tanks came into view as the dropship unloaded its rocket pods and mini guns, over a dozen targets were completely destroyed before they had passed by. Three fighters peeled off from the rest and headed straight for the dropship. They unleashed their own guided rockets.

"They have locked onto us, deploying counter measures and returning fire." Burning pyrophoric and smoke streamed from the back of the dropship. Two sets of Vulcan cannons attached to the top of the Dropship spun around and hosed the pursuing fighters.

One of them didn't even get a chance to evade as the heavy fire shredded the plane. Two missiles connected with the flares and detonated. The third exploded feet from the back end of the drop ship and the fourth, skimmed their right engine. The blast turned the side windows of the cockpit opaque as the glass tried to shatter.

"Too close, that was too close." Terrin shouted mostly to himself. Both of them heard the rattle of gun fire across the top.

"We have to go lower and drop our cargo off without us." Terrin nodded as it was their duty to transport their cargo to safety and this was their only choice. They skimmed a mountain on the rapid decent. They were a mere two hundred feet of the ground when the radio system kicked back.

"Command, come in!" Terrin screamed into his headset.

"This is command; please explain why you are so off course."

"We have taken heavy fire, there is an army heading towards the forward base in sector 15600."

"Can you finish your mission?"

"No, we have taken too much damage and will crash. We will drop the Coffin first to make sure our people have the best chance. We will be dropping in sector 15478. I repeat, we are going down in sector 15478."

"Thank you, pilots, you are what makes us. Blood and honour."

"Blood and honour Command," They shouted in unison.

"There's a hill coming up fast. Give them something to think about." Korts said and dipped the nose and aimed for it. Just as they were level, Terrin dropped a ground mortar. The surface of the hill blew upwards with tons of rock and debris.

The fighters pulled upwards as the dropship dropped down the other side. Both fighters unleased another set of missiles before the Vulcan guns tore one fighter in half.

"Counter measures out," More flares filled the sky but two missiles got through. One struck the top of the dropship and the other hit the back.

"Both Vulcans are gone, back thrusters are gone and the main fuel cells are critical. We are going to blow in the next minute and there is nothing to shoot at up front." Terrin screamed over the noise as some of the side window gave way and air rushed into the cockpit. Korts turned on the intercom.

"We are dropping the coffin in twenty seconds brace yourselves. Blood and honour soldiers, remember us." Korts set the ejection sequence and ignored the automated warning.

"We have to get rid of that son of a bitch or our people are dead."

"We have nothing left, unless you want to try and tombstone the bastard?" Korts said and Terrin nodded with excitement, if you were going out, you might as well do it in style.

"I'm disabling all safety protocols so it won't try and correct itself." The heads-up display flashed red and sirens blared as the dropship was now only thirty feet off the ground. Terrin shouted at Korts. "I had a meeting last night!"

"I'm guessing it was good!" Korts shouted.

The dropship decelerated and released the entire section that the troops were contained in. It dropped away and the coffin hit the ground and rolled.

"Oh yeah, he was fucking lush".

"Did I know him?" Terrin nodded with a huge smile, "you, lucky bastard!"

Both of them burst into laughter as they pulled back on the controls and fired the counter Boosters, these overheated instantly and threw out plumes of white smoke. The dropship kept level but turned upright within the thick white cloud.

The fighter pilot's reaction was only less than a second behind but with the rapid slow-up and unthinkable manoeuvre, she couldn't turn in time. The fighter flew straight into the drop ship and exploded with a scream of metal and ignited fuel.

The coffin rolled and bounced over hundreds of feet and only stopped when it hit a rock face and broke apart.

Chapter 29

The frontlines hadn't shifted in over three years, it was a stalemate of gunfire, but this, like everything else, was going to change with brute force and violence. The Bellatorum had grown tired of waiting and decided to force their opponents' hand. They wanted the capital of Draka and they would spill so much of their own blood to get it. They swamped the battlefield with troops and machinery. The grunts were sent in, first to 'weaken' the enemy, and the rest of the army would follow.

The weakening of the opposing army was by simple means. All they did was to throw enough organic at them so they could possibly run low on ammunition. There was no other use for them as these people were deemed cattle, and it was unethical to eat them. Even so, the subject of cannibalism was always open to debate.

The combat medic known to his squad mates as Med had been stationed at this particular frontline for only a year. In this war, everywhere was a front line. Med was bigger than most medics, he stood a good six inches above most people. He also spent quite a lot of his time in the gym. A number of his squad mates asked him why he was so bulky. His answer was always the same 'if you guys weren't so heavy, I wouldn't need to work out'.

The squad he was part of had only been in a handful of skirmishes in this time, but all of them had been hardened by battle since the start of the last war. This was until they received the confirmation that the grunts were to be sent in and them to follow. He checked all of his equipment more than once. He didn't want any mistakes on his part and took any extras that he could. His squad, with a number of others were tasked to escort a column of tanks and two legged mechanical walkers, these are commonly known as Mechs.

Med glanced to his left, then his right. He was amazed how many people were stood here. No one spoke as they listened to the roll of thunder that resonated from the battle in front of them. Med looked up at the cloudless sky, for every boom he heard, another person was already dying. The soldier next to Med caught his attention and they exchanged a look.

"You can hear the exchange of fire from here," the soldier said and adjusted his helmet.

"Those poor bastards that got sent in first, won't last long," Med replied. He had tried to help wounded Lows before but they were normally executed without a second thought. For this action alone, Med was put in confinement for 6 weeks, the enemy and Lows were not to be helped.

"Hey, keep the chatter down and do your damn job." Dimitrios called from the back. Med turned and looked at his squad leader.

"Yes sir!" Med turned his gaze back to the black smoke as it started to reach towards the sky.

And you can kiss my black arse.

They could see the columns of smoke caused by burning phosphorus and napalm in the distance. The Mech that was fifty feet to their left turned its guns to the sky and opened fire. It took out two of the three inbound mortars. The third one ricocheted off the closest tank and detonated in the air. The vehicles started to increases their pace and charged in to fray.

"This is it, move forward and shoot anything that isn't one of us," Dimitrios shouted. They weren't alone, this was a small part of an invasion force that stretched forty miles wide. Med advanced with his squad, two soldiers instinctively moved in front of him to act as a meat shield.

Each squad had two medics assigned to them, one primary and one secondary. The primary did most of the work and was only supported when necessary. The primary was deemed through service and skill level, and Med was their primary.

They reached a desolated town with a scattering of buildings. They crested the ridge that broke the town into two halves and all hell broke loose. Enemy fire, RPGs and mortars filled the sky. Two of their walkers burned in liquid fire and one tank was completely upturned.

"We have over extended, bunker down and return fire. We have claimed this land!" Dimitrios screamed at his squad. He felt the impact as something struck the centre of his chest. He gave the brass-coloured bullet that had flattened on his armour a look of disgust.

"Son of a bitch," he raised his gun and fired.

Each soldier had a job and they did it to perfection. The engineers threw out expandable shields and anti-rocket defences. A couple of the heavy gunners prepped their launchers and started to pick their own targets.

The enemy swarmed the already damaged buildings in front of the squad. Med kept his eye out for injuries and everyone covered each other. More tanks and Mechs rolled past them and pushed forward. Almost at the same time two soldiers dropped to the floor under heavy fire.

Med pushed towards them, he emptied one magazine, ejected it and reloaded with another. The anti-mortar turret to his right flashed red at him to announce it was out of ammo a second too late.

There was a loud whistle and then an explosion ripped him off his feet. His body was tossed through the air and smashed off a low structure. He tumbled down a slope and into the sludge at the bottom.

*

Med must have blacked out as he came to, face down on stone and mud. He heaved himself onto his knees with a grunt of pain. If there wasn't a part of him that didn't hurt, he hadn't found it yet. He thought he could see a group of people in the distance, in his semi-concussed state, he rushed towards them.

His legs gave out a number of times, each time he pushed himself up and forced forwards. He managed to get to the group and ducked against a low wall. His vision was hazy but the Boosters in his blood did their job well. They reduced the swelling in his brain and cleared up his vision.

It could have been much worse if his helmet hadn't taken most of the impact. That was when he realised, he was crouched among the dead, these remains were not part of his squad.

These were the grunts that were sent in first, he glanced round to see if any could be saved but his services could not grant life here. It seemed some type of high explosive had gone off close by. The higher ups didn't even give these guys armour to wear.

Where the hell is every one? Med thought as he scanned every possible surface, in front and behind.

The young man that was crouched against the same low wall gave him a startled look. Med looked at him twice, he was covered in so much mud and gore that he blended in with the surface of the wall. His blue eyes were the only part of him that shone through the thick coating.

Med was about to call to this guy when he stood up. He fired two rounds into the closet enemy as they came over a hill. He engaged two more before Med got a chance to add to the hail of bullets. Med was impressed with his speed, and the fact he was wearing no armour but was still wanted to fight.

"Is this your squad?" the guy nodded, "Why are you still here if this is what's left of them?"

"Too many threats upfront. I'm not allowed to go back." He responded as Med checked his radio and tracker.

"Guys come in?" Med looked behind him as the scanner was taking its time to reboot.

"Where the fuck are you?" His squad leader screamed down the radio. Med's tracker finally decided it was a good time to pick up their blips. The small screen gave him a direction to go and a distance counter.

"I was laid low for a minute. I'm heading to your location now. It's going to be a fight to get over there."

"Just advance we have cleared a path." Med heard multiple shots and explosions from the other end of the feed.

"I am engaging hostiles as I speak so, it is not clear. I repeat, it is not clear."

"Just get over here!" Dimitrios screamed again and the radio went dead.

"Son of a bitch," Med turned to the guy, "What's your name?"

"V," Med waited for more, but there wasn't any. He gave V a funny look without even thinking about it.

"Ok V, you have a choice. You can stay here and do what grunts do and die in a ditch or you can be my puppy and get my sweet arse back to my squad."

"I will take the second option." V's voice sounded like he was reading from a script and not thinking about anything else.

"Good, your priority it to keep me safe at all costs, is that clear?"

"Yes," V nodded in acknowledgment.

"Then let's get the fuck out of here. Stick to my leg and cover my arse." Med took a huge breath, "Let's go!"

Med stood up and rushed towards his squad. He glanced behind him and half expected V to still be sat behind the wall, but he was right there next to him. Where Med looked, V covered the rest.

Twice they fired past each other. V saw a woman in badly worn battle armour supporting a large tube on her shoulder. She stepped around a lump of blasted building with it and aimed at them.

"RPG!" V shouted before he shoved Med forward. The rocket propelled grenade shot between them and detonated with a shower of shrapnel against a low wall. V fired and the woman screamed as she tumbled backwards. V knew something struck his side but couldn't say anything about it.

"Good job, they should be just over here," Med said, V nodded his response. "You don't say much do you?" V shook his head. They ran around a burning building and jumped past a barricade and landed next to his squad. Med straight away pulled supplies from his harness and started to treat the wounded.

"Good to have you here, we thought you were dead!" A female soldier shouted at him and raised a clenched fist. The rest gave a roar for their returned Medic, the squads secondary breathed a small sigh of relief.

"V, go cover them" Med pointed and V turned to join the line. He was greeted with mixed looks. The soldier Med had begun to treat for gun shots to his legs looked between the two.

"Who the hell is that?"

"A lost puppy, he saved my arse twice, so he's good." The soldier nodded, but was still confused about the situation. Either way, he chose to accept what Med had said.

The battle raged for several hours, the soldiers took turns on the line but V wasn't replaced and remained where Med had sent him.

*

"Listen up people," Dimitrios shouted over the surrounding noise.

"The mobile base is moving forward so we hold here until it arrives. Extend out and make sure we are clear for its approach."

Everyone stood up to check the area. "Med centre on me and bring, whoever the fuck that is, over here." Med walked over to him.

"V over here," V stood from his position. He jogged over to the pair and stood to attention. The wound on his side had mostly stopped bleeding, but still oozed into his already disgusting clothing.

"A grunt? Why is he here?" Dimitrios pointed at V.

"I needed help to get back to the squad sir."

"Where is your squad, soldier?"

"Dead Sir," V said with a frown. The facial expression was not made by his own will.

"What were your orders?"

"To fight or die, either eventuality is acceptable," Dimitrios shook his head.

"What were you doing out there, what was your task?"

"I don't know sir."

"Well done Med, you brought a retarded puppy to the party," Dimitrios began to slow clap his hands, "good job," Med turned to V.

"Where were you trained and at what station?" Med made an attempt to make V look less stupid.

"I don't know sir" Dimitrios held his hands up and shook his head again.

"You must know where you got your equipment." Med was getting worried for his new puppy. V looked down at his weapon and back at Med.

"I don't know sir"

"How do you know your name is V, for fuck sake?" Dimitrios was about to lose his temper. V looked down again and pointed to the letter etched into his uniform.

"Great, what a waste of time, that's not even his name. You didn't find a soldier you found a worthless Low." Dimitrios drew his side arm. Med stepped in front of V as Dimitrios raised his arm.

"Sir, he is accurate and quick. We can always use support like that."

"What are you saying?"

"He can be my puppy and he will be my support."

"Then he shares your food allowance as he is not part of this squad." Dimitrios holstered his pistol with more force than was necessary.

"If he becomes a problem or gets in the way, you will be responsible."

"Yes sir," Med saluted his squad leader. Dimitrios looked at V like he was some shit that was stuck to his shoe. As Dimitrios walked past, he shoved V out of his way but V didn't seem to notice. Med waited for Dimitrios to walk a good distance away, as he barked at other members of his squad.

"He may be my squad leader but fuck me that guy is a prick. Right, let's take a look at you because no one's memory is that bad." Med pulled out a small flash light and shone it into V's eyes.

"What was the first thing you can remember about today?"

"Walking down the straight with the rest of my squad."

"That would have been about five hours ago."

"Yes sir," V stared forward.

"Firstly, never call me sir, I'm not an Officer and don't plan on being one," V nodded. As V stood there, Med pulled open the front of his ruined shirt. V had a small shard of metal embedded in his side. He took a closer look as blood oozed out of the wound.

"V, when did this happen?" V shrugged at the question.

"From before." Med cleaned the area and sealed the wound; the shard hadn't gone too deep.

The soldier that had the leg wounds raised himself up onto his elbows.

"You know they 'clean slate' the grunts before they send them out. That's so if they are captured, they cannot give over any information."

"Yes, I know that's a fact but it can't be permanent or they wouldn't reuse grunts that don't get massacred." Med took a double take of the soldier and then looked down at his legs. "Why aren't you up yet?"

"I'm not sure. I can move my feet but my toes feel numb. I'm also getting sharp pains that start in my feet and run up my thighs." The soldier turned his feet to one side then the other.

"I will have a look at you in a minute but I will tell you this." Med poked V in the chest. "This guy is not a normal grunt. Half of them can't even hold a gun properly and this guy has been trained very well," Med checked his eyes again.

"Yeah, he is on some serious shit, this is going to take some time to work out, or I could try this." Med filled a syringe with a mixture from his coloured vials.

"Give me your arm," V raised his left arm and waited. Med injected the concoction into him and took a precautionary step back.

"Right, let's give this time to flush his system." V went ridged and tipped backwards with a gargle.

Chapter 30

Marcus awoke to the smell of blood and the feeling that more than a few people had given him a heavy kicking. At first his mind floated and he thought he was at the rough end of one of his sessions. It took him more than a few seconds to realise that he was not in his bed or on the floor next to it.

As the feeling in his arms told him they were swinging above his head he knew this was far worse. The roof of the Coffin was now the floor, and it was a good four feet below him. The local volume seemed to kick in and he heard the screaming for the first time. He glanced to his left and right and started to understand what could have happened.

The Coffin had been broken into at least three parts. His seat wasn't that far from the open air. From where he was, he could see the back end of the second section and the long side of the third. He wrestled with his seat harness but it wouldn't unclip, so he pulled out his laser scalpel and sliced through the straps.

He should've put more thought into getting down as the final strap snapped, he fell. One of his arms caught in the strapping, as it wrenched back he made a complete backflip and landed flat on his face.

"Well done Marcus, you dumb bastard." He swore to himself before he forced himself onto his knees. He looked up at the soldiers still in their seats. Some were still unconscious but more than a few hadn't made it through the crash. They had been beaten to death by parts of the Coffin that had broken away in the impact.

"Marcus, get me down from here." Marcus looked round for the source of the voice. He spotted Danny as he waved his arm around. Marcus stumbled as he tried to walk, his balance felt way off. He wasn't sure if the chemicals in his blood were still having an effect or something had hit him on the head.

His helmet felt heavier than normal so he undid the strap, it slipped off one side of his head without much effort. A twelve-inch lump of metal had imbedded itself deep into the plating. Luckily for him, if it had penetrated only a fraction more it would have been inside his skull.

"Hold on give me a second!" Marcus heard more people calling his name. "Danny, where's your arm?" Marcus asked in disbelief. A portion of the Coffins hull had broken through and taken Danny's metal arm clean off at the shoulder. Without his sense modification being installed, the damage to the limb wasn't even noticed.

"Good question, get me down and I will look for it." Marcus cut his straps but supported his weight so he didn't make the same mistake and end up on the floor.

"Get everyone else down first, then look for your arm."

"No worries," Danny pulled a short blade from the sheath on his calf and got to work.

It didn't take long to get most of the soldiers down but some would have to be left behind. The troops supported each other as they clambered out of the remains of the Coffin.

Carlos called to his squad and gathered them in one place. This was some distance away from the wreck, on a flat piece of ground.

"Anyone that is still breathing get over here. Sue! Glad you're ok. Can you contact anyone from Command and find out what the hell happened"? Sue pulled at her back pack and checked her equipment.

"None of my gear is damaged but I cannot reach the base. I am, however, getting traffic from the frontline. It appears they have pushed into the capital of Draka. The surrounding area should be clear."

Carlos briefly chewed at his bottom lip. He had no clear instructions and any mistake on his part could cost him more of his people. If they stayed where they were, he was certain the enemy would send their own troops to investigate the crash site. The only choice he had was to move towards the frontline and regroup at one of the mobile bases. That in itself would be a problem as the terrain in front of them was a sea of jagged rock and scorched earth.

Marcus had cleared his wreck of survivors and brought them into the open. Most of them were ok apart from a couple minor fractures and a lot of small cuts. A number of soldiers had retrieved the remaining bodies out of the chairs and laid them in a row.

In this section of the Coffin alone they had lost five. He had checked each body for a pulse just to make sure they had passed; he then started the process to liquidate them. He searched each one for their vial of corrosive wash.

The chrome cylinder looked like a thermos flask that would keep a drink warm. Each cylinder had a bright yellow bar that run around the top of each one. Marcus slipped on a vapour mask and was about to crack open the first cylinder when Carlos walked in.

"Marcus!" Carlos shouted. Marcus stopped and turned, he pulled the mask off and waited.

"I will get one of the other guys to do that. Go check on everyone outside once more, I think a couple are playing down their injuries." Marcus thought about it for a second and couldn't help but to agree.

"Ok, I have put all of the ammo and guns in a pile that I could find. I wasn't sure if they were being liquidated too. Just so you know we couldn't find Danny's arm, we looked everywhere." Marcus indicated the pile of hardware with a nod.

"We will take what we need and get rid of the rest. We can't let any of our tech fall into their hands." Carlos looked to the two soldiers, "don't forget to take their tags, they will not be forgotten," both of them saluted.

Carlos scanned the bodies for anything his squad might need. Marcus handed the thermos and mask to the closest soldier and made his way to the rest of his squad. The soldiers looked round to him as he entered the clearing. Marcus clapped his hands together with a toothy smile.

"Right, who needs medical treatment because once we are moving it's too late." No one raised a hand or even made a noise.

"I have been ordered to check each one of you anyway so tuff shit on that one, so get your arses out." The larger part of the squad that had worked with Marcus before gave a round of laughter, the rest just looked at him blankly. Marcus gave each one a check over and from his point of view found nothing of significance.

While he was performing his duty, he couldn't help but smell the corrosive wash doing its work. It took less than a minute for it to reduce a body and all of its equipment to molten slag. It was said many times that no one would be left behind, but he had seen the puddles of slush after many a fire fight.

The sole point of it was to give the enemy nothing to work with from guns, explosives, or even the soldiers blood that may contain Boosters. Even heavy equipment was treated the same way. If a tank could not be salvaged, then it was to be destroyed and scattered across the battlefield.

Two soldiers walked from each section of the Coffin and saluted Carlos. There was only a brief exchange of words before he called for the attention of the rest of his squad.

"We will remember the names of those pilots. Korts and Terrin did what they could to get us on the ground and died with honour. Our fallen have been taken care of and the remains of the Coffin have been set with explosives. We will leave here and head for the frontlines. If Command do make contact, then our orders will change. We cannot continue with our current task and we cannot go back to our base as it has been compromised. Do you have any questions?"

The air was silent, not even a bird or insect was anywhere nearby. The surrounding area had been bombed more times than Carlos knew. Marcus smiled to himself, squad leaders didn't ask their troops anything, they screamed orders. Marcus knew that certain members of the squad would see this as weakness. One soldier put his hand up.

"Yes, what is it?" Carlos tried to assert his authority with a point.

"Could we head back and catch the enemy force from behind?" It was a good question and Carlos nodded to himself before he cleared his throat.

"If most of the heavy weapons had not been lost in the crash, we would counter attack. We don't have enough weapons left that can help in attacking tanks or heavy armour. That's enough talk, everyone get up and let's go."

There was a low mumble followed by the echo of not-too-distant gun fire.

"Move, move, move!" Carlos shouted. Everyone jumped to their feet and ran for the rocks. Carlos pointed at the same set of soldiers, "stay behind and watch the site for five minutes. If no one arrives then leave, but if they come then detonate the Coffin early and follow afterwards. Keep me updated on coms." Both of them saluted.

"Yes Sir!" They split up and ran to find cover. Carlos led his squad up a rocky pass and away from the crash site. Marcus followed up the rear and looked back just in time to see them disappear.

Good luck lads you'll need it. He checked the pouches on his harness. He didn't have as much as he wanted but considering they had survived a dropship crash; he could have had a lot less.

They hadn't been on the move for any more than a couple minutes when they heard the Coffin explode. A fire ball rose over the closest gathering of rocks, lumps of metal flew overhead. Carlos whistled and the group picked up the pace.

At thirty second intervals, Sue checked her coms but she received nothing from Command. She thought about giving up when her equipment blew out a sudden blast of static.

"Sir you need to hear this," she called to Carlos. He waved on his troops and backtracked to Sue. She pulled a second headset from her backpack and handed it to him. As soon as he put the headset on, his face changed.

"What the hell is that?"

"That sir, is another nation's language, but it sounds more like a chant repeated over and over again". Sue felt sick as she said it, as this was unheard of. Their coms were believed to be beyond secure. No one could break into their encrypted signal. The voice stopped and was followed by peoples screams then it started over again.

"On our coms? Are you recording?"

"Yes Sir, everything is recorded."

"Are you sure you are not picking up a cross signal," Carlos asked. Sue glanced down at the digital screen that was strapped to her forearm and shook her head.

"No, sir, this is the signal that Command should be on. If the enemy are monitoring our signals, then they will know exactly where we are."

Carlos shook his head in disbelief as this situation just got a whole lot worse. The two soldiers that had stayed behind sprinted around the last corner and saluted.

"How many are coming for us?" Carlos called to them.

"They have no flyers but there are many ground units. The tanks can't follow us up here but I counted over a hundred soldiers."

"The Charons must be pissed about their Capital being assaulted."

"The people behind us are not Charons, Sir. They are not wearing their colours and they move and fight differently. I do not recognise anything about this force."

"Well who the fuck are they?" Carlos said but neither of them knew. Carlos tapped at his ear piece.

"Turn off all communication equipment we are going silent from here."

He took a couple steps forwards then turned back to the two soldiers.

"Go down the line and make sure all these are turned off," Carlos pointed to his ear piece.

"Yes Sir," they saluted and jogged after the rest of the squad.

"It's no short distance to the front line, is it?" Sue asked and turned off her equipment.

"We are not part of that operation so there was no reason for us to be close by. It's about forty miles give or take a couple." Carlos knew it was going to be difficult just to get over there.

"That's a long jog," Carlos nodded with agreement.

"Could be worse," Carlos said with a small attempt at a grin.

"How could it be worse?" Sue asked.

"We could be dead," they exchanged a look and carried on.

*

Several hours had past and they had seen no hide or hair of the enemy. Sue wanted to turn on her equipment and try and reach Command, but the risk was not worth it. They were already too far to head back to the base so even if Command knew where they were, they would have to wait for emergency pick up. Carlos hissed and they all took a knee.

They formed two lines as they walked down trails and round mountains of blasted rock. Carlos hissed again and the squad moved as one. This forced stopping and starting, repeated itself a number of times as Carlos thought he heard something in the distance.

He had started to doubt himself and thought that maybe he was hearing things, or his mind was playing tricks on him. The land they were in was dead and nothing was out here with them. He hissed and the squad stopped, it was that same exact sound that he heard before.

He thought it was an engine but he couldn't quite make out what it was, or even guess at what it could be. He signalled to one of his engineers to scan the area. The engineer pulled off his bag and assembled something that looked like a metal detector, when it was ready, he aimed it at the sky. The engineer's eyes played back the signals straight into his brain.

He glanced over to Carlos and shook his head. Carlos was about to scold himself when the engineer gave a frantic wave and pointed upwards. Carlos gave the signal and the squad dispersed, anything that could give them cover, they dived into. Some pressed themselves against walls that had an overhanging ledge or any large rocks near-by.

Carlos pointed at one of his heavy gunners and she pulled the launcher off her back and made sure it was loaded and ready to fire. They waited for something but none of them knew what it could be. Carlos looked over to his engineer and shrugged. He held his device higher then pointed to a mound of rocks.

Carlos turned his head in the general direction and had to think about what he saw. It was dull metal foot about three feet across, followed by what looked like a two-foot-wide spiders' leg. Then a second mechanical leg rose over the rocks and thus followed the body of a spider tank.

Carlos had seen these before but not this stealthy, he also did not recognise the markings on its side. Four mini guns were mounted on its head and two 80mm cannons protruded out of its back. The large head that could easily fit two people swayed to one side then the other.

The engineer looked down at the screen on his arm and this thing was not on his sensors. The only way he could detect it was the small amount of noise each foot of the spider made when it touched the ground. Carlos tapped his gun three times and anyone that saw it swapped out their magazines for heavy armour piercing.

As one changed their magazine, the people closest to them did the same. One member of the squad was not as concealed as the rest; the spider may have picked out an arm or a leg but they would never have known. The head turned with a quick snap, the mini guns spun up and sprayed the area. Two soldiers went down under the immense fire power.

"Fire!" Carlos screamed over the roar of the mini guns. Every squad member unloaded from their position and a hail of armour piercing rounds struck its head. The launchers fired their rockets and the spider was knocked sideways with the force of the explosions and rolled down the rocky surface and out of view.

"Move!" Carlos sprinted out onto the path and his people followed.

"They know where we are, Sue, get on the comms and try to raise command."

She turned on her equipment and the signals were crystal clear. Two of the soldiers that were closest to the fallen grabbed their corrosive canisters and poured them over their bodies. Their armour and flesh dissolved as quickly as pouring boiling water over ice.

"This is Run Squad seven, Command do you receive me?"

"This is Command good to hear you are alive. What is your situation?"

"Our dropship was attacked by an invading force headed for the forward operating base in sector 15600. We are under fire and request emergency assistance!"

"The enemy force has been repelled. We have you sighted by satellite and we will." The signal seemed to crackle and fizz before it came back, but this was someone else.

"It's a graveyard out there, isn't it?" Sue stopped when she heard the male's voice, another soldier almost crashed into her from behind.

"Who is this?" Sue regained her composure and sprinted towards Carlos, she handed him a head set.

"You will never find out who this is, as all you fucks, will be dead within the hour." The voice sounded monotone like it was made by a machine. The connection failed and went silent.

"Did you get through to Command before our transmission was breached?" Carlos asked.

"I think so, they said that we had been spotted by satellite."

"Did you recognise the accent?"

"No sir," Sue said with a shake of her heads.

"And how the hell does he know our language?" Carlos didn't know what to think as he'd never encountered this before.

"I pray that they send hornets. Another Spider tank approaching from the front!"

This one moved quicker and seemed to scramble over the rocks with ease. It aimed its back cannons at the troops and unleased two shells. The squad got smaller as more explosions blew apart their rocky cover. The first heavy trooper was gone but the second took aim and made a good hit on one of its front legs.

The metal work separated at the joints as it tried to remain upright, the trooper reloaded and fired again. The rocket hit it square in the face. The impact caused it to topple forward and down the rocks towards them. The heavy gunner turned away from the Spider Tank and ran back to his equal.

The shell must have landed right next to her as her body was twisted and broken, but at least it was a quick fate. She was gone and he would pay his respects but he needed her launcher ammunition first, he drove his hands into her backpack for more rockets.

Carlos, followed by most of his squad, rushed the damaged tank. They fired at the control hatch to try and break the seal to the cockpit. He wanted captives but he could smell burned metal and flesh, the rocket had done its job a little too well. He waved at his engineer and he jogged over.

"Scan that wreck before it's all burned away. We need to find out as much about this thing as we can." He signalled to his squad to make a perimeter, they dispersed to cover all of their lines.

Marcus seemed to have a lot of work on this mission, it seemed to go one of two ways. He either had nothing to do and then spent the time thinking about food or his next chemical session, or the mission went to hell and he didn't stop.

Most of the injured had bullet holes but that was simple, you bypass the bleed, plug the hole and seal the wound. One lost an arm and another was missing a hand, but he dealt with each situation. He had to hide his smile, even with all the bloodshed he was having a good time, at least he wasn't bored.

The most important thing was that he was left to do his job, and that's what he liked. The only thing he was concerned about was the likely point where he would need to take blood from some soldiers to give to the others. It seemed odd to him just how protective people were of their blood. It didn't matter as a body produced more than enough to function.

"Right, how does that feel?" Marcus asked his latest patient. The soldier looked down to the stump that used to be her hand. She felt no pain from the area but being able to hold a gun correctly would be awkward.

"No problems other than the fact I have no fingers."

"That I can't help you with. To be honest, I did have a quick look but I couldn't find them. Keep an eye on that, if it starts to bleed or the pain comes back in waves you have to tell me." She nodded at him and he stood up, Marcus had a quick stretch and felt the muscles in his back creek and crack.

A soldier was about to pour wash over the body of another.

"Wait, I haven't checked her yet!" Marcus walked over to the body as the soldier shook his head.

"Is there a problem?" Marcus asked.

"She's dead, look at her, you can't help with that."

The soldier pointed to the fallen. Her armour had been blown off her front and her intestines had pooled next to her waist; her face was a bloodied mess. Marcus knew she couldn't be saved but if there was time he could help in another way.

He knelt down and placed two fingers on her neck and waited. Marcus looked up at the soldier and slowly shook his head. He could feel his face start to redden as he bared his teeth.

"Then explain to me why I can feel a fucking pulse, back away with that or at least put the lid on."

The soldier screwed on the lid and waited. They all knew that Marcus could flip so it was better to leave him be. Marcus placed the palm of his hand on the back of her neck and connected his mind with hers. He could see her torment and hear her cries.

With the sheer force of his will he smothered her mind and drew away the pain and panic into himself. He couldn't communicate but she could feel he was there. She knew this was her end but with his help she was content. To Marcus this process felt like it went on forever but in fact only lasted seconds. Marcus took away his hand and sat back.

"Now, you can do your job." The soldier tapped his chest, roughly where his heart was. This was meant as a sign of respect, but also could be taken as an apology.

"Don't worry about it. I just like sending people on, knowing they aren't screaming." Marcus stood up and turned away. Everyone was preoccupied so he turned back to the soldier.

"I'm going for a piss round that corner." Marcus pointed at a boulder and the soldier nodded. Marcus smiled and walked around the rock, he turned towards it and unclipped his armour. He stood there and waited. His mind started to replay the dead soldiers last moments, these were mixed with other memories that had bled through the connection.

This was a side effect and each person that could practice the connection dealt with this in their own way. Some would meditate or use breathing techniques; others would become reliant on chemicals. There were many ways to ground yourself but being able to keep another person's memories out of your own was always a challenge.

Marcus nodded to himself and used his own tried and tested method. He smashed his forehead into the hard surface in front of him, this made no difference, so he brought his head back and did it again. He only stopped on the fourth strike when he felt blood run down his nose and his mind cleared due to the pain. He pulled a reflector out of a pocket and looked at himself. The gash wasn't too bad so it was quite quick to clean himself up and seal the wound.

"Marcus!" Marcus heard Carlos shout so he leant back and looked round the rock.

"I'm taking a piss over here!"

Carlos walked over to him.

"Are you doing ok?"

Marcus smiled at him and shook himself off before he zipped up his armour.

"I'm good, please tell me we are not doing the 'talking about my feelings' are we? I really can't be arsed." Marcus wiped his hands on his legs, he would make a mental note to sterilise them later.

"No," Carlos pointed to the sealed wound on his head, "that wasn't there ten minutes ago."

"Oh, right, yeah," he looked down and kicked a lump of rock. "I tripped over that when I came round here. I'm fine, there's no lasting damage and I don't have concussion. I didn't want to say anything before because I feel like a dick about it."

"No problem, we have contacted Command and they are sending in a dropship and hornets to pick us up."

"Did they say how long?" Marcus asked but their conversation was cut off by a blinding flash and earth-shattering explosion. The ground shook and some piles of rocks and rubble collapsed nearby. Marcus grabbed hold of Carlos's arm for support.

"What the hell was that?"

Carlos felt himself go cold; he knew what that noise was even from here. A distant memory flashed in front of his eyes and he couldn't help but close them for a second.

"That was some distance away but I know that was a tactical nuke. Can you see where that came from." Carlos called to his engineer.

"It's sector 15600 Sir."

"Are you certain?"

"Yes, they, they nuked us."

"Where did Command say the Dropship was coming from?" Marcus asked as he yanked a device from his harness, he clicked it on and the black box lit up and started to buzz.

"I'm picking up radiation and it's getting worse; everyone take two blues now!" There was a mass rummage as everyone dropped their bags to find their capsules. Marcus always knew where his were and cracked open the silver pack. He popped two of the blue ones into his mouth and swallowed. They were larger than the average pill so it was a slight struggle to get them down, he chased them with a gulp from his canteen.

"Fuck me this is bad. Back to plan A, we head towards the frontline." Carlos waved his squad on and they all ran as fast as they could.

Chapter 31

The capital city of Draka had been secured mere hours after the initial push. The people that tried to fight back were killed, and the ones that didn't were taken. The mobile base had advanced all the way up to the city walls. These mobile bases were huge armoured boxes covered with more weapons than what most armies could muster.

For being over a mile wide, it was amazing how fast these structures could move. Unlike the smaller attack bases, these could house thousands of personnel. The Boosters roared as the huge structure steadied itself and numerous legs rotated out of the bottom on huge hydraulics and set down on the ground.

The area around the mobile base turned into a hive of activity. Temporary buildings were erected, these were living quarters, toilets, bars, but all of the storage and supplies stayed inside.

After the initial shock of the mixer entering his blood stream V seemed to be ok, but his mind was the same. He followed orders to the best of his ability and didn't ask questions. Med wasn't that fussed as he had a personal escort where ever he went and knew he could rely on V, for the time being anyway, things could always change.

Dimitrios had been given the order to stand down so he directed his squad to the temporary buildings. He didn't give a shit what anyone else did, he just wanted to have a drink. Three Officers walked straight towards them in full battle armour, you couldn't tell if they were male or female, but they all had their own markings. This was so each squad leader knew their Officer.

"Stand to one side, Officers coming through." The squad split down the middle and saluted. The lead Officer stopped in front of Dimitrios and the other two followed suit.

"You did good work today." The Officer's voice sounded robotic through the helmet.

"Thank you, sir."

"However, a number of the kills in your area are not recorded by any member of your squad. How is this possible?"

"That would be him," Dimitrios pointed at V, "he is Med's responsibility and he was instructed to leave him behind. He found the grunt on the battlefield." Dimitrios smiled to himself as he had avoided all possible back-lash. Med on the other hand, had to force himself to remain where he was and not punch his squad leader in the side of the head.

You back-stabbing son of a bitch.

The Officer walked over to where Med was stood and looked V up and down before poking him in the chest, pretty hard. He stepped back with the force and stood to attention.

"You are coming with me, now." The Officer spoke to Med but tilted its armoured head towards V, "and bring him along. Stow your weapons before we enter the base."

"Sir, may I recommend?" The Officer gave Dimitrios a sideways glance and held up their hand. "Sorry sir, carry on."

As the Officer moved on, closely followed by the other two, Med looked straight at Dimitrios and mouthed the words.

"What did I do?"

Dimitrios smiled and shrugged at Med.

You prick. Med had wanted to say it but that would have ended badly for both of them.

"Come on V, walk with me." Med said as he shook his head and trailed after the Officers. The other members of his squad watched him go.

It was a long walk to the main entrance of the base. There were many other ways to get inside but this was the closest to the Officer's section. Med almost stopped as they came close to one of the newly build bars but forced himself to walk past.

The Officer waited as they handed in their weapons and continued to the Officer's quarters. The Officer entered a room and walked into the closest corner before she stepped backwards out of her armour. The mechanical armour's plating shifted and moved with the low hum of gears and motors.

The suit she wore under her armour didn't leave much to the imagination. She turned and sat herself behind a wooden desk. The desk itself was older than everything else in the room. Her jet-black hair was pulled tight behind her head. Before she could speak or the door behind them shut, Med saluted and immediately tried to talk his way out of this situation. Whether he thought he was in trouble or not made no difference.

"Officer Faleama, this is all a simple misunderstanding. I was separated and needed support and he was there so…" She held up her hand.

"How are you, Med?" Faleama said with a smile. She crossed her arms and sat back into her chair; it was a very nice chair.

"Regarding the current situation, I'm fine, sir."

"Is Dimitrios still being a Kank?" Med winced at the word.

"He can be a bit aggressive sir."

"That's not what I asked."

"Yes, he's being a dick."

Faleama smiled, she always liked Med, it seemed everyone liked him.

"You are not in trouble," Faleama pointed at V, "Where, and how, in all of this world, did you find him?"

"On the outskirts of Draka, he was part of a grunt squad that was wiped out. I got separated from my squad and needed assistance in getting back to them. I asked him to support me and he said yes. He doesn't talk much but he saved my arse twice."

Faleama got out of her chair and got right up to V's face. Wherever in the room Faleama walked to, Med averted his eyes.

"Someone of this calibre and training and they send him out as a grunt, what a waste." She took a long look into his eyes.

"They've wiped him too, have you tried to give him anything?"

"Yes, I gave him a flush but it had no effect."

"It's lucky you didn't kill him," she stared into his eyes once more, "you will ignore us from this point onwards until I tell you otherwise. That is an order, do you understand?"

"Yes sir," V saluted and his eyes seemed to glaze over.

319

Faleama walked back to her chair and tapped at one of her three screens. Small pieces of cloth had been cut and laid on the surface of the desk. This meant there was no danger of them scratching the wood.

"What's his real name?"

"It's Vandeaga 454376AHF."

"Isn't all of this data saved onto his file? Every grunt gets their own file." Faleama spun the screen so Med could see it.

"He is not a grunt and his file has been deleted. All that is left is one letter, V."

"Why didn't the flush work?" Med asked because the flush shot always worked.

"It's not a chemical that cleans the mind and blocks memories. It's too risky because of rejection and damage to the brain, they use a certain type of Booster. The flush didn't work because the Boosters rejected it, which in some cases is so forceful an effect, it will make the person's brain burst out of their ears. If you had used a Body Clean Shot, he would have definitely died."

"A Booster can do that?" Med had never heard of this and was damn sure he shouldn't have been told now.

"Yes, it is reversible but the required shot is very hard to come by, unless you work with the grunts as their keeper." Med sighed to himself, if an Officer wasn't going to get it then he wasn't. She walked over to her armour and unclipped a hidden section. Faleama pulled out a vial of clear fluid.

"It's strange I came by one of these months ago and I can't tell you why I kept it."

"It that the shot?"

"Yes, it's strange how this world works. I always thought I would need it one day." Med stood to attention again and

Faleama gave him an odd look, this was at least the second time he had saluted since entering her office.

"Sir, may I please ask a personal question?"

"If you must."

"Why do you feel the need to protect this one?" In that moment Med realised with a snap, what he had said and to whom. Med struck an even more formal salute.

"I have no right to be speaking to you in this way, nor do I need to know this information that is above me. I request that you give me leave for I am just a combat medic," Faleama smiled.

"That's why I like you Med. Now this information will stay between us and that is an order." Med forced himself to replay what had been said in his head, and after a minute he closed his mouth. He was certain he said he didn't want to be involved.

"He was part of the soldier experiment at one of the academies. To make the next generation of enhanced soldiers, or that was their plan at least. It was a huge screw up from the beginning and the Artificial Intelligence that controlled most of the facility was a mess." Faleama pointed at Vandeaga.

"He was reported to me as dead, which is why, I volunteered to come back to the frontline. I'm going to assume his details were purposefully edited to make sure that I was given this misinformation. Do you follow me so far?"

"Yes, but weren't most of those test subjects clones and why does he matter?" Med patted Vandeaga on the shoulder. Vandeaga didn't even look round as his mind had gone somewhere else.

"You know it is impossible to have children once you have had Booster implants."

"Yes, or pass over infection."

"He is my son and—" Faleama stopped at Med's outburst.

"Well, fuck me sideways," Med didn't intend for those words to pass his lips. He slapped the back of his hand against his mouth. He moved it aside just enough for him to speak.

"I'm sorry sir." Faleama blinked at him a couple times before she continued. Med always made a point of apologising for the silliest of reasons.

"That's fine. It is rare for someone to conceive with Boosters but it's possible for anyone to have offspring. I had the child and he was taken away."

"Sorry, but how can you be sure he is your son? Why has he not reacted to any of this? Because if that was me, I'd be like, what the fuck?"

"When I walked into that dorm room and saw him for the first time I just knew. He is the spitting image of his father. I thought that maybe he was a clone but I had his blood work analysed and it came back positive. There are codes left within clones so they can be verified back to the original source. I'm not saying he wasn't cloned himself, but he is the original. He has not reacted because I ordered him to ignore us so the Boosters in his blood have effectively put his brain into standby."

Med waved a hand across Vandeaga's face, he didn't even blink.

"Wow, that is creepy. If two Officers do have a child, then that must mean that the child could be born already enhanced to a certain extent at least." Med had never thought about this before.

"That is possible, nothing definitive came back regarding his blood analysis but you never know. He does have a natural gift to absorb information." Faleama turned the screen back and tapped at the glass.

"Why have you involved me in this?" Med shuffled his feet slightly. He just wanted to go and get a drink.

"I wish to protect him as best as I can." Faleama stood up and paced behind her desk.

"I'm not a parent, that is not how we are made, but regardless, he is my son. We also need to keep this as simple as possible so you must swear to me that you will never tell him who I am. It will cause him to act differently which could put him, and me, in danger, is that clear?"

"On my blood and even in death, those words will never pass my lips." Med saluted like it was his last, these words were not thrown around meaninglessly. When spoken out loud they were an oath, an oath that would never be broken.

"He will be given a chance but I cannot directly intervene." Faleama said before she handed Med the vial of liquid.

"Take him to medical and ask them to perform a physical as he is now part of your squad. I will change the details as you have requested and it has been recorded as such." Med opened his mouth to protest but closed it again.

"Hand this to Tina and no one else. Tina is the lead down there and will know what to do. I'm still owed a few favours." She walked back to her computer and began to rapidly tap at the keyboard. Med looked between Faleama and Vandeaga more than once before he found the ability to speak.

"Ok, right, I guess I will be going then. Come on V we are heading to medical." Med took a couple steps towards the door, but Vandeaga didn't move.

"Wake up Vandeaga, it's time to move, soldier," Faleama shouted at him. He jumped to attention.

"Yes sir," Med repeated himself and Vandeaga started to follow him to the door.

"Med," Faleama stopped him, he would give anything for a drink, just one shot would do.

"Yes sir."

"Just call him Van. Vandeaga is an unusual name and I want him to stay unnoticed as long as possible. I have updated a profile which he will now use, it was an unused number 454367AHF. Protect him and he will protect you in every way he can."

"Yes sir," the pair almost made it to the door before they heard the commotion in the corridor. Faleama rushed to the door and yanked it open. She shouted at a Tech as he jogged past.

"What the hell is going on?"

"The mobile base in sector 15600 has been nuked, sir." Faleama pulled back as she must have heard him wrong.

"What? That's not possible, how the fuck did they nuke one of our bases and who was it?" She almost grabbed him by his collar but stopped herself.

"I don't know sir, but all of our defences are being triple checked and recalibrated. Other than that, I have no more information."

"Thank you, get back to work."

"Yes sir." The Tech jogged down the corridor as Faleama turned to Med.

"Get him to medical quickly. The security here is going into overdrive and we won't get another chance. I have already updated his file." She glanced past Med as an Officer shouted at her and she replied with an aggressive tone, "I'm required elsewhere."

"Sir, Van, let's go." Med pushed Van out of the door and down the corridor.

*

Base commander Reece had called an emergency meeting for all Officers. They flocked to the operations room and saluted before each took a seat. Their mechanical armour gave off low murmurs and clicks. Faleama walked in and saluted. Reece leant round another Officer to make sure he was clear on what he saw.

"Officer Faleama, it's good to see you. May I ask where your armour is as it appears it is not on your person." As Commander Reece spoke his voice was elegant, almost royal in tone and etiquette. Faleama stood to attention in her thin body suit.

"Sir, this is more important than the need for armour. Unless anyone here wishes to try and stab me then I will be fine." Reece's large frame rocked slightly as he laughed to himself, his well-groomed beard matched the motion.

"Very good Faleama, please take a seat. Now we have been informed that the Base in sector 15600 has been attacked."

One Officer looked like he was about to speak but without even a sideways glance Reece held up his index finger.

"Satellite imagery has confirmed that it was some form of missile that contained an advanced nuclear payload. We, however, do not know how the strike got past all of the base's defences. Do you have any questions?"

"Could there be survivors inside the base? It should withstand a direct hit."

"Only if the blast shields had been deployed and from the imagery, they were not. We have tried every signal that we have and there is no noise coming from that sector. Also, the type of weapon used was beyond dirty. The techs have picked up huge amounts of radiation in the area. This means that even scrubbers would take more than ten years to get close to the base. Sector 15600 is now set to dead zone status, whatever was there, is gone."

"Was there any communication from the base prior to the attack?" Faleama asked.

"They had reported a possible invasion force headed their way. While one of their Dropships was on mission it reported the enemy movement, but soon after the transmission was sent the Dropship was shot down and the base went quiet. Over a period of three hours, we also lost all satellite communication so we have no idea what happened leading up to the strike. We know where the dropship crashed and we also know where the survivors are headed."

"How did we lose the satellites for three hours?"

"That is a known problem and is being looked into by Command. Every sector at points is having blackouts."

"So, we will never know if they find anything about it then?" One of the Officers muttered to himself. Reece slowly looked over to him as his face changed to a dead, cold look, and he shook his head. No more was said on the matter.

"We have to be alert. The techs are checking all of our systems for problems and we will be ready for anything that happens. My base will not be taken down by a mere nuclear weapon or some orbital drop."

"Where are the survivors from the Dropship?"

"The group are headed towards the frontline. We have sent a Dropship and Hornets to their location. This was arranged by Command before the base was hit."

None of this makes sense, there's just too much defence. Our bases would never let a missile of any kind through. It would be taken out miles before it was even within visual range. Faleama shook her head at the thought.

"If that is all then we all have our jobs to do. Blood and honour my Officers." Commander Reece saluted with the fierceness of duty and pride.

"Blood and honour, Sir!" The response was as one voice, the salute was the same.

*

Med walked through the doors to the medical wing. He had never been in a hospital before, but this was mostly the same. Except the staff made more noise than the patients.

"Could Surgeon Merker, please report to room six and seven!" The voice blasted over the internal system and a couple members of staff looked towards the closest speakers. A set of side doors burst open as a woman marched through. She stripped off her bloodied overalls on the move and handed them to her assistant.

He passed her a clean set that she threw over her head and front. Her pure white eyes darted across every patient that she passed. These coloured implants were purely cosmetic, just so they would match her hair. The bloodied clothes were thrown into a side shoot and disappeared. She shouted at a number of staff as she passed.

"The two in room one are ready to be transferred to recovery. Hello Med, how's the arm doing?"

"It's fine thanks to you." Med called after Merker, as she strolled up the corridor. She gave him a thumbs up and disappeared around a corner. Med approached the main desk as staff and dollies whizzed past. The man behind the desk took his eyes off his computer long enough to acknowledge that Med was stood in front of him.

"What is it you require?" He used that tone where he wanted to help but he was too busy to care.

"This soldier needs a physical. He has been transferred to our squad and I was told to ask for Tina."

"Tina, is busy at the moment. Anyone can perform a physical so I have put him on the waiting list. He will be seen shortly."

"I was told to ask for Tina."

"As I have already stated, Tina is busy dealing with all the injured that are being rushed through these doors." Med held up his hands to stop him from talking.

"Not a problem, where should we wait then?"

"There is a room back up that way, it has waiting room printed on the door, you can't miss it." He pointed back the way they came.

"Thank you, I will let my Officer know that you kept us waiting." Med pushed Van and they started to walk away.

"Hold on, who asked you to speak to Tina?" Med stopped and turned.

"Officer Faleama told me to ask for Tina, but it's ok we can wait. I really don't mind." Med said those last words with a knowing smile. It still surprised him what power Faleama's name held.

The man held up his hand then tapped at the side of his head, then at the computer.

"Tina, I have one of Faleama's asking for you. No, I didn't find out. Ok, I will let them know." He glanced at Med then back down at the computer and tapped at the glass.

"Wait in check room four, Tina will be along shortly. Go to the end of the corridor, then turn left, forth door on the left."

"Thank you, come on Van." Both of them turned and walked up the corridor. Med heard muffled screams from a number of the rooms as they passed. He found room four and pushed Vandeaga through the door and there wasn't much in it. Two chairs, one table and a cabinet full of chemicals.

"I could have some fun in here." Med smiled to himself but felt Vandeaga's eyes staring at him.

"Don't look at me like that. I don't know what is happening either, just grab a chair and sit down." Van pulled up the closest chair and sat down.

Med had paced the room more than a dozen times before he heard footsteps getting closer to the door. To Meds surprise, a large man entered the room.

"I hope this is important, as I am very busy." Med looked him up and down. He was a big guy, his shoulders were wider than Meds and he was at least a foot taller. He looked more suited on the frontlines than in a medical facility.

"And you are?" Med asked with a very confused look.

"I'm Tina and Faleama told you to speak to me?"

"Tina?" It still hadn't sunk in quite yet.

"Yes, you think only soldiers have problems when it comes to picking a name?"

"Sorry, but that completely threw me."

"It won't be the last time, so what is it you need? I'm really busy."

"Oh, shit, sorry, he needs to be given this." Med held up the Vial.

"Is that a cleaner?" Tina asked but Med's expression said 'maybe, I have no idea'.

"He was a grunt on the front-line and—" Tina held up his hand.

"I don't want to know, but to give him this shot we are in the wrong room. Follow me please." They left the room and proceeded down the corridor. Tina held open a door and let them in first. They were now in a room filled with computers and machinery.

"He will need to be hooked up to that machine," Tina said with a heavy-handed point. Med knew what it was and started to attach the probes to Van's head and sat him down into the chair.

"Right, secure him into it," Med looked down at the metal arm and leg restraints.

"Is this necessary?"

"Oh yes, if he reacts badly to this then he will attack anyone present. There is always a risk of an outburst. It's how the Boosters in his system work."

As he clipped them in place the metal looked like it turned to fabric and gripped onto Vandeaga's wrists and ankles.

"He's secure."

"Good, now this needs to be inserted into his arm." Tina held up a needle and tube, the tube was connected to the machine.

"Is there fluid already in this?"

"Yes, the shot is thinned out before it is injected. If we don't then the cleaner would melt his arteries before it even got close to his heart. If it did, then we would be picking him up with a shovel." Med stared at the needle for a second.

"Why am I doing all of this?"

"Because, we are not supposed to be here and every action I take is recorded. If anything goes wrong, I have not touched any of the equipment." Tina said with an air of assertiveness. Med took the hose from Tina and pushed the needle into Van's arm. Tina tapped at the console and pushed the vial into a glass cylinder connected to its side, "here we go."

Tina pressed a button and stood back. Med watched him and also stepped back a safe distance. The machine buzzed as the fluid drained from the vial and the clear liquid turned black. It was only moments before the fluid run into Van's arm. The pair of them stared at him and exchanged a look.

"Is this normal?"

"We should have seen a reaction by now."

Van's body bolted forward, if it wasn't for the straps he would have shot out of the chair. His eyes widened so far they looked like they were about to burst out of his head. His jaw opened like he tried to scream but nothing came out.

"Now is THAT shit normal!" Med asked, Tina just shook his head.

"Maybe," Tina answered as Vandeaga started to shake.

"What do you mean maybe?"

"I've never cleaned a grunt of Boosters before. It's normally done in a separate department."

"You're telling us this now, after you shot that shit into his arm." Van went limp in the chair and they rushed to his side. Med checked his vitals while Tina checked the computer and the machine.

"It looks good this end," Tina said with a sigh of relief. Vandeaga opened his eyes and slowly turned to Med. "You might want to put this under his chin." Tina tossed Med a container that looked like a waste paper bin. Med placed it in front of Vandeaga's face. Before he had a chance to say anything, he started to dry heave at first. Mouthfuls of black sludge splashed into the bucket, after more than a normal stomachs worth of fluid, he stopped. Vandeaga rested back into the chair, he didn't have much choice while he was strapped to it.

"That couldn't have hurt any more than it did, what is that stuff?" Van said as Med took the container away.

"That is what Boosters become when they are flushed from the body. Well this type anyway, most are permanent or only upgradeable. It's not a pretty sight is it? How are you feeling?" Tina asked as he tapped at the computer screen. The restraints loosened with a low humming sound.

"I feel like I have been hit by a Slab, more than once."

"That's normal for what you have gone through, but you two need to leave as this is not a recorded procedure."

Tina turned off the systems and tipped the sludge down a side drain. Med helped Van to his feet and they headed for the door.

"I don't need to tell you this but I will. Do not talk to anyone about what happened here. If anyone does ask about your recovery you tell them, you don't know."

"Thank you, Tina." Van held out his hand and Tina shook it with a hefty grip.

"Helping out Faleama is never a problem." They parted ways and headed straight for the front doors. As they passed the main desk the assistant gave them a wave.

I just want to get out of here. Van thought as they approached the desk. Med didn't look concerned as he leant against the counter.

"Did he pass?" The assistant asked, Med gave him a toothy smile in return.

"He made it look easy. Is it me or has the physical got tougher? I don't remember it being that intense."

"It has been improved somewhat; you didn't give me his number." There was a moments pause as Med turned around to look at Van. His eyes went wide as he tried to think of what Faleama had said.

"Oh yeah, sorry," Med turned back, "it's 454367AHF, my fault."

"That has all been recorded, have a good evening." The assistant released them with a nod and Med raised his hand.

"You too". They turned and walked out the main doors.

"I never got a chance to thank you. You saved my life out there," Van said.

"Don't mention it because you covered mine as well. What is it like to be on Boosters like that?" Med asked as they breached the command base and into the open air. Van took a lung full, it felt good.

"Just imagine being given a set of instructions and not even being able to speak unless it was in response to a question. I couldn't even tell you my name. I'm just lucky and unlucky at the same time."

"How so? Wait, before you answer we are going to the bar because I need a drink." Van smiled and this one felt natural, but it didn't last.

"I'm here, I lived through the battle but I watched so many just walk into oncoming fire, just because that was what they were told to do. Or, weren't trained to do any differently," Van shook his head. The Boosters must have messed with his memories as he could only see still pictures of what happened. He felt himself start to turn pale. Med gave Van a sideways glance.

"I think you need something strong too."

"That sounds good to me."

Chapter 32

Carlos had pushed his squad hard and fast since their base was struck. Marcus and the remaining Tech kept their devices working overtime. Marcus had stopped them at one point to make sure everyone took another dose of the blue tablets. The blue tablets prevented radiation from damaging the body. The chemicals clumped the radiation particles together and passed them through the system, but the process was quite painful.

"Marcus! Can you come here for a second?" Danny shouted from behind a bush. Marcus jogged over and stopped given the situation he was presented. Danny was leaning against a rock with his dick in his hand and a facial expression like he was chewing a wasp.

"What's wrong?" Marcus asked but Danny didn't open his eyes.

"It feels like I'm pissing razor blades and its fucking blue." Marcus looked down at Danny's hand.

"He looks fine to me."

"No, my dick isn't blue Marcus. I'm talking about the piss. It's blue and it hurts." Marcus tried to hide his smile but only for a second.

"Yeah that's normal, just shake it off and you will be fine. It is going to hurt like that for a few days."

"What! I can't do this again."

"It's either this or radiation poisoning, and I think you would rather deal with this than the latter."

"Good point, can you help me because I almost got him stuck in my zip the last time." Marcus helped Danny clasp up his armour and walked back from behind the bush. He saw that everyone was out of sight and they were on their own.

"Did you tell anyone you were going for a piss?" Marcus shouted at Danny.

"No, I forgot."

"You prick, we are being left behind, grab your gear." Marcus dug his radio out of his pocket as he never wanted the head implant. "Marcus and Danny are following so don't leave us behind. We are coming up behind you!"

They ran up the path and saw the last of their squad in the distance. They increased their speed and rounded the last corner. Marcus and Danny both dropped to the floor as a shot snapped past them.

"What the fuck are you two doing? You could have been killed." Carlos screamed at the pair. Marcus pushed himself onto his knees.

"I shouted down the radio about a minute ago, did no one get that?"

The squad looked at each other as Carlos signalled to everyone to check their positions. The engineers radio crackled.

"Sir, that voice is back," she said and handed Carlos the head set. Carlos almost placed it to his ear and stopped.

What the hell are we doing?

"They are tracking our signal, turn off your equipment now!"

They never saw where it came from but the rocket impacted amongst the squad. There was a deafening blast as Marcus was blown backwards. He connected with a rock wall; he would have been fine but he never replaced his helmet. His skull made a crunch as he bounced off the solid surface.

His brain tried to black out from the pain as he skidded across the floor, but his Boosters forced him to remain conscious. He scrambled for his bag as blood poured past his left eye, that's when he realised, he had gone blind in his right.

He ripped out the scanner and flipped the screen so he could see himself. The scanner showed him a multi-layer image of himself, he could see bone, muscle and even nerves if he turned the dials. His right retina had detached and a section of his skull had fractured.

I should be dead. But he wasn't and only because of his Boosters. The microscopic machines worked a long side the chemicals to keep him alive. However, they couldn't stop the flow of blood on their own, so he was going to have to operate on himself. He pulled out all of his instruments and tried to ignore the screams directed at him.

"I have to stop myself from dying first, give me ten seconds for fuck sake." The screams didn't stop as he got to work on himself. Marcus had to do everything backwards, with his arms over his head and from a reversed image but he did it. He stopped the bleed and sprayed the fractured bone with a bonding spray.

He could have fixed his eye but he couldn't waste any more time on himself. He did however have to take something for the pain, so he prepped an injector. He could only give himself enough to take the edge off, any more and it would impede his abilities. He pushed the device to his neck and squeezed the trigger. He felt it instantly and tried to stand but his balance was gone. He felt an arm wrap around his and lift him to his feet, he looked up at Danny.

"Where do you need taking to?" Danny asked.

"Our people need me, where's Carlos?"

"He's gone mate, whatever that was, hit him first before it touched the ground. Our engineer got it too."

"Those bastards knew to target our leader, what's everyone doing?" Danny looked around and couldn't believe some of them where just crouched down with their eyes on the floor.

"I don't know what they are doing, Marcus."

"No one is giving orders?"

"No Marcus, everyone that could is dead."

"Then take charge and get them into cover."

"I can't do that; I'm not made to lead."

"Carlos said the same thing to me at the depot when the shit hit the fan. Get all the injured into cover and I will keep them alive. You will keep us safe." Danny slowly nodded with understanding and then started to shout at the top of his lungs.

"Anyone that is able, drag the injured into that cave mouth. Where are my heavies?" There was only one left and he called back. He placed both of his bloodied hands on his leg where it stopped above his knee.

"Get your launcher ready as soon as you can, I'm guessing there are more tanks coming. Everyone else shoot at anything that isn't us."

Danny was amazed at just how quickly the other soldiers accepted his orders and began to move. When they were out of the open Marcus got to work. He did his job but some of his people were already gone before he could get to them.

"Danny! Has anyone got signal flares?"

"Show of hands, who has flares left on them?" He counted six. Danny knelt next to Marcus and whispered to him.

"Why do we need flares?" Marcus almost snapped at him but held his tongue.

"We have no way to communicate with Command. They are meant to be sending a Dropship and Hornets. We may have to wait for them and show them where we are, with a flare."

"Got it, thanks for not treating me like an idiot."

"I'm an arsehole Danny, but I'm not that much of an arsehole." They all heard the unmistakable noise of a Dropship. Before anyone could say otherwise. A soldier launched a flare into the sky.

"What are you doing?" Marcus shouted, "we don't even know if it's one of ours."

Over a ridge less than 500 feet away a dropship did appear and it wasn't friendly. The main guns on the front started to rotate in the squad's direction. The heavy gunner forced himself onto his knee and fired his launcher. The rocket missed by miles and exploded on a rock face.

"I didn't compensate for the leg." He said as he forced another rocket into the back of it and took aim. The Dropships guns fired, but so did he. The rocket forced it to take evasive action so the spray of bullets missed the squad. He threw the launcher down and rechecked his bag.

"No good, I have no more left."

All of them readied their weapons but each one of them knew they would have no effect at this range or even on the dropships armour. The dropship turned and started to fly towards them for easier kills.

"Here it comes. Blood and honour!" Danny screamed as they all fired. Marcus still tried to treat the wounded even though he knew this could be his final act, but it's what he did, it's what he was made for.

The Dropship took aim and fired, but almost instantly an explosion erupted from its right side. Its damaged engines drummed with power as it tried to keep level but it took a second hit. The engines flared then burned as it rotated out of control. It struck a mound of rock at speed and broke apart with a deafening blast.

"What the hell is going on?" Danny shouted. Two Hornets snapped past and started to engage targets that the squad could not see.

"Fire a flare, fire a flare!" Another soldier shouted and two burning balls of green were sent sky ward.

"There it is," The heavy gunner pointed at their ride home. The remains of the squad grabbed their gear and waved at the Dropship.

More explosions echoed from behind the mountains of rock as the Hornets fought a battle of their own. The dropship touched down and lowered its rear doors. Four more combat medics rushed out to support the wounded. Everyone was dragged on board including any dead members that hadn't been washed.

Marcus slumped down into a seat and listened to the engines start to rev up. He pulled out his scanner to check up on his eye but was amazed to see the remains of a bullet lodged in the device. He looked down at the smoking hole in his bag then back up to Danny.

"You were lucky," Danny said with a point and a laugh.

"Yeah, I think I was," Marcus replied as a voice boomed over the intercom.

"We are leaving straight up, so strap in. One hornet is down and the others reserves are low so this is going to be a hot take off."

There was a massive tug of G-force as the Dropship went from a stationary position to vertical in under four seconds. It sounded like someone had thrown stones against a metal wall as their armour was riddled with gunfire.

Marcus closed his eyes for a second. When he opened them the bloodied remains of Carlos gave him a mangled smile from the opposite seat. There wasn't much left but the parts that were not connected still floated like they were.

Why do you show me these things when I'm safe?

Marcus shook his head and ignored the dismembered arm that had appeared and started to wrap itself round his ankle. Then he thought of something that made him smile. Everyone that knew about his little chemical problem was dead. He shouldn't have smiled but he was going to have a party tonight and with anyone that wanted to join him.

Chapter 33

Van followed Med through a number of doors until they walked into what he thought was a canteen. It was the same as any other he had seen with metal tables, chairs and a couple counters. He had never seen a bar before with a man and woman serving drinks and a wall lined with optics of all types of coloured liquids.

A number of the personnel that were already seated had a good look at them as they walked past. Med didn't even notice as he had stopped caring a long time ago. There were a number of tables reserved for Officers but these were empty.

Med walked over to the counter and placed his hands on the top. He smiled at the woman behind the bar. She met his gaze for a second before her eyes fixed on the work surface.

"What are you having?" Med asked and gestured to the moving pictures on the counter. Van scanned them for a moment and gave a shrug. The entire top moved with images of all types of drinks and food.

"I have no idea what any of this is?"

"I will start you off easy then." Med tapped a picture of a glass size then a description. The woman nodded and grabbed a glass and started to fill it with a brown liquid. When she placed the glass on the counter Med tapped a second set of images. "That's yours, mine is on its way."

"What is the difference?"

"If you drank that," Med pointed at the blue liquid in the smaller glass, "without Boosters, it would knock you out for a day."

"That bad, is it?"

"No, it tastes great but it's powerful. Grab that and follow me as we need to have a long talk." The woman went back to her original position and stared at the counter. Van looked back at her before he followed Med over to a booth that sunk into the wall. Two female soldiers were already sat at the table in mid conversation.

"Excuse me, could we have this table as I need to have a talk with my friend?"

One of the soldiers looked round with a face full of thunder and she was about to scream an obscenity but realised it was Med stood next to her. Her clenched teeth very quickly turned into a very pleased smile.

"Hello Med, good to see you."

"Good to see you too, Siena."

"Is this talk going to be serious?"

"Oh yes, I need to explain some life lessons to my friend. You know how I feel about open tables." She leaned back into her chair and rested her hands on her thighs.

"I will make you a deal. You agree to a meeting later and you can have the table." This brought a smile to Med's face.

"You say it like I would even consider saying no, it's a deal." Siena smiled and stood up. The other female followed suit. Siena stepped towards Med and whispered into his ear.

"Believe it or not but my friend is very shy and doesn't like to ask herself. Could you help her out later?"

"If she is happy with that arrangement, then sure," Med whispered back. Siena looked past Med's shoulder and the female soldier smiled and nodded once.

"Yeah, she's good," Siena said, the smile on Med's face hadn't faded.

"Looks like I'm having a busy evening." After the day's battle, this was the perfect way for Med to relax.

"Yes, you are, see you later." Siena and her friend moved onto another table with their drinks and continued their conversation. Med sat down and gestured to the opposite chair. Van sat down with a confused look on his face.

"What's that look for?" Med asked as he sipped his drink and sucked air through his lips. "What's a meeting?"

"Please tell me you are joking?"

"No." Van scrunched his eyebrows together.

"You were not even told about that?" This time Meds mouth stayed wide open.

"I have no idea what you are talking about."

"The term means an agreement for sex."

"Oh ok, between male and female."

"No, anyone and everyone can have a meeting. It depends on how you feel at the time, or who you want to feel at the time. It is considered quite rude to reject an offer with no good reason."

"What if you are not into that?"

"Then that's a good reason, wait," Med waved his hands, "that's not why we are here. Faleama has asked me to basically look after you and I have no idea who you are."

"I don't remember her saying that." Van looked down at his drink and tried to think. "I don't remember much of that conversation at all?"

"That's the Boosters, they were what blocking what you could take in. Right, tell me about yourself and try not to leave anything out." Van took a long breath and took a minute studying the top of their table. It was grey, and other than a couple smears it was pretty clean.

"Only if this stays between us, and I don't want to bring it up again."

"That's fine by me."

Van told his story of the dorms where he grew up and then the academy. He said everything he could remember about the complete mess that was his training and the people that were lost. He felt like he could trust Med so he even told him about Chrisa and Taradin.

He choked up a little when he came to the arena part of his tale. Just saying Larooa's name made him angry, he wished he was there to watch Taradin take his punishment. He laughed as he revealed how he cheated the final test and received a pass and a fail.

"That is messed up, so you didn't want to be a leader then?"

"Giving orders that could cost someone their life is not me. At least that place was almost deserted when I left. I hope no one has to go through that again." Van said as Med pulled a wry smile.

"I hate to say this but there are hundreds of those facilities. Most of them are built out here so no one can see what goes on. You are one of thousands that get tested on and that will never change, because that is what our people do."

"Why do we fight, why is this all happening?"

"That is a good question and the answer is simple. We fight to protect our people."

"That's it? And who are the enemy?"

"That is what we are told and that is what we live and die by. Anyone that threatens our people are our sworn enemy. That is how it has always been. We are all messed up in our own way. You couldn't even say that most of us are stable but as long as we get the job done, Command don't care."

"Who is Command?" Van took a mouth-full of his drink, swallowed and looked down into the glass. Maybe he just needed to get used to it. Because, right now, this tasted like shit.

"They are the people that make all the decisions. They give out the data that the armies follow. We do nothing that isn't analysed or planned a thousand times. This is where you need to listen to me and understand what I am saying. If you stand next to a medic in battle, you are at the most danger. The enemy know what we do and how good we are at getting our people back on their feet. We are priority targets and they will shoot through everyone to get to us. You'd be glad you missed the days when they gave medics different coloured armour. We lost so many of us back then." Med drifted off for a second, he came back with a slow shake of his head. "So, you cover me, but don't get too close unless I say so. Also, everyone doesn't need to know that you are back to normal. The rest of my squad thinks you are a retarded puppy so let's keep it that way for as long as possible."

"Thanks for that," Van shook his head at Med.

"Don't get upset, it just happened that way. Faleama said you could be targeted so one-word answers and keep to yourself. Also, you have a new number, I know it's going to be a nightmare to forget your old one but it's 454367AHF."

"Yeah you said that before, I think I recognise that number."

"That might make it easier to remember then." Med drained what was left of his drink and winched.

"Damn, that's good. I will say don't be a dick about it. You know just be respectful and keep an eye on Dimitrios. That arsehole likes to execute people, and he can if given a just reason. The problem with that prick, he always manages to find a 'just' reason. If you want to know something ask me, because if you fuck up and you haven't, then it's on you."

"Why is he a squad leader then?"

"Because, he gets the job done and that is all that matters out here." Med looked down at his empty glass.

"Your round," Van smiled and stood up.

"What do I do?"

"Walk up to the counter and point at the size of glass first and then at what you want. I will have the same but you pick what you want but keep to the stuff on the left side of the list. Save the other stuff for when you have been given your Boosters. Also, don't talk to the woman behind the counter because it's forbidden. She cannot understand a word you say to her anyway."

"Why?"

"She's a conscript, either she works here or gets sent somewhere else. There are a lot of worse places to work and they wouldn't put one of us behind there."

"Why not have it automated?"

"I've never thought about it. It's just always been like that." Van stopped and turned back to Med.

"Can I ask you something that might seem a little odd?" Vandeaga wasn't sure how Med would take it as everyone else he asked didn't seem happy afterwards.

"Sure." Med had already thought that this day couldn't have gotten any weirder anyway.

"How old do I look?" Med blinked at the question and thought about it.

"You look about eighteen maybe nineteen, why's that?"

"Only a couple years ago I was told I was thirteen."

"Have you grown much in those two years?" Van shook his head. "Then you are either well-developed for, what? Fifteen now? Or, they tried to keep as much information from you as they could. By the way, welcome to the Blood shield, it's always good to have another member." Med patted his chest in a welcoming salute. "We fight and we protect our people with blood."

Van nodded and walked towards the counter, he looked lost, like a small child in a supermarket. Med rubbed his face with his hands.

Why does this type of shit always happen to me?